OMNI

KR JACOBSEN

CRIMSON BLADE PRESS

CHAPTER 1

Ryan Sutter arrived at work a minute or two early, just as he always did. The two hours before the public was allowed to enter was a quiet, peaceful time; with the rise of the internet, the idea of the library as a silent bastion of study was no longer applicable.

Clear skies, temperate weather, and a cool breeze—a standard Southern California morning—greeted him when he went outside to empty the book drop. Five years at the library and now in his mid-twenties, Ryan wasn't sure his Liberal Arts degree was doing him much good if he was still emptying book drops. Perhaps he should go after that Master's and be a librarian.

Treasures from the weekend filled the aged metal box: books, DVDs, and even the occasional dirty, abused lumps of paper that people considered donations because they were loathe to throw them out. He shrugged as he placed a couple of donations onto a cart. They'd be in the trash soon enough.

Budget cuts and layoffs left the staff somewhat thin, and as Ryan rolled the cart back into the building, he remembered the days when the staff had been more than double in size. Thanks to the cuts, they'd all become closer.

The smell of coffee—fresh and bitter—stole his thoughts and overpowered the usual smell of dust and paper when he took the cart to the circulation desk to check everything in. Thomas Vasquez was deep in mid-drink and smiled as he placed his coffee mug on the scratched wooden counter.

"Fresh pot back there. It has your name on it."

Ryan laughed. "I don't think so."

"You'll give in one of these days. You really don't know what you're missing."

"Might as well just get an IV and put the caffeine straight into my bloodstream."

"Like all those sodas you drink are any different."

"At least they don't taste like bitter, dirty water."

Thomas laughed and they checked the items in.

Ryan left the counter and started shelving. Bradbury here, Goodkind there, King and King and King here, and so it went for some time. He emptied the cart and rolled it back to its storage place. As he set the cart in its spot, red light strobed through the library. Ryan left the cart and navigated the shelves to the front doors.

Lights blazed through the sliding glass doors as though vehicles were nearby, but there were no places for anyone to park so close to the library's entrance. Thanks to the fountain, paved walkway, and trees outside, the space immediately outside the door was clearly meant for pedestrians, not vehicles.

Yet as he looked out, he was sure it was headlights he could see shining through the mildly tinted glass. One of the vehicles, for surely it had to be, turned toward the door and Ryan suddenly found himself staring at the glare of headlights.

"What the hell…" Ryan approached the door and the lights hit the glass at just the right angle to be blinding. Bodies cut across the light, momentarily dimming the glare. It looked like the police. But why would the police be gathering around a library, especially when it wasn't even open for the day? Certainly no one had called to complain about the internet crowd that gathered in the early hours. They may have irritated him, but they generally kept to themselves outside and didn't cause problems.

Ryan turned from the front doors and hurried around the circulation desk and into a side door. He followed a short hallway and turned into the back work area. Voices came to him from the break room around the corner and he entered just in time to see emergency vehicles zip by with lights flashing but no sirens. Cassie Cox and Thomas turned their heads to follow the vehicles as they vanished in the direction of the building's front.

"What's going on out there?" Ryan said. "There's a bunch of cops right outside the front door, and one even parked there."

Neither of them turned to regard him, but Cassie spoke quietly.

"I... I think some of the police have their weapons drawn."

"That's not standard issue for patrol, either." Thomas took a drink of his coffee without looking down at it and continued to look outside. He held the mug in both hands like a sacred object. "That one's carrying an AR-15. Definitely not standard issue for patrol." He took another sip, his gaze intense as he stared out of the window.

Ryan looked from one to the other then outside again. A couple of police cars stopped and officers emerged from either side carrying shotguns and assault rifles. The pairs went different directions, and it looked like one was headed for the front of the library before they passed out of sight of the window.

"Do you think there's something going on at city hall?" Ryan put his nose up to the glass and turned his face to look to the side, past the park to city hall, but he couldn't see anything through the sea of vehicles and bodies, and the flashing lights.

"Something big, whatever it is. Those guys don't suit up like that to get a sleeping bum to leave the park."

Thomas stood there, calm and matter-of-fact with his coffee, as though the police showing up armed was an every-day library occurrence. Cassie, however, shook slightly. Her eyes darted as she looked out of the window, her arms wrapped about herself.

Ryan opened his mouth to offer a comforting word, but stopped and turned when unrecognized voices came from somewhere outside the break room. Cassie and Thomas seemed intent on watching the window so Ryan went to the door and looked out. Cops, several of them, were walking through the back offices in that irritating way that cops have when they think they belong somewhere they don't. They spoke on their radios at the same time and he couldn't pick out their conversations. However, they appeared to be making their way toward the break room.

One of the cops shoved past Ryan to get into the room. Ryan fell back a step and bumped into a wall, and he withheld his protest when he saw some sort of submachine gun in the officer's hand. Thomas's words ran through his head.

Another of the cops walked into the room and went to the window, a submachine gun hanging on a hook at his side. The officer that shoved past Ryan looked up at the library employees. "We're taking over this building. Get your coworkers and bring them to the back where we'll give you more instructions."

That shook Cassie awake. "What's going on? Why do you need the library?"

"Ma'am, please gather your coworkers." He then pointed to where the fax machine and printer stood just outside of the break room. It was one of the few open spaces in the back large enough to accommodate a sizable gathering.

Cassie looked at the officer but he turned to the window. Someone said something on the radio, something in code, and the officer responded in similar fashion.

Ryan left the room with Thomas and Cassie close behind. They stopped once they were several feet away from the break room and in the cube farm. Cubicles stretched past them beyond the printer and fax and turned the corner to fill out the rest of the staff area. The other officers that had come with the first two apparently kept going through the back as they were nowhere to be seen.

"I don't like this, guys," Thomas said. He still clutched his coffee in both hands.

Ryan looked back to the officers in the break room. They had their backs to him as they stared out of the window and spoke over their radios. Ryan nodded and turned back to Thomas and Cassie. "I'll get the rest. Maybe you'll overhear something and figure out what's going on."

Thomas only nodded in response as he looked back at the break room.

Ryan left them and navigated the cube farm to the locked door that opened to the library proper. The door had a tall but narrow window in it, and through it he could see something happening in the library. Upraised guns passed through the stacks. Ryan opened the door and the sound of orders being issued from the stacks came to him. He was about to walk through when he saw his coworkers. Natalie, Amelia, Donna, and Pauline being marched by the cops toward the door behind the circulation desk, guns pointed at their backs.

Ryan sucked in a breath and closed the door, careful to make sure it latched quietly. He watched for another couple of seconds until they were out of sight of the door's window then turned to go to the break room. Thomas and Cassie needed to be warned, and then what?

What would they do? Who were these guys? What the hell was going on?

Ryan stood there, dumbfounded, but voices dragged his attention back to the present. His other coworkers had made it to the back and he heard Thomas shout and heard the distinct sound of a mug shattering on the floor.

Ryan ducked and crept forward to see. He edged out to the cube farm's aisle and followed it until it turned the corner. Still hunched down, Ryan peeked out. Thirty feet away, his coworkers stood with their hands and faces against the wall, the officers with guns pointed at their backs.

The cops were speaking, but their voices were low and Ryan could only pick out a few words.

"One more?"

They knew he was still in the building.

"Find him."

Ryan turned and moved as quickly as he could while keeping his head and body low. He turned the corner then stopped once he reached the end of the cube farm. He poked his head out and looked right. Through the tall window in the door, someone walked by, gun in hand, head moving back and forth as he scanned the building. Ryan pulled himself behind one of the cube walls, heart pumping.

Shit. Guys behind me and guys out there.

Ryan looked left and decided. He pushed off the wall and ran straight through the door into the storage room. He had his hand on the crash bar to the outside door but stopped when he heard voices just outside. He risked a glance through the peephole and was greeted with a fish-eye view of two officers talking to one another.

He took his hands off the crash bar and turned around. He needed to run back into the staff area and try another direction, but he heard the side staff door open and could envision his impending doom at the end of one of those submachine guns. Ryan looked around the room, at the scattered boxes and large trash cans, old furniture and other assorted things they really should have thrown out years ago, and he realized the ceiling was partitioned. A broken office chair to his left provided inspiration and he made straight for it. He mounted the chair, pushed up one of the ceiling panels, and hoisted himself in, but not without some trouble.

Though he had visions of himself climbing into the ceiling only to fall through like some dumb criminal on a TV show, he was lucky because pipes and conduits ran just above the other side of the off-white ceiling panels, some of them coming from or going to what looked like an HVAC unit nearby. Whatever it was, it looked heavy and had several diagonal braces of thick metal that were attached to something that vanished further into the darkness of the ceiling above.

Ryan had to maneuver around several pipes, but he just managed to squeeze himself in and balance on a fist-sized metal pipe while holding onto some support brace or another. Grace wasn't his priority at the moment. The HVAC fan spun fast and whined. It was loud enough to cover his awkward movements. He pushed the panel back into place, but with one hand wrapped around the support brace and his legs splayed over the pipes and conduits that ran through the ceiling, he wasn't able to slide the panel all of the way over. He could see a quarter-sized section of the storage room's wall through the gap.

Sound came up to him moments later—it sounded like someone was banging around in the storage room—and he heard someone say, "Nothing." Another couple of seconds passed and he realized he was alone with the whir of the HVAC fan.

Time became a fluid concept, impossible to guess at while he waited and tried to determine what he should do. At the moment, he was mainly concerned with staying hidden, his feet balanced precariously on a metal pipe and one of the support braces, and his hands wrapped around more of the braces to keep himself from falling through the ceiling. The fan eventually shut off and the quiet filled in the emptiness. Ryan rested his forehead against the back of his hand as he tried to sort the images and sounds that played in his head.

Why would the police be taking over a library, and why did it look as if they were taking the employees prisoner? And what about what Thomas said, that the guns weren't standard issue?

Ryan shuddered involuntarily at the thought. Why would the police come in with nonstandard equipment? Were they expecting a terrorist threat? The idea was ludicrous and he wanted to laugh, but was it really so crazy? Hadn't he seen the officers enter, big guns in hand, weapons at his coworkers' backs?

Then the thought hit him: What if they weren't the police? What if they were terrorists, or at least a gang, dressed as the police?

Ryan's hands went cold and he squeezed them tight around the support brace. The slightly rounded edges dug into his skin, but he didn't pay the pain any attention.

If they weren't the police, that could mean anything.

Another minute passed then the silence was suddenly broken by a loud pop. A scream followed it almost immediately, and he realized it wasn't a pop, but a bang. Another bang, another scream. Bang, bang. Still screaming. Bang, bang. Silence.

Ryan, forehead still against his hand, squeezed his

eyes shut and tried to block it out. His stomach churned and his hands lost strength. His grip began to slip but he caught himself. Ryan forced his eyes open and looked at the bit of light the ceiling panel gave him. He couldn't make out anything in the storage room, but everything was so blurry it didn't matter.

Panic flared up and his breathing came faster and heavier. He knew what the sounds meant and didn't want to think about it, but he couldn't stop himself. His coworkers, his friends, they'd all been murdered. Six friends, six shots. And he was hiding in the ceiling like some rat while they died.

Ryan held on even tighter to the support braces until the panic dried up. It left him exhausted and raw. A cold sort of logic, pure survival, kicked in.

He let go with one hand and fished his cell phone out of a pocket and flicked it to life. Why hadn't he thought of it earlier?

The screen was bright and disorienting in the darkness. After a few moments his eyes adjusted and he went to dial, but he noticed that the screen said he had no service. Coverage was usually excellent in the building. Was it because he was in the ceiling, surrounded by pipes and wiring of all shapes and sizes?

Ryan had to try anyway. Since he was using his cell phone he knew he needed to call the local police, so he flipped through his contacts, touched the right one on the screen, and waited. He put the phone to his ear and heard nothing for several seconds, and then three short beeps.

Damn. He tried 911 anyway, but the same thing.

Three short, mocking beeps.

He turned off his phone, turned it back on and waited, but there was still no service. He needed to tell someone, needed to discover what was happening, but that wasn't going to happen while he was in the ceiling and he dared not drop down to the storage room. That meant he had to wait longer.

Ryan choked back a cry of frustration and shoved his phone into his pocket. He tried not to think of those six shots and the screams. And the silence.

The time on the phone said 2:38. He'd been in the ceiling for more than five and a half hours. Every muscle in his legs ached, as did his abs, back, and neck. He wasn't sure if he could move or if his limbs were locked into place. Only his arms and hands still worked, but his shoulders hurt and his hands were threatening to rebel from grasping the braces for so long. Ryan put his phone away then shook one arm and hand out while still holding on with the other and then switched. It helped, but he desperately wanted to be out of the ceiling, and his bladder fully agreed with the idea.

He waited several more minutes then realized he couldn't hear anything. The fan wasn't running and it sounded like nothing but emptiness. They couldn't have all left, could they?

Ryan lowered himself to the hole in the ceiling and pressed an ear to it. Nothing. There'd been sounds — voices, booted footfalls, the occasional loud crack — since a few minutes past the gunshots. But now there was nothing, and for some time he realized.

Ryan pulled the panel away and light flooded his world of darkness. Hands still gripping the braces, he lowered his head and peeked around the storage room. It was still the same collection of cardboard, shelving units, broken chairs, and other junk. Ryan pulled himself back up and sat there looking into the storage room for several long moments.

Ryan decided it was time to look around. He took a deep breath and lowered himself. His feet and legs tingled with the motion and he bit back a grunt of pain as they were forced out of a position they'd held for so long. The chair that had been below him had been toppled, and Ryan dropped down to the floor with a grunt. He stood up, doubled over with his knees bent for a few moments as he tried to get his limbs to cooperate.

Ryan took another deep breath and stood straight and felt his back and neck pop in several places. He was going to hurt tomorrow, assuming he made it through today.

All was still silent in the storage room. He walked to the outer door and looked out of the peephole. Nothing. He blinked and looked again. Still nothing. He pulled away from the door and went to the flimsy inner door. His hand shook while he hesitated, but eventually he opened the door a crack and looked through. He couldn't see anything except the cubes.

Door still open a hair, he pulled his phone out and checked again. No signal. Strange. He put it away and opened the door a little more. Still nothing. Ryan opened the door enough to squeeze through and he burst out and made for a cube. He looked around as he half-ran, half-crouched, but he didn't see anyone or hear anything.

He stopped for a few seconds in the cube—Lorraine's, he noticed, only today she was on vacation for the next three days—and waited for his heart to slow a few beats or to at least stop the blood rushing in his ears.

Once he could think and hear clearly again, Ryan looked to her desk and the phone that sat there. He snatched the receiver and dialed 9-911 then put it to his ear. Silence. He flicked the switch to disconnect the call and listened for a tone, but it was silent.

Shit.

Ryan replaced the phone on the cradle then leaned out along the floor and risked a glance either way. Still nothing, still quiet. He was beginning to think the place really had been abandoned. Ryan left Lorraine's cube and went to the staff door that opened into the library. He put himself flat to it and looked out of the tall window at an angle, and then ducked and popped up on the other side to look the other direction. The lights were still on, but no one occupied the building.

Ryan left the door and started down the cube hallway, at first slowly and in a constant crouch, but as he turned the corner and could see the break room ahead, he gained speed and confidence that no one was around. He certainly would have seen or heard something by now, but he hadn't.

He slowed for the last fifteen feet and didn't look to the corner and kept his eyes forward, but some primal urge insisted he look. He resisted for as long as he could, but at length he looked to the corner where he'd last seen his friends and coworkers and saw rust colored stains on the floor.

Tears threatened to overwhelm him again but he blinked them back and turned away. He didn't need to look at the stains to know what happened or to honor their memories.

Ryan walked past the stains and into the break room and practically ran into something that didn't belong in there—a large, steel drum with some electronics on top. He took a deep breath and then looked at a screen that was mounted on the lid.

It was an iPod and its display showed time counting down. The iPod sat in a speaker dock and wires ran from the back of the dock into the drum. The screen read fifteen minutes and change to go. It didn't take a large stretch of his imagination to guess what the thing was.

For a moment, a brief one at that, he entertained the idea of disabling the bomb. Then the moment passed and he knew that he needed to run, that there was no possible way, save total dumb luck, he would ever disable the thing.

Ryan drew his eyes away from the drum that reminded him of Oklahoma City and looked out of the window. The last time he looked there'd been emergency vehicles outside, but now they were all gone. He moved closer to the window and looked over the park where numerous emergency vehicles were hastily parked.

He furrowed his brow as he looked then remembered there was a bomb slowly ticking away behind him. He left the window and went into the library proper and forgot that he should, perhaps, be stealthy. Ryan entered the circulation area then walked around the counter through the swinging gate all the while scanning the large, open areas. Still no one, still quiet. His eyes, however, settled on another bomb, this one square in the middle of the children's section, itself in the center of the building.

He always thought that the children's section should have been in a different location, but this was a rather rash way to change it. Curiosity compelled him forward and he moved to inspect the bomb.

It was much the same as the other, something like a fifty-five gallon drum with a small collection of electronics and wires on top of it. The timer was down to thirteen minutes and it continued to subtract the seconds. Ryan rubbed a hand over his face. How many other bombs were in the building? Even if he hoped to take care of one, who knew how many more there were?

About to leave, Ryan scanned the building again from where he stood and saw something he missed the first time. At a distance, he wasn't sure what it was, but it almost looked like a shoe was in the children's computer area. He left the bomb to its ticking and walked around the shelves and was now sure that it was a shoe, only it wasn't by itself. He knew that shoe, a brown loafer, and before he turned the corner he knew he was going to see Thomas on the floor.

Ryan stopped and turned around; he didn't need or want to see more. They were all there in a heap and blood was caked on the backs of their heads. He didn't want to imagine what their faces looked like if the backs of their heads were that bad. Tears came again and this time there was nothing he could do to stop them. He focused on his tears in an attempt to ignore his suddenly churning stomach as he walked to the front door.

He wiped tears away then looked and saw more rust colored stains on the floor near the front, and as he turned the corner to see in front of the door itself, he saw more bodies. He didn't recognize them, and it didn't look like they had been executed, but he didn't want to see them regardless.

Unnoticed until now, the smell of it, of all of it, of death hit him. It prompted a whole new attack on his stomach and Ryan had to turn away and close his eyes and plug his nose until he was ready to deal with it again.

The doors were closed and blood was streaked and spattered against it. His shoe made an awful slurping noise as he lifted it and took a step forward and realized that the pool of blood was so massive that he was already standing in it.

Whatever was happening had turned into a surreal nightmare that only got worse as the doors automatically slid open to reveal further horrors. More bodies and blood were outside the door and a lifeless arm, still attached to a man with several large, dark red holes in his chest, flopped into the opening made by the door.

The weather was still beautiful—shocking clarity and blue skies overhead—the perfect antithesis to the blood and horror of the library.

Ryan hurried outside, careful as he stepped over bodies and blood, and tried to ignore the sound of the doors repeatedly opening and closing on the corpse's arm. He looked around and realized he hardly recognized the front of the library. Bodies, blood, tire marks from the vehicles that had been there this morning; it was anything but the downtown branch library he used to know. And then there were the bombs.

The last thought got his legs moving and he went straight for the parking lot and his car, but he stopped in midstride as he turned the corner. Below him, past the few steps that led to the parking lot, two sides engaged in a stand-off. Emergency vehicles dotted the parking lot, with a couple of ambulances in the middle and police vehicles on his left. Those farthest away from him looked like police officers, a dozen at most and perhaps some of the same ones he'd seen this morning. They crouched behind the numerous police cruisers. He wasn't sure, but he thought it likely that they were far enough away from the library that any large debris wouldn't hit them if they were still there in the next ten minutes.

Closer to him, however, were a half-dozen people dressed in black. At first he thought they were wearing suits, a Matrix-like thing, but he realized they wore dark clothes more akin to what SWAT would wear. He studied them then changed his opinion; it looked like body armor, something out of the North Hollywood shootout he remembered from when he was a kid. The black armor bore no insignias, nor did the black vehicles—large SUVs—that they hid behind.

Ryan stood and watched, transfixed, but no one moved. He thought it odd, that there should at least be some shooting since they were all armed, but each side was just huddled behind vehicles for protection.

17

One of those in black nearest to Ryan looked to be speaking into a concealed radio. He stood and pointed in Ryan's general direction. Ryan stared for a second, dumbfounded, then ducked around the corner, his heart pounding. He turned to run but stopped when he heard a vehicle coming from the direction he turned to. This was strictly a pedestrian area, but that hadn't stopped the cops, or whoever they were, earlier that morning.

The panic passed and he burst into motion, but he threw himself against the front of the library as a black car, a BMW or an Audi, came roaring around the corner and cut right across the front of the building, heedless of the blood and bodies. The tires squealed and bounced and Ryan looked up to see the car plunge into the parking lot from the walkway. It drifted to a stop with the car's passenger side broadside to the police officers. The driver door opened and a man, this one definitely wearing a suit like an agent from the Matrix, stepped out of the car.

Intrigued, Ryan didn't realize he was walking back to the corner of the building until the man looked his direction, raised a hand, and Ryan stopped in mid-step. It was as though Ryan ran into some physical barrier, but nothing blocked his way. Ryan's eyes grew large as he looked for what had stopped him and saw nothing, yet something had definitely stopped him. It didn't make sense and his brain ignored the impossibility of it as it tried to cope.

He remained there and watched as the agent adjusted his jacket, turned and exchanged a couple of words with what were apparently his cohorts. One of the men went to the back of an SUV and pulled out a handful of cylindrical devices and passed them to the others while the agent stood around and supervised.

As one, the men and women took their devices and threw them each in a different direction. The sunlight glinted off them as they soared through the air, and one came toward Ryan, but stopped several yards short. Almost as one, a series of small explosions cut through the uncomfortable silence, and then it became obvious what they were.

Smoke erupted out of the grenades and billowed forth in great voluminous clouds that suddenly obscured everything from sight. One moment, Ryan could see the police on one side and the black-clad men and women on the other, and in the next instant, they were gone. Ryan took a step back, then another, suddenly afraid of what might happen. All was quiet again except for the hiss of the grenades as they spewed forth smoke, then Ryan jumped as gunfire rattled out and shouts hit the air. Bullets pinged off vehicles and walls, and Ryan dropped to the ground and covered his head. He knew he should have run, should have run far and never stopped to look at the parking lot, but the only thing he could picture now was a bullet slamming into his back, so he shivered on the ground and hoped nothing would hit him.

The seconds passed in hours and he opened his eyes. Still gunfire rattled out and nothing hit him, then there was a pause. This was his moment, his chance to get away. He stayed there, unable to move, unable to believe he could escape this nightmare. No, he could make it. Ryan got up to his knees before he dropped back down again.

The unmistakable sound of glass exploding was combined with the harsh screech of metal on metal. Ryan covered his ears from the sudden cacophony. Though he still couldn't see through the smoke, it sounded as though a few cars just collided with each other, only he hadn't heard any engines. Screams and cries rent the air, a horrible backdrop to the gunfire, then the awful screech of metal and shattering of glass sounded again.

All was eerily silent. Fractions of the smoke cloud drifted away and allowed him to see glimpses of the carnage he could only hear; Ryan knew that something had happened that he couldn't explain.

The agent stood alone in the parking lot and surveyed the damage. Multiple cars were twisted and smashed, resting on their hoods or on other cars. One of the vehicles, an ambulance, was on its side and in the middle of the police cars, and Ryan could see legs sticking out from underneath it.

It made no sense. How could the vehicles have displaced themselves? The agent was wearing a suit, nothing more, and carried no weapons as he slowly looked over the wreckage before him. He nodded, turned around, raised his right hand briefly, and started back toward those wearing the black body armor.

They popped out from behind their vehicles and opened fire on the others. The police officers, the few who weren't crushed under cars, were caught completely unaware. Bullets ripped into their ranks and they fell to the ground, and only one managed to cry out in pain or surprise.

The agent ignored the bullets that whizzed by him

and looked over at Ryan. Ryan blinked and felt his heart pound in his chest. The paralysis that had struck him immobile vanished, and Ryan knew he had to get out of there.

"Shit!" Ryan rushed to his feet and started to run, but something hit him from behind and threw him forward. He stumbled for a couple of steps and managed to regain his balance, but it hit him again and he fell forward. Ryan collapsed to the concrete, arms and legs akimbo. Skin scraped away from his hands. Ryan looked back, but there was nothing behind him, not even the agent. Confused, but even more scared, he scrambled back to his feet ran. He risked a look back and something slammed into him yet again.

This time he was looking back when it hit him, but there was still nothing there. He twisted and fell onto his back and his head bounced off the concrete. Despite the pain and confusion, Ryan knew that nothing had hit him, yet something had.

His brain was on the verge of mutiny, and now Ryan suddenly found breathing difficult as the air was knocked out of his chest and he struggled against the pounding in his head. He propped himself up on his elbows and looked up and saw the man in the suit emerge from the wispy strands of smoke, headed his way. He didn't understand, yet he did all at once. There was nothing he could do to get away from that man, whoever he was.

Survival was a strong instinct and Ryan tried to get up again, but some great invisible weight pressed against him and flattened him to the ground. He pushed and kicked and punched, but the barrier didn't budge. The agent was only twenty feet away now and Ryan renewed his frantic attempts to free himself, but it was futile. Dress shoes entered his field of view.

"Who are you?"

Pure panic sent adrenaline racing through his body and his mind no longer tried to rationalize what he had seen and heard. Instead, he tried to figure out a way out of another insane situation. Only he couldn't move, though nothing prevented him from doing so.

Something hit his foot and he looked up and ceased his struggles. The agent stood over him, a severe look on his face. He was older than Ryan had first thought, maybe in his fifties with deep lines on his forehead and by his eyes. His hair was still dark but showed grey at the sides, and he had a neatly trimmed silver Van Dyke.

"I believe I asked you a question, son."

"Ryan. Ryan Sutter." Ryan fumbled for the badge clipped to his shirt and tried to hold it up, but the invisible barrier stopped him.

"Ryan Sutter." The agent turned his head and Ryan had the distinct impression the agent was listening to something or someone. He turned back to Ryan. "You'll need to come with us."

"I don't want any trouble. I didn't see anything. I couldn't see anything." Ryan's eyes darted about. "Those guys, the police, they killed my coworkers. I just want out of here."

"That is not an option. You will come with us."

The man started to bend, arms out, but he stopped and turned his head slightly.

Ryan stared at the agent then realized why he'd stopped. Music. And it was coming from the library. In the moment, everything, the weird bending of reality, the merciless, impossible slaughter of the police, his own terror at the sight of this strange man, became meaningless because he remembered.

"Oh shit! They rigged up — "

Wagner roared to a climax then the world became light and sound before it melted into darkness and silence.

Ryan had a glimpse of the genesis of an explosion, heard the first inkling of the sound, but now he could see and hear nothing save the white before his eyes and the ringing in his ears. The world seemed to pause and time became an insoluble mass that he couldn't see or make his way through. Seconds could have passed, or hours, while he lay there dazed.

He blinked several times and realized that he could see again and that a cloud of dust obscured his vision, only he wasn't inside it. A clear circle outlined the ground around himself and the agent, and no dust or debris was inside of it.

As the dust began to settle, Ryan looked to the library, but it hardly resembled the library he knew. Through the dust, the walls had become a set of jagged, broken teeth.

He looked around, his head lolling to one side, and took in pieces of the carnage around him. Bits of wall and other things littered the ground. He looked up and saw the agent standing there, arms outstretched, a look of severe concentration on his face. Ryan suddenly realized that the weight that had been pressing down on him was gone and he tried to stand, but found his body wasn't cooperating. The man turned to him and said something, at least Ryan thought he said something because the agent's lips moved, but Ryan couldn't hear anything.

Ryan continued to try to stand, but the agent suddenly kicked him down to the ground. Ryan slammed back into the ground and the impact stole the protest from his lips. In an instant, it was replaced with a scream as the library's roof burst through the cloud straight at them. The section of roof grew in size as it closed in until it was big enough to block out the sun over them. Surely it was large enough to crush them with ease, but it stopped a couple of feet above the agent and shattered. Chunks of roof flew in every direction. The agent shook under the impact and groaned, but he remained standing and nothing passed through his invisible barrier.

Several more pieces, smaller things, rained around them, and then only the dust remained. The agent waved his arms about and the dust flew as though propelled away by giant fans.

"Okay?"

Though he was dazed, Ryan realized he could hear again, sort of, and looked up and nodded.

The agent nodded back. He extended a hand and helped Ryan to his feet.

"You could have given me more than two seconds of warning about that."

Ryan shook his head and gave what he hoped was an apologetic smile.

"Come along."

The agent grabbed his shirt and started moving.

Ryan fell into step behind, unable to halt the momentum. His body placed one foot before the other and he staggered along as he looked around dazedly.

They emerged from a cloud of dust into the parking lot and the agent stopped for several seconds and waved his arms forward in great, sweeping arcs. The dust swirled up and away and left a small tunnel through which they could see.

The black SUVs were covered in dust and debris and they sat on their sides. Holes, large and small, dotted the side of one SUV while fluids leaked out of the bottom of the other. If the vehicles had fared that poorly, he could only imagine what must have happened to the people.

"Fuck!"

Ryan looked away from the vehicles and the agent took off at a sprint toward the parking lot. Something about being away from the strange man left Ryan feeling vulnerable and he hurried to catch up, his bruised knees and legs complaining the whole way. The agent stood surveying the scene. Debris, much of it large and heavy, covered the parking lot. The people in black body armor couldn't have survived this.

"Motherfuckers!" The agent raised his arms and one of the SUVs began to shudder, but he quickly dropped his arms and it rested back in place, fluids leaking onto the parking lot. His shoulders heaved as he stood there staring at the vehicle.

Ryan blinked and pretended he didn't just see that. "Hey, I'm sorry. They killed my friends, too." Ryan took another look around at the remains of the library and the parking lot. "What's happening here?"

The agent turned to face Ryan and Ryan took an involuntary step back. The agent's face was red, his eyes wide, his nostrils flared.

"What the fuck does it look like, kid? It's war."

"War?"

"You're not dumb. You can see that."

"But, I mean, what's really happening? Who are these people? And who are you? How are you doing these things?"

"Who do they look like? They're the government."

"Government?" Ryan looked around again.

"So are you." He took a step forward.

Ryan backed up a step. "Hey, I just work in a library. I don't know what any of this is."

The agent looked Ryan over and seemed to consider something then nodded. The muscles in his face relaxed. He extended his hand.

"I'm Malone, and I'm a cleaner. And you just got yourself in the middle of a big, fat revolution."

CHAPTER 2

Malone's car was buried somewhere under a pile of debris and dust, but Malone cleared it off, and though the car displayed dents and holes galore, the engine fired right up when Malone approached it. Both doors opened and Malone hopped into the driver seat. Ryan swatted broken glass out of the passenger seat then eased himself in.

Lights and switches filled most of the center console and some sort of metal covered the inside of the doors and panels. Even the floor was covered in the same metal, and when he looked up, he saw more of it, along with a thick roll cage that crisscrossed the roof. The cage extended down yet somehow didn't manage to impede the entering and exiting of the car.

Malone gunned the engine and Ryan hurried to get his seatbelt on — a five-point harness.

It was almost too much, and Ryan forced himself to focus on something other than the questions that raged unanswered. "I bet it didn't come this way from the dealer."

"Perceptive."

Ryan looked over and shrugged.

"I've never seen anything like this."

"Kid, if it's just the same, I have some thinking to do. I'll give you the tour later if I have time, but we both just lost comrades in the war. Maybe you should keep that in mind."

"I'm sorry, I just…" Ryan blew out a sigh and turned his attention outside. How was he supposed to deal with what he just saw, never mind what he'd already seen and heard that morning? It was too much.

The noise from the wind blowing through the windowless car made it difficult to talk anyway and gave Ryan something else to focus on. They turned off a street and looked to be heading for the freeway. A few moments later, Malone turned onto the two-lane highway that led to the freeway. The minutes passed and Malone steered the car onto the freeway. They merged into traffic and zigzagged their way through at speeds that would have made most Southern California asshole drivers blush.

"I don't mean to be harsh, kid." Malone had to yell to be heard.

"The name's Ryan."

"Things just haven't been going well, kid. Look, when we get back to command, you're going to give them a report. I'll try to fill you in afterward but I make no promises, alright?"

"Yeah."

What else could he say? And what was the talk about revolution and war? Ryan looked at Malone out of the corner of his eye. Malone was focused straight ahead as he cut off one motorist and another as he continued to break numerous driving laws. Revolution and war weren't simple words to be thrown about, and if anyone wanted to start either, there were a lot better places in the world, never mind a lot more important, than his Podunk town to start something. Sure, San Vicente was nice, but it was small and insignificant compared to, well, most everything.

Ryan tried to push the questions aside as he looked out of the window and watched them leave the city. He must have fallen asleep—no small task in the wind tunnel—because the next thing he remembered was that the city was gone and they were on an empty stretch of freeway he didn't immediately recognize. He fished his phone out of his pocket and saw he still didn't have phone service, but thanks to one of those expensive GPS apps, he didn't need a cellular signal to see where they were. He touched an icon on the screen, waited a few moments, and then it popped up. They were somewhere on the 14 and there was nothing around for miles.

Ryan looked over at Malone and back to the phone and then looked around outside. It looked as though they were passing through a canyon, with desert filling in the rest of the space all around them. Malone took the next off-ramp anyway.

They drove down some road that hugged the mountains and paralleled the highway for some time. Malone slowed the car as they went around a corner then stopped in the middle of the road.

"You can put that away now. This isn't on any map."

Malone reached out to the center console and flicked a couple of switches and the mountainside opened.

With the morning's impossibilities safely tucked away in the corner of his mind, they leapt back out and threatened to overwhelm him. "No way." Ryan put a hand to his head and stared straight ahead.

Trickles of dirt and a small cloud of dust puffed out as the mountain began to open. A large concealed door, big enough for a semi to drive through, maybe even two, opened inward in the mountain and Malone eased the car in. He stopped, flicked a couple of switches again, and the door closed behind them. He waited until it was completely closed before he took them further inside.

Ryan looked to his phone and watched as they drove into the middle of nature as far as the GPS was concerned. A few moments later, he lost the satellite signal and put the phone away.

"Who are you guys?"

"We're the government."

"But—"

"The other government. The shadow government."

"You mean like in those conspiracy theories? Like the Illuminati?"

"Not quite, but close enough for now."

They drove through a tunnel complex. Concrete surrounded them on all four sides with a ceiling tall enough to stack a few of those black SUVs on top of each other and drive through. Lights shone from the ceiling at even intervals and left large puddles of yellow light, enough for one to walk by if one so chose. Malone kept the speed at a gentle thirty miles per hour.

"So you're like a backup government should something happen to the primary one?"

"You're pretty perceptive, kid."

"And you're admitting to this stuff? You're not worried?"

Malone turned his head and smirked then looked back to the road.

"No, I imagine not." Ryan's heart jumped. "Are you going to kill me after I give my report?"

"Me? No."

Ryan swallowed hard, but he needed to ask. "And the shit you were doing? How? What was that? Tell me it's a gun or device or something."

Ryan waited, but apparently Malone had nothing more to offer. Ryan stared straight ahead for several long moments as he tried to decide if he should unbuckle his harness and dive out of the car.

"Don't worry about it. Look, you're not a bad egg and we don't kill people. They're the ones murdering innocents, alright?" Ryan nodded in response but Malone apparently didn't notice. "Alright?"

"Yeah." It didn't do much to settle his worries or answer his questions.

The following minutes passed in silence until the nondescript concrete gave way ahead to a more distinctive dark metal wall with a guard post on either side. Malone stopped the car. A guard in dark body armor armed with an assault rifle approached the car. Another watched from the left side, while two more watched from the right. And they watched actively, Ryan noticed.

"What happened, Agent Malone?"

"They blew the library to hell."

"Damn it." The guard said something under his breath. "The others? We haven't heard anything."

Malone shook his head. "I lost communications with the blast, and they were caught in it."

"Bastards!"

"We'll get them."

"Yeah. You better go. They've been itching for a report since we lost contact."

The guard went back to his post and a large section of the wall slid open to allow the car access. Malone drove them in and they were greeted with more concrete on all sides. They passed a couple of branching tunnels along the way and went straight to the end.

"They didn't even ask about me."

"Why would they?"

"You guys don't care about prisoners?"

"Prisoners?" Malone barked out a laugh, a single syllable that echoed through the tunnel.

They stopped at a dead end and Malone got out of the car, engine still running. He angled toward a door at the end of the tunnel and Ryan hurried out of the car to catch up.

"Not a peep until you're addressed. Got it?"

Ryan nodded, and when Malone stopped and looked at him, he nodded again.

"You're not a bad egg."

Malone stopped at the door and produced a card from a pocket in his jacket. He swiped it through an unmarked slot in the door. A beep issued from somewhere and Malone opened the door and walked in.

It was another nondescript hallway with another door at the end fifty feet away. At this, Malone stopped and placed a finger over an unmarked spot on the door and another beep issued, the door opened, and they walked in.

Another nondescript tunnel awaited them with a door even further away that Malone stopped and put an eye to some unmarked spot to gain admittance.

"I wouldn't be surprised if you have to give blood for the next one."

Malone stopped, stared at Ryan, and then barked out his single syllable of a laugh and continued on. The next door at the end of the hallway opened by itself as they approached to reveal what looked like a crazy data center with flashing lights and screens all along the walls.

Desks filled almost every part of open space in the room, small utilitarian things with just enough room for a flat-panel monitor, a keyboard and mouse, and a few sheets of paper to fit on them. Men and women sat at the desks, the workstations arranged in long lines that stretched from one wall to the next. A few more people navigated the sea of desks in the large room, heedless of the maze they were traversing. The sound was somehow controlled and comforting, the familiar sound of clacking of keyboards, clicking of mice and low voices speaking into telephones. It reminded him a little of the library. Ryan pushed the thought away.

Malone walked right into the room and down the center of it to an area sectioned off with smoked glass at the end. They had to walk this way and that to make their way through the mass of people and desks that threatened to overwhelm the massive room. Malone opened a glass door at the end and turned right. He walked into a room where five people sat around a semicircular table. Ryan stopped behind Malone and peered about the room at the monitors and TVs on the wall, the laptops on the table, and the sharp, angular men and women behind them.

One of the men looked up from his laptop with only his eyes and peered over his glasses. He looked at Malone then looked briefly at Ryan.

"We've heard the result. What happened?"

"They bombed the library. Nothing but rubble and dust remained."

"Yet you lived."

"No shit."

"And you managed to find the lost puppy?"

Malone reached back and pulled Ryan forward. He stumbled over Malone's foot but Malone caught him and straightened him. Ryan blushed and looked closer at the men and women. They reminded him of the men and women in control of the county library system: in the fading years of their career, bored, and with the severe look of self-importance.

"What am I supposed to say?" Ryan looked from the table to Malone and back.

"Tell us what you saw, please, so that we may continue with your visit."

Ryan looked back at Malone, but the agent paid him no heed. Ryan shrugged. "I don't know what I saw. A bunch of cops and paramedics all pulled up to the library, some swarmed inside, murdered my coworkers and planted a bunch of bombs and then lost their asses when this guy," Ryan jerked a thumb at Malone, "and his friends wholesale slaughtered them, although I'm still a little sketchy on what happened."

The man's eyes went to his laptop and traced side to side as though reading. After several long seconds, he looked back up at Ryan.

"The man leading the law enforcement officers, what did he look like?"

"I have no idea. He could be standing here now and I wouldn't know. He was a cop. They look the same: short hair and a mustache."

The man seemed to frown, but the movement was so minimal Ryan wasn't sure, and he looked back at his laptop.

Malone nudged Ryan from behind.

"You don't remember anything about him? Short?

Tall? Color of his hair? Sound of his voice?"

Ryan thought back and vaguely remembered the abrupt cop who invited himself into their break room. He seemed to be the one in charge, but he couldn't remember many specifics.

"Some guy burst in with dark hair and a flat top barking orders. You don't see that much anymore when they shave everything else off but leave it just on top."

"Did you notice anything that may be unique to him, a tattoo or a scar?"

Ryan thought back to those few seconds in the break room. He hadn't been paying close attention to the cops, because they were the cops and they weren't supposed to do things like that. But he seemed to recall a scar, small, just under the guy's right eye and parallel to it. He said as much to the severe man.

"Did you see him again after that?"

Ryan shook his head. "I don't know if he was in the parking lot. Hell, I don't even know what I saw." Ryan could feel his pulse quicken and he took a deep breath to steady himself.

Malone cut in. "No, he wasn't. I remember those who were and I didn't see him there. I wasn't aware he changed his look, though."

The man at the table gave the slightest nod and looked at Ryan. "You're sure he was the man in charge?"

"I'm sure. He was a dick, and he's the one who ordered the others to find me."

"You didn't tell me how you got away, kid."

"You didn't ask."

"Gentlemen, now is not the time, though I admit I

35

have certain suspicions about the convenience of this young man escaping to provide information, little as it may be."

That pissed Ryan off. He thought he was doing them a favor and they had the audacity to insult him after the hell he'd just been through?

"Hey, you asked me and I gave you what I saw. I'm a little raw, okay? The police executed my coworkers. The fucking police! You got that? And this guy," Ryan pointed at Malone, "I don't know what the fuck he does, but the laws of physics apparently don't apply to him. Then he tells me we're in the middle of some damn war, and you and your suits sit behind the table acting all superior and accuse me of what? Being a spy? Is that what you're implying? I just want to get home to my family and scrub this shit from my brain, never mind what tomorrow brings."

"Son, your tone is unacceptable."

"And so is yours!"

Malone placed a hand on Ryan's shoulder but Ryan shrugged it off.

"We're trying to help, alright, kid?"

"Hey, I appreciate that you saved me, I do, but I'm done here. They want to mock my friends being murdered?"

Ryan gave one last look to the people at the table, waited a moment, and then turned and left the room.

What a bunch of arrogant assholes. If they were supposed to be a super secret powerful shadow government, why did they need him to know what was going on?

"Kid, wait up."

Ryan was several steps down the hallway before he

stopped, but he made a point to not turn around.

"Kid, those guys are just doing their job. I don't like them and they don't like me, but we tolerate each other. I haven't lived this long not to have learned a thing or two about life, and right now you're acting like a petulant brat."

"Why'd you even drag me here, Malone? You had to have known I didn't have whatever the hell they wanted."

"Hey, I have no idea how or why you were out there. You could have just been coming in on your shift or you could have been there all morning and found a way to escape those guys. Either way, if you have information, it helps."

"I told you what I know, and I don't even know what I believe."

"Hey! It's good, it'll help. We didn't know that he changed his hair and grew a mustache."

"Sounds like you guys are the epitome of the old joke: government intelligence."

"Kid, you have no idea. We're hurting here. We've lost men and women, good ones at that, and we're severely outnumbered. There's only so much we can do."

Ryan nodded at Malone. He felt as if he should apologize for acting like such an ass, but damn it, he was angry and hurting and confused and they weren't helping matters. He sighed and took a deep breath.

"So how do I get out of here? I'd call my folks but I can't get a signal."

"And you won't for a long time."

"Why not?"

"Walk with me. I'll tell you what I can."

Malone led him back through the office then the series of hallways.

"This is it, kid. This is the start of the war. You've heard of things here and there for the last twenty years and been told it's terrorists this and terrorists that, but that's not always the case."

"Like nine-eleven?"

"No, that was definitely terrorists. I'm talking about other things. Subway bombings, satellites being knocked out of orbit, power grids failing, cables being cut, that sort of thing."

"So, the government we pay our taxes to is trying to kill us and keep technology away? That's stupid."

"No, but there's certain factions within the whole that think they can do better, and now they're showing themselves and getting rid of those who oppose them."

Ryan laughed at the idea.

"So why bomb a library? If I hadn't been there, I wouldn't believe it happened."

"That wasn't the sole target. What else is over there?"

"A couple of other government buildings. Meeting halls, traffic enforcement, city hall."

"Yeah. They were going after the mayor."

"Of a small town? Why?"

"This is a test to see how effective they are. It'll be everywhere. We don't know when it's really going down and there isn't shit we can do about it. It'll be happening in the smallest town of Shitshoveling, Arkansas and in places you have heard of, like New York."

"I don't buy it. There's no way. That's too many people. There's no way that millions are involved in this conspiracy."

"That's the beauty of it: most don't know they are. You heard of Operation Valkyrie?"

Ryan shook his head.

"Kids today, no appreciation of history. Back in the forties, some Germans thought they'd rid the world of that bastard Hitler. You know Hitler, right?"

Ryan shot him an ugly, unamused look.

"So they thought they'd take the bastard down, and then they'd take Germany over by using Hitler's own plans. Operation Valkyrie was a contingency plan to secure the country should Hitler die. They rewrote the orders and assassinated Hitler, or at least thought they did, and then used Valkyrie to have the reserves institute martial law. It backfired when they figured out that they fucked up and Hitler was just fine and the SS squashed the coup. Poor bastards paid dearly, but you have to respect the balls on the guys."

"Lovely. So you're saying there's an American Operation Valkyrie going on now?"

"Something like that, only instead of martial law, it's martial chaos. And these guys don't have noble intentions. This is just the first step. The guys you saw today, some were probably legit and some weren't. But the guy we want, he's pretty high up."

"Shouldn't he be in LA or New York or DC or anywhere else?"

They reached the last door in the hallway and walked out into the tunnel.

"He grew up here, kid, so it's special to him. He wants to bring the pain to this place, and it looks like he has. He brought in a small squad. Fifty guys, maybe a hundred, and they're responsible for the shit happening around here now. The real police are responding to threats and claims of bombs and just doing their part, but when they're told all sorts of lies about what's going on, they're bound to get a little trigger-happy. Joe Cop isn't responsible for this. It's these sick fucks who killed your coworkers and everyone else around there. And they're not all Americans. It's a big world, kid. You might be surprised to find what lurks in the government when you turn the lights on."

A car was waiting for them in the tunnel, the sound of the engine idling bouncing off the walls around them. It looked the same as the previous one, only this car could have just rolled out of the factory. No one stood near the empty car, but someone had to have known they were coming, unless they also had some technology that summoned cars. He snickered at the thought, and that he could find humor given his hellish day. He got in the car and buckled the harness.

Malone turned a quizzical look on him. "What's so funny?"

"Nothing, really. Odd to find humor when everything happening is horrible."

"It's called coping."

Malone put the car in gear and slowly pulled away.

"So where are you taking me this time?"

"You said you wanted to go home."

"What about old man Ebenezer? He made it sound like I'd be staying a while."

"Nah, you told us what you knew. It's time to go."

"That's it? You just take me home? No agents stalking me, wiretapping my phone, reading my email?"

"Nothing to tap or read. I'm telling you, kid, this is real. Enjoy life while you can. Besides, it's not like anyone will believe you if you tell them, right?"

He had to admit that Malone was right. If he tried to tell people what was going on in town, or told them about the interesting — it somehow felt less crazy to refer to them as such — abilities that Malone had, they'd laugh at him.

Ryan snorted and looked out of the window, but the plain concrete wall was boring. At least he was finally going to get home and see his family. He was worried about them and what they must think had happened to him.

He looked over at Malone, a study of concentration as he drove. Malone's pupils suddenly contracted. Ryan's heart jumped. How much worse could his day get?

An explosion rocked the tunnel ahead. The entire tunnel complex shuddered in response and dirt and grit drifted down from the ceiling. A moment later, the shock wave slammed into the car with a thunderous boom and threatened to throw it around. Malone held the wheel tight in both hands. The agent slammed on the brakes and spun the car.

Ryan strained to find the source of the commotion, but it was all tunnel as far as he could see. "What the hell was that?"

"Bad company."

Malone watched for a second in the rear-view mirror then stomped on the gas. The engine roared and the car lunged forward.

"Is that those guys from earlier? Did they follow us here?"

"That's them, but there's no way they followed."

Ryan heard something, some chatter, and he looked over at Malone. For the first time he noticed something in Malone's ear, a transmitter perhaps.

"Tunnel's breached, returning to base." Ryan knew Malone wasn't talking to him. "Negative. Nothing on radar and six is clear for now." More chatter. "On the way."

"Malone?"

"Your trip home may be slightly delayed. We need to get back to the base and protect the council."

"'We'?"

"Yeah, we. That means me, and you're coming with."

The base, as Malone called it, was just ahead, but the door that led inside and to the long hallways suddenly flew off its hinges, a jet of fire right behind it. The blast erupted into the tunnel and superheated air whooshed by.

Malone turned the wheel hard in response and the car came to a screeching stop broadside to where the door had been. The idling engine filled the momentary silence with its quiet rumble.

"Come in." Pause. "This is Malone." Another pause. "Does anyone read me?" Malone looked to the dash and pressed a button on what looked like a standard car radio. The speakers chirped in response.

"Zeta has been breached. Repeat, Zeta has been breached. All units respond." Silence.

Malone looked around hurriedly. "Shit. This is bad." Perspiration formed at his temples.

"Malone? What's going on?"

Malone looked to the door, down the tunnel, then to

Ryan. "I think we're knee-deep in shit, kid."

Malone stomped on the accelerator again and took off down the tunnel, but he cranked the wheel hard and turned down a tunnel Ryan hadn't noticed the other times they passed by. The plain concrete walls seemed to form a singular wall, and he realized it must have been intentional for just that reason.

Lights passed by overhead in a blur as Malone navigated the slightly curvy tunnel then stomped on the brakes as they neared a wall. He feathered both gas and brake and drifted them around a corner and into a large parking lot where maybe a dozen black SUVs and two other cars sat, including the damaged one they had driven there. Malone drove right by them and headed straight for the far wall.

"You're running away? You're just going to leave all those people inside? And what about in the tunnel? Why don't you just go wave your arms around and kick these guys' asses?"

"Kid, you don't get how it works. Those up front are toast. If they're hitting our base, it's not the bush leaguers. And those inside? If they're smart, they'll get away. There's rat tunnels in there I don't even know about."

"But you're just leaving them."

"Yeah, and I'm a super soldier so I should go destroy them. That stunt at the library drained me. I've got nothin' left, but I've got my wits. We'll get out, don't worry. Besides, those guys didn't make it to the council for their looks or personality. They were all agents at one time or another, too."

Ryan tried not to worry, but another explosion shook the underground complex and he found it difficult to be so confident.

Malone stopped in front of the far wall and hit a couple of switches in the center console. Part of the wall gave way in front of them and slid back and to the side. It was dark inside, but Malone pulled forward when he could fit the car through. He hit the switches again and watched the rear-view mirror intently.

"Shit!"

He suddenly mashed the gas and they took off in the tunnel. The only light to be found was from the car, and Malone was going entirely too fast for Ryan to feel safe given the narrow passageway.

"Hit that blue button, kid."

Ryan looked at the console but didn't see any blue buttons.

"No, inside the console at my elbow. Hurry! I have to pay attention here."

Ryan opened the middle console and looked around. Inside, way at the bottom, there was a singular button, and in the darkness, it could have been blue. Ryan hit it anyway. He heard a loud pop and metallic rattle, then a few seconds later, another pop and rattle.

"What'd that do?"

"Spike strips. It'll slow them down. Maybe."

"They're following us?" Ryan looked back, though he couldn't see anything beyond the car.

"They saw us go in here."

Malone reached down to the center console again and hit a couple of switches without ever taking his eyes away from the tunnel ahead.

"Hurry." Malone whispered it as he hit the switches a second time.

The pattern of the headlights changed ahead and

Ryan realized that it was because they were nearing another wall. Another secret door was opening, however, Malone wasn't slowing for it. Ryan gripped the seat bolster hard and pushed with his feet against the floorboard as though he might stop the car before the impending impact.

The door slowly opened, sliding into the wall from right to left, and they raced toward it until they were finally right on it. Malone moved the car as far to the right as he could. The door still wasn't open all of the way and they were on it. The car protested with a screech of metal and a shower of sparks as they just squeezed through, but they emerged on the other side.

Malone turned the wheel and the car kicked up dirt in seemingly every direction. The agent dropped a hand to the center console and hit the switches again and kept them moving.

Ryan, his heart jackhammering against his chest, looked over and realized that Malone's side mirror was missing. They were in the desert somewhere and Malone drove on until they jumped onto a little road that cut through the landscape. They drove for some time in silence. Ryan's heart gradually slowed as it became clear they lost whoever was following them.

What a day. Ryan pulled his phone out, but he still had no service. The clock on the phone said it was now evening; he hadn't realized how much time had passed.

"Your trip home has to wait. They'll be out there looking for us and they know our cars."

Ryan looked over at Malone then put his phone away.

"So your base. What happens now?"

"It's gone. We have a leak. I tried to warn them, but

no one listened to me."

"A spy?"

"Something like that."

Ryan felt a sudden buzzing in his head, and sound, as if he were underwater, filled his ears. He thought he was drowning as the sound of the water became so pervasive around him while his head continued to buzz, but he realized he could still breathe. Even as he began to calm from the realization, pain, sudden and harsh, burrowed into his temples. He couldn't hold back a scream. Images raced through his head while the pain stabbed at him and water flowed all around him. People moved in a blur and their voices came through the buzzing and water. The numerous voices were all run together and sounded as if they came from old records played at the wrong speed, some slow, some fast.

Then just as suddenly as it hit him, it passed. It was as though nothing had happened, except that his heart slammed against his chest and his pulse pounded in his ears.

"What happened? You okay, kid?"

"I... I don't know." His voice sounded weird to him but he felt normal, aside from his heart and pulse. "I think I had a seizure."

"Seizure? Describe it."

"My head started to buzz and it felt like I was drowning. Water was moving all around me and in my ears. I saw people and heard voices. It was crazy, like throwing so much paint against the wall it's nothing more than a blur of color and sound."

"Focus on the people."

"How? It's—"

"Just do it. Focus on one of them."

Ryan put his head in his hands. Malone was crazy. Didn't he understand there was nothing to focus on? It was just pictures, sounds, nothing specific. A hallucination brought upon by the day's events.

Ryan looked up and his eyes blinked rapidly though he wasn't looking ahead. The vision came again, fast and overwhelming, but he forced himself to pay attention and it slowed. Water flowed around him while his head buzzed again, but this time he focused on the vision.

At first he didn't understand anything, perhaps it was too slow, then he saw people, four of them, and they were gathered in a small room. A single light bulb hung from the ceiling, as though a utility closet, and two men spoke quietly. Ryan stared hard; he recognized one of the men from those he had met at the base today, but the rest had their backs to him. One of the men with his back to him seemed familiar. They continued to speak and seemed to be making an arrangement. The one he could see asked when he could expect the arrival, and the other answered just after dusk.

They shook hands and two of the men who were standing there—guards perhaps—opened the door and walked out. The two men in conversation exchanged a few more words, and then the one with his back to him turned and Ryan could see his face. It was the same officer he'd seen in the library, the officer he'd been asked to describe.

Ryan snapped out of the vision and looked at Malone. Malone was staring at him intently.

"What'd you see?"

"I... I think I know who your traitor is."

CHAPTER 3

All was silent in the car and Ryan realized he was waiting for Malone to bring the car to come to a stop. Slowly turning his head, he found Malone staring at him expectantly. Beyond Malone, the desert they were driving through sat perfectly still. He hadn't realized how dazed he was.

"Tell me what you saw, kid. Take your time. This is important."

Ryan nodded and took a deep breath. "Four guys, all meeting in a small room, but only two spoke. I think the other two were guards. One of them was the guy you mentioned, the one at the library."

"I'm following you." Malone had the look of one who had just taken a bite of something new and wasn't sure if it was a good experience.

"The other guy, I don't know him, but I saw him. Today. He was at the table in your base."

Malone's left eye twitched. "Which one?" His voice was strained.

"The one at the far end of the table, to the left."

"Describe him."

"Those old guys all looked the same. Old, pointy noses and glasses." Something came to him, and he snickered despite Malone's glare. "The one with the nasty sore on his forehead."

Malone slammed a hand against the steering wheel and stared straight ahead for several seconds before meeting Ryan's eyes again.

"You're sure about this? What'd they say?"

"I only heard part of the conversation, but they were talking about when to expect 'a package.' Sore Guy asked and the other guy told him just after dusk."

"The visions are seldom wrong." He appeared to be speaking to himself more than to Ryan. "They don't judge, they don't lead, they don't instruct. They just show what happened or may happen. But shit, this can't be."

Malone turned back to the windshield, his eyes focused somewhere far beyond. He clenched his jaw tight.

"What was that, Malone? I don't know what the hell happened, let alone know what any of this means." Ryan rubbed his face with his hands and looked out of the window as though the desert might contain answers.

"You just had a vision, kid. A bad one for me and the agency. I've suspected Fisher for some time now, but I never had any proof."

"I wouldn't call some drug-like trance proof."

Malone looked over and put the car in gear. "Kid, you have no idea, but I think you're going to learn."

"What's that supposed to mean?"

"There's a reason I didn't let you run away, kid. I haven't been entirely honest with you. My name, what we're doing, I didn't lie about that, but I lied about why I took you. Now you know why."

Ryan tried to speak but stuttered out something unintelligible. This was too much. First, Malone threw cars with, what, his mind? Then Malone stopped a bomb blast with his hands. And now Ryan had a vision. He was wholly unprepared to handle this sudden change in the expectations of reality. He shook his head and, for the moment, focused on what Malone had said, that Malone knew this would happen.

"How did you know I was going to have a vision?" It came out harsher than he meant, but he didn't care right then.

"You remember the guy who called you the 'lost puppy?' You're a latent."

"Latent what? What is this? Some sort of Star Wars crap?"

"Always with the Star Wars. It's something else, but we have a more immediate problem. Hope you're strapped in."

Malone stomped down with his right foot and the car jumped forward. Ryan looked in the mirror. A black car in the distance approached from the secret exit they had used. Something flicked in and out of the mirror and Ryan turned to see out of the rear windshield. He had to duck a little, but a black helicopter was closing on them quickly.

"Uh, helicopter?"

"Got it, kid. You might have to deal with it, though."

"Me? I don't know how to throw cars with my..." Ryan waved his hands around.

"I have a more conventional plan if it comes to it."

They tore through the canyon roads and blind corners as though it was a race, and perhaps it was. It wasn't that Ryan had anything against spirited driving, but what Malone was doing was purely suicidal. Another car, or worse, a semi could be coming around the next corner, but Malone didn't seem to care or even think about it the way he charged ahead.

The sun vanished behind the mountains, heralding the beginning of sunset. As they rounded one corner, the freeway on-ramp, still a couple of miles ahead, came momentarily into view. Several blind corners still awaited them, but after that they could jump right on the freeway. Malone had already proven he could cover ground quickly on that.

Dirt and gravel suddenly shot up in tiny bursts around the car. A distinctive pinging sound accompanied each burst and Ryan didn't have to turn around to know that someone was shooting at them.

"You play video games, kid?"

"What? Yeah, why?"

Malone pressed a couple of buttons and the glove box door dropped open. Instead of the usual storage area, a small joystick and a lever were mounted to the inside of the door, while an LCD screen filled the rest of the space. A loud pop sounded from behind them. Ryan turned around and found he couldn't see out of the back because the trunk was open, only it wasn't flapping with the airflow over the car. Though he could barely see it through the thin opening the trunk's cutout provided against the back of the windshield, a machine gun sat mounted on a short pole in the trunk.

"No way."

"Shoot, kid. We won't make it to the freeway like this."

Ryan looked back to the glove box and swallowed. The stick was plain enough, the sort you'd see for a flying game, only basic and with just a couple of buttons.

"He's at seven o'clock."

Ryan grabbed the stick and pushed gently. The view in the screen changed, only it whizzed by. He took a deep breath and tried again, this time using much finer movements, and he found the helicopter, only he lost it as it banked sharply. He pulled on the lever and the camera zoomed out, but another round of pings sounded from the road around them. It lasted for several seconds and Malone braked hard then accelerated and drove all over the width of the road. The shots kept pinging down and missed, but the last few bullets ripped through the back of the car.

Ryan realized he had shut his eyes as he waited for the assault to pass. The pings stopped and it didn't seem like anything was going to ricochet and hit him in the head.

"Ignore it, kid. Wipe my ass! Hurry!"

Ryan focused on the screen again and Malone told him where the chopper was now. It only took a couple of seconds to find the chopper. Ryan took a deep breath and held it. He pulled the trigger.

A succession of loud bangs, something that would scare Rambo, erupted from the trunk of the car. Ryan jerked the stick back in response to the gun's report and watched as the chopper dropped out of sight all the while the gun roared. Whatever was in the trunk, it meant business. Ryan quickly recovered, stopped firing, and pushed the stick forward and found the chopper again. He squeezed the trigger again, this time braced for the report of the machine gun. The gun announced each round in rapid succession and Ryan zoomed in. It was difficult to tell with darkness about to fall, but he thought one of the rounds might have actually hit the helicopter.

The chopper banked hard and Ryan zoomed out and managed to keep it on the screen, but not in the reticule. However, the helicopter pulled back and Ryan shot another burst at it, just to be sure.

"Good shooting. We're almost there."

Malone steered the car onto the on-ramp and joined the freeway. He poured on the speed while he weaved in and out of traffic. Several drivers pulled over before he ever got close, but still the helicopter followed from a distance.

"What about the car on the ground?"

"We're doing 160 now. We've lost the car, and at this speed, we'll lose the chopper. Those aren't built for speed."

Ryan looked out the side window and realized that everything was a blur. Holy shit they were moving fast.

"Uh, Malone? The gun in the trunk?"

"Right." Malone hit a couple of buttons again and the glove box folded itself up and the trunk slammed down with a shudder.

Air whistled through bullet holes in the car's roof near the back, otherwise everything was quiet for several minutes.

His heart was again running a race and Ryan wondered if there was a limit to how many times a day one could go through life-threatening situations. Surely, four times in a day was pressing one's luck.

Despite the relative quiet, Ryan kept looking back to make sure they were getting away and found that the chopper was getting harder to see as night moved forward. Soon, he wouldn't be able to see it because it had no lights on.

"What's the plan, now?"

"We don't have a choice but to go back to San Vicente and figure it out from there."

"Looks like the helicopter is breaking off."

"He's trying to beat us to the off-ramp. He might."

Malone pushed his foot down in response and the car sped up even more. Traffic ahead was light and they were making excellent time, but their path involved turns where the chopper could fly straight to intercept.

They passed cars at an alarming rate of speed and Ryan snickered as he thought of what the CHP would think if they drove by one now, then he remembered they were likely dealing with other problems.

The thought of those other problems prompted him to consider the city and its potential safety. They were in a race to get to the off-ramp, assuming it wasn't already occupied, but somewhere beyond that off-ramp was a veritable nest of hiding places.

Ryan looked to the southeast and noticed for the first time that the city was darker than usual. Though San Vicente was not a major metropolis and there were no skyscrapers to light the city's skyline, the usual array of lights should be seen for miles. Even the lights from houses and street lamps should have been clearly visible against the backdrop of sky. Instead, Ryan could count the number of lights he could see with his fingers, and they looked small and insignificant, never mind overwhelmed, in the vast darkness. It was as though the sky had swallowed all the light and left only pieces, like crumbs, to twinkle in the darkness. If civilization had crumbled and only scattered remnants remained, this is what he expected it would look like from a distance. The dark sight of San Vicente, his town, the only place he ever really called home, was unnerving. In fact, it was downright creepy. He gave an involuntary shudder and pulled his eyes away.

"What's going on? Why's everything so dark?"

"They moved forward with their plans. This is their small-scale test. Cell towers, down. Power grid, down. Telephone, cable, gas, everything down. It's like the wild west, only with machine guns."

"But there's still some buildings with power."

"Generators, unless they messed up." Malone paused. "I'm guessing they didn't."

Ryan imagined what might be happening in the dark town. Without power and communications, they must have been wondering if it was anything from a major infrastructure failure to World War III. What must his friends and family be thinking? Had they heard about the explosion at the library? Were they safe at their place of employment or at home?

Ryan pulled out his phone and it still insisted there was no service. He considered turning it off to conserve what remained of the battery, but there was no guarantee when it'd even work again, so did it really matter?

"There's a charger in the center console. Get what you can while you can."

Ryan shrugged. "Thanks."

The charger Malone spoke of was a match to his own phone. Ryan stared at it suspiciously before he plugged the phone in. Funny how Malone had the right charger when some manufacturers still insisted on using a proprietary plug.

As if responding to his thought, Malone pulled an identical phone out of his jacket and showed Ryan.

"Happy coincidence."

Ryan snickered and wondered if it was government issued.

A traffic jam ahead forced Malone to slow the car. A line of cars in the rightmost lane sat stationary while the rest of traffic trickled by them. A single off-ramp connected the freeway to a two-lane highway that led into town, so perhaps there was congestion with people trying to merge onto the surface streets, especially if there was no power on said streets for traffic lights.

Malone slowed even more as they approached the line of cars then veered right into the emergency lane. Several cars honked but he ignored them and kept going. A sign informed motorists the off-ramp to San Vicente was a mile ahead. The seconds continued to tick past as Malone slowly drove forward.

They had covered most of the distance to town when Malone hit the steering wheel with his palm. "Shit. Take the wheel."

"What?"

"Take it. I need to clear a path."

Ryan grabbed the wheel and did his best to steer from the passenger seat with the harness holding him in tight, but the perspective was confusing. He tried to hold the car straight, but it took on a noticeable list that he had to keep correcting.

Malone, meanwhile, disconnected his harness and rolled down his window. He turned cruise control on and leaned out of the window.

"Hold it for a few more seconds."

Ryan held the wheel and noticed what Malone must have already seen: a roadblock of police cars ahead. Lights rotated and flashed, reds and blues and yellows and oranges. He tried to focus on where the car was going, but he kept looking at the vehicles, expecting to see someone holding a weapon somewhere.

"Hey!"

Ryan looked over and realized the car was drifting dangerously close to the traffic on their left. He straightened the car and waited. Motion in his peripheral vision demanded his attention. Malone pulled his hands back and then shoved them forward.

Almost on top of the roadblock now, two police cars suddenly jumped back, as though a giant wedge had slammed into them. They jerked back, hard, and with brakes that squealed in protest. The cars only moved as though someone had put them in reverse and stepped on the gas then stepped on the brake a second later, but the distance between them looked just wide enough for Malone to squeeze their car through.

Malone climbed back into the car and grabbed the wheel. He accelerated and aimed for the gap.

Men appeared from behind vehicles and raised guns and opened fire. Bullets slammed into the car and flew by. Ryan ducked as much as he could with the harness still holding him, but he damn near screamed every time he saw another dent appear in the windshield. Whatever it was made of, it was more than bullet-resistant like most "bullet-proof" glass.

The car rattled as bullets pelted it and they were right on the broken roadblock. The police officers ducking behind the cars jumped away at the last moment. Metal screeched as the sedan punched through the break in the line. Malone's sedan charged through like a professional running back breaking through a defensive line of high schoolers. The impact hardly slowed them, not even enough to set off the airbags — assuming the modified car even had them — and they shot down the off-ramp.

Malone put his arm down—Ryan hadn't even realized it was up—and bullets dropped onto the dash with a loud jingle. The glass hadn't stopped the bullets after all. Those weren't dents in the windshield; they were holes. Malone was pale and sweat rolled down his temple and forehead.

"Malone, you okay?"

"I'll make it." His voice was quieter than it had been and he stared forward intently.

The drive along the connecting road was quiet, though once they hit the city they had to go around another roadblock, but this one wasn't prepared for traffic coming from the other direction and there was room to dodge by on the side.

They plunged into town and found that traffic was light. Along the way was the occasional police roadblock with a line of cars trying to get through, but these were mostly at major thoroughfares. They managed to turn down enough side streets and alleys that they emerged in a neighborhood Ryan was unfamiliar with.

Though sweat trickled down the side of Malone's face and he was shaking slightly, he managed to guide them to a nondescript house in a nondescript neighborhood that was completely dark except for occasional pinheads of light in windows. A few people stood outside talking to one another, but it looked like most were either inside or not home.

Malone pulled into the driveway and pointed at the garage door a couple of times until it clicked with Ryan. Malone passed him a key and Ryan hurried to undo his harness then hopped out and opened the garage door. It was an old wooden thing with a padlock across an old-fashioned lock that had rusted over some time ago.

Ryan opened the door and the headlights illuminated the inside of the garage. Aside from a refrigerator near the back wall and a couple piles of tools, the garage was empty. Malone drove the car in and killed the engine. Ryan pulled the door down to the accompaniment of squeaky springs. Though the car was off, the headlights continued to provide light. One of those fancy things where the lights turn off automatically, he mused.

Now that they appeared to be safe and indoors, Ryan turned his attention to the refrigerator. He opened the fridge and cold air rolled over his skin. A few bottles of beer near the back caught his eyes, and as a bonus, they were still cold. He grabbed a couple and waited for Malone to get out of the car. After what felt like an hour, Malone emerged from the car and ambled around the front of it. Ryan offered him a beer, but Malone shook his head.

"Don't drink."

"Me either, but it seems appropriate."

Malone was shaking his head before Ryan finished. "No, you don't understand. You can't drink. You're no longer latent."

"Because of whatever this is," Ryan pointed vaguely at his head with a bottle, "I can't drink?"

Malone nodded.

Ryan shrugged, tucked one bottle under his arm and popped the cap off the other. "After my day, I don't think one will be enough." He took a long drink—how long had it been since he'd eaten or had anything to drink?—and didn't stop until he'd emptied half the bottle.

"Suit yourself." Malone walked past him and to the door that looked to lead into the house.

Ryan stood there, aglow in the beer's aftertaste, and noticed the door had a number pad for the lock. Malone punched a few buttons then walked in the dark house. The headlights on the car cut out and Ryan decided he should probably go inside as well. Malone apparently wasn't waiting because Ryan heard the door close and he looked into absolute blackness.

Ryan remembered his phone and put the unopened bottle of beer into a pocket before he stumbled his way over to the car, free hand leading, and eventually found the passenger door. He opened it, grabbed his phone, and followed Malone inside with his makeshift flashlight.

The door opened right into the family room where he could see the front door to his almost immediate right and one that looked like it went to the backyard to his left. A hallway in front of him led deeper into the house and he opted for that route, taking the occasional drink along the way.

The house was small with a few bedrooms off the hallway and an apartment-sized kitchen at the end. Malone was there, fridge open, and in the middle of drinking straight from a carton of orange juice.

"Classy, man. I might have wanted some."

Malone flipped him the bird and kept drinking until he emptied the carton. "No worries, now."

Ryan laughed and took another drink of his beer. "So is this your place or what?"

"Hideout. Agents use it when they need to dodge someone or perform interviews."

"Interviews?"

"Two and two, kid."

Ryan nodded and took another drink. "So is there food in the fridge?"

"Knock yourself out." Malone walked off, something in hand, and Ryan rummaged through the refrigerator until he found something that looked edible, an unidentified sandwich in a plastic bag.

Malone sat at a table in the family room when Ryan came back. The agent leaned back in the chair that faced the window, his jacket draped over the back of the chair. The curtains were open and starlight seemed to outline Malone with a light glow. In the moonlight, it was obvious just how exhausted Malone was. Hair stuck to his forehead and bags pulled at his eyes.

Ryan pulled a chair out, set the bottles down. He unwrapped the sandwich and took a bite. It was awful. Stale and tuna, two things he hated. He put it down on the table and went back to the beer instead.

"So what's your story, Malone? How old are you? How'd you get into this?"

"You're pretty nosy, you know that?"

"So old you don't remember?" Ryan smiled.

"I'm old enough to be your dad, kid, but this isn't Star Wars." Malone smiled, but only briefly. "What's your deal, kid? Why are you so cavalier about this? Most people can't handle being in these situations, never mind multiple times in a day. And then there's the whole 'throwing cars' and 'vision' thing." Malone made air quotes using an index finger.

Ryan shrugged and took a drink, but he couldn't suppress a shudder. "You have to deal. I don't know what the hell is going on or what's going to happen, but you've been on the level with me, so I'm just pushing forward. I'm trying not to think of all the heinous shit that's happened today and trying not to worry about my family. I know it's bound to catch up, but right now, do I even have a choice? I mean, if I don't, I'll—" He could feel what semblance of control remained on the verge of crumbling and he took a deep breath.

"That's good, kid. It'll save your life someday. You have to focus on what's happening now and just do what it takes. I wasn't always that way."

Composed again, Ryan said, "I find that hard to believe."

"I was a pushover when I was younger. I was indecisive." Malone paused and studied Ryan for a breath. "I was on a mission with another cleaner and he was the same way. We had to split up, and what I was doing was easy enough, but he had to make some snap judgments and didn't. He panicked, second-guessed himself, and got his team killed. I promised myself I wasn't going to be like him and I'd do whatever it took to make sure of that. It took time, but I haven't been him and won't be him."

"How old were you?"

Malone looked over at Ryan then back out of the window. "Younger than you are now, I'd wager. I joined when I was eighteen. A little like joining the army, I imagine."

"The army drives tanks; they don't throw them."

"Indeed."

Silence and darkness filled the room. Ryan didn't even want to think about it, but he needed answers to some questions.

"What's going on, Malone? On the level, what are you and what am I?"

"On the level?" Malone sighed and said something under his breath. "I called you a latent before. You were, but now you're innate. That means the power manifested in you."

"You say it like it's matter-of-fact."

"Isn't it? You're the one who had the vision."

"But what is this? Why's it happening?"

"I'm not sure I can explain that." Ryan glared at him but Malone shrugged. "I don't have the whole story kid, just the pieces I've been told. It goes back to some experiments in World War II. Some scientists messed with people and chemicals and things and bam, it's like the comic books."

"I don't buy it. There'd be more of it out there. There'd be videos on the web."

"Let me finish, Mr. I-Know-Fucking-Everything."

Ryan looked down and took another drink.

"The suits funding the research predicted exactly that, so they canned funding. Project Silver Bullet was cancelled."

"But?"

Malone smiled. "But someone else decided to continue the research. He claimed to be doing some bullshit research, something about raising cows with more meat, but he kept most of the original scientists on board and continued the research.

"They made progress and even managed to determine when the ability would be passed on and when it wouldn't. I don't know how they figured that out, but someone high up knows. That's why I was told to find you. It was serendipity that saved your ass today because we had no idea this town was going to get an enema."

"So why wait until now?"

Malone shrugged and leaned back. "I'm just a grunt. I don't know why you didn't hit the radar sooner."

Ryan took another drink and set the bottle down slowly. If the powers were somehow related to top secret government testing, how did he end up with them? He wasn't sure he was ready to know just yet and changed directions.

"So are you going to teach me how to do what you do? Throw cars, I mean."

Malone looked at his wristwatch then stood and walked to the front door. He opened it and turned to Ryan.

"Maybe, but I don't think you're ready to learn just yet."

Ryan opened his mouth to ask why not, but an unsettling feeling struck his stomach. It quickly grew, a bubbling sensation like someone was brewing a witch's concoction in his stomach. The sudden nausea blindsided him and he understood why Malone opened the door. Ryan knocked over his chair in his haste to get outside and he just made it to the threshold when his stomach ejected its scant contents.

The pain and suddenness doubled him over and he dropped his beer to the ground where it clattered and rolled away, all the while Ryan vomited.

Once the vomiting stopped, Ryan sat with his hands on his knees and alternated between coughing and sucking in air for a while. The smell of vomit burned in his nose and his throat felt as though he swallowed steel wool. He finally stood, glared at Malone, and went inside and lay down on the couch.

"I did warn you."

Ryan swore at Malone but it came out as an unintelligible mumble. He put his hands to his forehead. Everything hurt.

Malone tsked. "It's poison. You can't have it. That's your body's way of fighting it off."

"It can't wait for the liver like everything else?"

"Nope. It interferes with things."

"Fuck me."

CHAPTER 4

Morning was a pleasant change from the last thing Ryan could remember. He didn't specifically remember falling asleep on a couch in a strange house, let alone with a blanket, but it was still nicer than the feeling of intense pain and nausea he last remembered.

He threw the blanket off and tested sitting up. Everything seemed in normal, functional order, only there was an odd sort of pulse at the edges of his peripheral vision. It was a subtle thing, but it was as though some infinitesimal light pulsed at either side. An odd sort of clarity accompanied it, a strange knowledge that he somehow knew things he shouldn't know, but he couldn't place what they were, let alone even begin to fathom how he might know them.

Ryan stood and found Malone in the same chair he was in the previous night. The sight of the agent — his jacket was still off and his sleeves rolled up as he slumped in the chair — was a reminder of the previous day's test of atrocities and sanity. The memories came back to him and threatened to knock him down, but Ryan took a long, slow breath and felt his heartbeat calm. He still wasn't dealing with everything that'd happened, but for now he could compartmentalize and function. That would have to be enough.

Ryan walked quietly down the hallway and looked into each room until he found the master with the bathroom.

He stopped at the kitchen on his way back and grabbed a small bottle of orange juice that had been hidden in the back of the refrigerator and wandered back into the family room.

"Feeling better this morning?"

Ryan nodded. "Much, but something's not right."

"No, it's right. You just have to get used to it."

"What?" Ryan remembered his vision from the previous day. The impostor cop with the dark hair came back to him, and even more, the man with the sore on his head infiltrated his thoughts. Even seeing Malone didn't make it all seem real, but that memory, vivid and clear, was enough to bring him back to reality. Something strange had happened to him, and now he had some kind of power. It wasn't a weird dream. He could feel his pulse quicken again, but he remained in control.

"Weird shit happened yesterday, friends were murdered, and I had a vision of your traitor. This is happening?"

"Sorry to say, but it is."

Ryan shook his head and looked away.

"I don't mean to be that way, kid. This isn't easy on me, either, but I know you must be really confused and hurting right now."

"You're telling me."

"For what it's worth, I'm sorry. I can't change what happened. I know I'm a little blunt, but I don't know any other way." Malone paused until Ryan looked back at him. "It'll be okay. You have my word."

Ryan nodded. "Thanks." He rubbed his eyes and forced himself to focus on the present. "So, uh, what now?" Ryan took a seat at the table and started on the orange juice. It seemed to settle him down a little.

"We wait. I'm trying to contact my people, but it's

difficult. We have to use HAM radio and anyone can listen to it, so it makes getting a message across tricky."

"Wind talkers?"

"Pretty much."

The morning passed quietly, except for Malone occasionally trying to contact someone on the big handheld radio he had. Every time he ventured to leave the radio on for a few minutes, the room would fill with chatter, but nothing he seemed to recognize as his compatriots. Malone turned off the radio after one such moment of listening and announced he was going outside to stretch and get fresh air.

The stale air in the house made it obvious that visitors weren't a common occurrence. Power had yet to be restored, and when Ryan turned on his phone a couple of times, he still had no signal. Even the wired telephone in the house provided nothing but dead air. All lines of communication truly were cut.

To further complicate matters in what was already close to a mind-breaking twenty-four hours, a burgeoning conscience was insisting itself upon Ryan. At least that's what he called it.

Ryan didn't quite understand what it was, but to call it an extension of his senses sounded close. It was almost as though he could see or feel things around him, yet when he looked at them or held them in his hand, everything felt normal. But there seemed to be something extra to them when he looked with his peripheral vision, almost like an aura that his mind equated with an inherent power to the item. Most things had little, but electronic devices had a more noticeable aura or field about them than, say, the couch or the table.

Malone came in and closed the front door and Ryan turned his head sharply away and gasped. A blinding glow surrounded Malone.

"What the hell is wrong with you?"

"Excuse me?"

Ryan kept his face turned away. "Why are you surrounded by light?"

"You're acquiring your sight. It takes some time to acclimate."

"'Sight'?" Ryan made air quotations.

"No, just sight. It's like any other sense."

"Well why are you so damn blinding?"

"There's a little juice running through me."

Ryan turned his head quickly and stared at Malone head on. It was far more bearable this way, though the edges of his sight were still illuminated by Malone's aura. Malone flashed him a sly smile then he looked at the table and picked up the radio. He turned it around in his hands then threw it at Ryan.

Ryan put up his hands instinctively and thought to block the radio. He heard it hit something, something squishy it seemed, and it bumped into his hands and fell into his lap. He looked up and knew that Malone had thrown the radio hard, but there it was, sitting in his lap like Malone had gently tossed it.

"What?"

"Baby steps, kid."

Ryan picked up the radio and looked at it. Rugged as could be, the radio was a couple pounds of metal and thick plastic. Ryan got up and placed it on the table.

Malone tapped the radio. "You extended your will to block it, though it was somewhat flaccid."

"Is that a dig?"

"Not at all. You were a latent until yesterday. Not everyone can throw a car, and not everyone can see things they weren't party to."

"So it is a little like Star Wars. You never saw Luke throw lightning around or choke anyone."

Malone sighed. "If you want to think of it like that, go ahead. We just have different talents, that's all."

"And mine is in seeing?"

"Perhaps. You'll have to wait and see."

Ryan glared at Malone but Malone showed no expression. Instead, he picked up the radio and tried to contact his superiors again.

Ryan wandered around the family room and pulled the drapes aside. The backyard was nothing but dirt, dirt, and more dirt. Presumably, whoever purchased the house originally got it that way from the builder and never bothered to do anything with the yard because who cares what the backyard of an interrogation house looks like? The thought was darkly comforting because it meant that at least one government agency wasn't spending needlessly, even if the house itself could be argued against.

A thump sounded behind him, the radio being placed on the table.

"Nothing," Malone said. "We can't wait here all day. We'll run out of food and water if nothing else. We'll move once night falls if I don't hear anything."

Ryan nodded and continued to look out to the backyard. Something had been bothering him since Malone had explained what was happening.

"Malone, do you think it stops with Fisher? What if it keeps going?"

"What're you saying, kid?"

"I'm not, but do you think he's the only leak in the ship?"

Silence for several breaths. "I've not seen or heard anything that makes me think otherwise, but it's possible."

"How'd you know it was him?"

"Little things, really. Looks he'd throw at people, the way he'd be speaking when he thought no one was listening, his body language. He just looked and sounded guilty."

"You didn't see any documents or witness any covert meetings?"

"I used my gut."

"So it's possible there's other things going on you don't know about."

"I don't like your tone."

Ryan left the window and regarded Malone. The agent squinted his eyes and stared back at Ryan.

"Who is this guy you keep referring to but won't name?" Ryan said. "The one who killed my friends."

Malone tapped his index finger on the table. "I'm telling you a hell of a lot more than I should. I could be in serious trouble for revealing even half of what I've already told you."

"Humor me."

Malone tapped again. "Fine. His name is James Sikes and he's a former cleaner. He left the agency years ago to do his own thing, only we had no idea his own thing was going to involve forming a terrorist cell."

"You didn't watch this guy after he left?"

"Of course we did! Who are you to question what we did or didn't do?"

Ryan held his hands up defensively. "I'm just asking. So how many people did he bring together? Hundreds? Thousands?"

Malone took a deep breath. "We don't know. He has fingers in damn near everywhere. Fire, police, military. I don't know how he did it, either. I know he started with the unions, but from there?"

"Was he your apprentice? You seem to have a connection to him past being a coworker."

"No. He was the guy I didn't want to be, the one who let his team get killed." A pause. "So what are you suggesting? Some big conspiracy theory?"

"I don't know. I'm just wondering. I don't see how this one guy could get his fingers in so many places without help. Sure, he made contacts in whatever you're in, but you want me to believe that he did it alone? No way. If what you said is true, if this guy is planning to bring this country down and institute his own rule, that takes a lot more resources than one guy has, even if he has Bill Gates's money.

"Think about it, who's better set up to take over the government than the shadow government? Sikes isn't working for himself or some gigantic, renegade faction. They're not the revolutionaries; you are. You're all being played."

"That's straight out of Valkyrie." Malone shook his head and walked off.

Ryan could practically imagine the man's thoughts. Malone mumbled something as he walked down the hall that Ryan couldn't make out.

"What was that?"

"I didn't say anything." Malone's voice came from down the hallway.

Ryan shook his head to clear his thoughts and sat on the couch. None of it made any sense, and he wasn't sure his conspiracy theory was any more believable than the shit Malone had shoveled his way, but it seemed possible. At least, it seemed possible if one considered it possible to throw cars around with their mind.

For one man to have made so many contacts, and no one to know anything about who they were or how he made them, it just wasn't possible. But one man acting as a face to an entity that already existed to take over in case of complete government meltdown? That sounded a little less unbelievable.

Ryan didn't hear Malone walk back into the room. "What you're suggesting is treachery up the ladder somewhere, maybe all the way up. My gut says you're wrong, but I admit it's possible, however unlikely or vile the thought is. But we have bigger problems than that now, like contacting my superiors and devising a plan to take this town back under control."

"And if you can't reach them?"

"We wing it."

He wanted nothing to do with any of this, but it didn't seem as though he had a choice. Besides, Malone was the only person he knew who could even begin to explain what was happening to him, let alone how to handle it. If he were going to be forced into something, some war that he wanted nothing to do with, he could hope that everyone he knew and loved was safe somewhere away from whatever was happening out there.

The thought brought a vision to mind and Ryan sat back and braced himself, but nothing came of it except for a cloudy picture of something indistinct.

"You have to learn control. You can't just go trying to see and hear and do everything right away. You'll kill yourself."

"I'm not trying to!"

"Then stop doing it."

Ryan threw his hands in the air and slumped on the couch. Maybe Malone wasn't so necessary after all.

Radio chatter broke through the fog of confusion and self-pity and he focused on it. Whoever was speaking was describing some event happening in town. Malone sighed right then and turned the radio off.

"Turn it back on."

"Why? I can't get anyone."

"I want to hear what's happening."

"Riots, chaos, the usual that happens when society devolves."

"I just want to hear someone else's voice for a minute."

"Suit yourself, but just a minute. Batteries don't last forever."

Malone turned the radio back on and the same person was still speaking. Ryan focused on the voice and imagined the speaker as a man in his fifties or sixties. He was clearly disgusted at what he was describing, a riot occurring at an electronics store across the street from him. People were looting the store, running out with TVs, DVDs, video games, stereos, anything they could get their hands on. A police officer drove by, but apparently saw he was outnumbered and left. No one had been by since.

"Hear enough?"

"Just another minute."

Another person chimed in and said the military was seen on the freeway. The National Guard were going to be setting up in town soon because the source of the trouble was apparently construction gone wrong, combined with a massive gas explosion that leveled a good part of the city's center.

"Time's up." Malone turned the radio off.

"The National Guard? Was he serious?"

"If the governor thinks it's a big enough disaster, they can grease wheels and call people in."

"Does Sikes have contacts in the Guard?"

Malone shrugged. "Sounds like we're going to find out."

"This is crazy, Malone. It's barely been twenty-four hours and the military is coming in."

"Valkyrie described martial law in less time than that."

"So, what, these guys are amateurs?"

"Hardly. The Nazis were at war. This isn't officially war. Yet."

"So do we just sit and wait?"

Malone looked annoyed at the question, but also thoughtful. "I'm not sure we can or should. Grab some food and water. We need to do some recon."

Ryan wasn't sure why the change in plans came about, but he was glad to be out of the house. Even though the car was more confining, he was witnessing firsthand what was happening in his town.

They drove out of the neighborhood. A few small groups of people walked along the street, though more peeked out from behind curtains. Most, it seemed, had the courtesy to stay inside and be good citizens. Those who didn't, however, were clearly up to no good.

A flipped car at the end of the street blocked the middle of the road while makeshift roadblocks—trash cans and a severely out-of-place piano—blocked the rest of it. Malone slowed as he came to the end of the block and a group of thugs strode toward the car.

Malone accelerated and one of the men was either brave or stupid and stayed in the road while the rest scattered. The man dove at the last second, but Ryan heard the unmistakable sound of something hitting the car. He looked back and saw the man spin to a stop on the ground. Several of the thugs raised their arms and opened fire with handguns, but the bullets flew harmlessly by.

Ryan turned back to Malone. An impassive look covered the agent's face. "You're nuts, you know that?"

Malone raised an eyebrow. "Am I? I wasn't the one standing in front of four thousand pounds of Kevlar and titanium."

"Where are we going?"

Malone steered the car onto the sidewalk and didn't bother to slow. He went around the piano and rejoined the street.

"We're checking out fortifications at city hall."

"You think they barricaded themselves?"

"That's what I'd do."

"So they take over city hall and then what?"

"Wait for the military to come in and take control of the city."

"You're buying my conspiracy theory now?"

"I'm considering it."

The inside world of the car was quiet—whistling

bullet holes aside—as they drove through town, but similar random acts of violence and mayhem interjected themselves at irregular intervals. Aside from looters and roving gangs, the city was eerily quiet. Traffic lights no longer flashed. No noise, no pollution, nothing came from the buildings. Most major intersections had roadblocks in the shape of police sawhorses and blockades, but there weren't many vehicles around to stop.

"Why aren't there news vans around?"

Malone stared straight ahead. "They can't get in."

"Bullshit. The media always goes where they want."

Malone stopped at an intersection and turned to face Ryan. "This isn't what it looks like to the rest of the world, kid. These aren't amateurs. They know how this works and they know how to get what they want. If what they want is a little bit of privacy before the world comes peeking in, that's what they'll get.

"Besides, this is a small town. You said it yourself, it's Podunk. If this was LA, you bet there'd be no way of stopping them, but a two-bit town? Time is something they can afford, at least for a little while."

Ryan wasn't convinced, but he had to admit that he hadn't seen anything that screamed media, and in those times Malone had the shortwave radio on, he hadn't heard anything about media, be it newspaper or television, being around. The kind of pull required to keep the television media out frightened him and gave him a new perspective on who they were dealing with.

"So how long do they have? They can't hide this from the world forever."

Malone shook his head and started the car off. "Can't say. Maybe the rest of today, maybe tomorrow.

If the National Guard is coming in, that's what I'd be worried about. We don't know whose side they're on."

Ryan returned to looking outside and tried not to think about the implications of the National Guard being under Sikes's control. He already had enough things to worry about, including whatever the hell was happening to him and worrying about his folks, that he didn't want to add this to his list of problems.

They reached city hall a few minutes later, though they approached from the back. The modern buildings, sleek and minimal in styling, appeared unbothered. Ryan strained to see the library, but other buildings blocked it. City hall itself looked intact, as did the other couple of buildings that filled the square. It appeared as though only the library had suffered the fate of a "gas explosion." Ryan realized he wasn't ready to look at the library and deal with the emotions it'd stir up. He quickly looked elsewhere.

Yellow tape and barricades cut off the entire square while a couple of police cars blocked the entrances into the parking lots. The officers weren't anywhere to be seen, but they were likely nearby.

Several large trucks were parked in front of city hall, their backs facing the building's entrance. At first Ryan thought they were all moving trucks, three in total, but one of them had a logo painted on the side that read B&S Disaster Recovery.

"They already have a cleanup crew at city hall? But the building is intact."

Malone said nothing and slowly pulled them closer to the square. They parked on the other side of the street, up a bit from the square and Malone turned the rearview mirror to study the scene behind them.

"Shouldn't they be parked in front of the library? And where's the gas company? If it was a gas explosion, shouldn't they have trucks and guys out here?" Ryan struggled to turn around in his seat to see what was happening behind them, and still Malone said nothing.

"So what is it? What do you see, Malone?"

"I'm not sure. I want to get a closer look."

Malone unbuckled his harness and slipped out of the car before Ryan even had his hand on the buckle release.

Ryan caught up to Malone and they crossed the street together. Malone kept sweeping his head back and forth and occasionally looked behind him. He seemed to be aware of who and what was around at all times.

If something wasn't as it appeared, if perhaps the police or the cleanup crew were really someone else, they could be walking into a bad situation. Though he'd only been around them yesterday, Ryan already had his fill of bombs and guns. He'd prefer to return those things to something he only saw in games and movies. The car was likely the safest place at the moment, but Ryan wanted to know what was happening. He stayed close to Malone.

They stepped onto the sidewalk and made straight for the square. Malone walked right over a line of police tape that had been stretched from one barricade to another while Ryan ducked under it. As Ryan popped up on the other side, someone walked around from the back of one of the nearby police cars. The hair on the back of his neck instantly stood up straight and his back tensed.

"Sir, you're going to need to leave immediately. This area has been sealed off from — "

"I think you'll find I'm allowed in." Malone pulled a badge from his jacket and flashed it at the officer.

The officer stared at the badge then turned to Ryan. "I need to see your credentials, sir."

"He's a specialist on contract that my credentials cover. The rest of my team should be here already." Malone started walking forward. "Can you direct me to them?"

"Sir, I've seen no one else from DHS."

"Then you haven't been looking hard. I'll be speaking to your superiors about this."

The officer stopped walking and instead turned and said something quietly into his radio.

"DHS?" Ryan whispered.

"Go with it, kid."

Malone had the I-belong-here-so-don't-fuck-with-me walk down pat and Ryan stuck by his side. He did his best to emulate the walk. They crossed into the parking lot and the library came into sight off to the side, but Ryan looked away again.

"Hang in there, kid. We're looking for friends here. We'll figure this out."

"You think there's other agents here?"

"It would make sense."

Ryan nodded but said nothing. They walked across a small park of grass and flowers as they approached city hall. Men carrying a variety of things came and went from the building to the trucks.

"Is this a good idea, Malone? I have a bad feeling."

"Are you seeing something?"

"No, but my gut doesn't like it."

"Don't sweat it. You're upset because you're back here. It's natural. I have this."

"I hope so."

They crossed into another parking lot without being noticed. They walked around one of the moving trucks and stopped just short of the back where a man in a Disaster Recovery uniform loaded a computer monitor into the back of the trunk.

He dumped the monitor into the truck and looked up at Ryan and Malone. He was one of the officers that had barged into the break room, but he wasn't the one that Malone's agency was looking for. Ryan remembered that face, and it seemed the man remembered Ryan, though the only clue was a momentary flash of recognition which he quickly hid by wiping sweat off his forehead.

Ryan felt a knot form in his stomach and his hands go cold. This was one of the men responsible for killing his coworkers. He looked around, but no one else was paying attention to them.

The worker took a step toward them. "You know you're not supposed to be here?"

Malone flashed his badge again and the man blew a short sigh.

"I'm looking for my colleagues. Where is your supervisor?"

"Yeah, I think I saw a couple earlier. Sup's inside." The man jerked a thumb behind him in the direction of city hall.

Malone nodded and started forward. He hadn't walked more than a few steps before Ryan whispered to him.

"He's one of the guys who killed my coworkers."

Malone looked back. "You sure?"

"Yes I'm sure. We can't just leave him, Malone. And what about the rest of these guys?"

"You don't look good, kid. You feeling alright?"

"No, I'm not."

A sudden pop smote the air followed by another. Something sliced into Ryan's arm and sharp pain accompanied it. Blood oozed out of what looked like a large, thick cut on his arm, only no one nearby held a knife.

Another pop sounded, followed almost immediately by a splashy sound of something impacting a wall of gelatin. Ryan turned to see a bullet fall to the ground. The man in the cleaning uniform aimed a pistol at him.

In an instant, rage, frustration, disbelief, and pain welled out of Ryan. This was one of the men who destroyed the library, who killed his coworkers. He was one of those who executed his friends one by one, left them to be blown into unidentifiable bits and pieces. He was, quite simply, a murderer who didn't deserve to live.

With no knowledge of what he was doing or even how, Ryan focused all of that negative energy on the man. Every bit of Ryan's being wanted that man to suffer, to feel the pain he felt.

The pistol began to shake in the man's hand and he fired another round, but the round went awry. The shaking started at his hand and went up his arm and to his torso and to the other arm, went down his legs until his entire body shook like a marionette dancing on strings to a drunken master.

Pressure built in his head and Ryan could only hear his pulse raging through his ears. He began to tremble, but still he focused on that asshole in front of him and all of the pain he felt.

Ryan's vision began to take on blackness at the edges and then it began to creep in. The man's head began to shake violently, and just as the blackness became a pinhole he was looking out of, Ryan saw the man's head snap forward and the worker crumbled to the ground. The pinhole closed and Ryan fell.

CHAPTER 5

Ryan didn't remember signing up to use his head as a punching bag, but it sure felt like he did. He opened his eyes for a second then slammed them shut and groaned. The light, though it only hit him briefly, was overwhelming. Even as it tried to come through his lids it was like his own personal sun shining right in front of his eyes.

He groaned again and buried his face in what he assumed was a pillow. Someone nearby was speaking, but he couldn't pick up the words. It sounded like a man's voice, but it definitely wasn't his dad. He didn't have any brothers, so who the hell was it?

As the second slowly passed, the extremity of his pain and disorientation eased. After what must have been five minutes, he felt able enough to pull his head up and look around. He opened one eyelid, slow and shaky, then the other.

The small room was somehow familiar to him, but at the same time, it seemed foreign. Wherever he was, he was definitely not in his room and not in his bed. It was a bedroom, but it wasn't his.

Boring white walls surrounded him on all sides. The bed covers were an unassuming blue and a small dresser occupied the far corner. A battery-powered camping lantern sat on the dresser, the source of the bright light. The strangest thing, however, was that he was fully dressed. He couldn't remember the last time he went to bed in the same clothes he worked in, because they were definitely his work clothes. Only they looked dirty and stained with blood.

Ryan rolled over and almost fell when he placed weight on his left arm. He grunted in pain and looked at the arm that had betrayed his simple request. It was wrapped in a long cloth bandage, and at least in one spot, the bandage looked a little pink, as though blood had soaked through. He untied the cloth and found the strangest looking wound, like something had ripped right across his flesh and scored an ugly cut, only it was too thick to have been made by a blade. He wrapped the wound again. Ryan grabbed the lantern and wandered to the door.

Now that he wasn't focused on his surroundings or the odd pain in his arm, he heard the voice again. It was intermittent and came from his left. He looked down the hallway to the right first—a tiny kitchen—then looked left. A man wearing a dirty white button-down shirt and dark slacks sat at a table with what looked like a giant walkie-talkie in his hand. Another lantern sat on the table throwing out bright light. The man seemed familiar.

Ryan stared at the man but couldn't place him. The sight of the unknown man didn't elicit any fear or dread within him, just curiosity. Obviously, this was the man's house, but why was Ryan here? He wasn't a prisoner, or else the man was so confident that Ryan was left unhindered out of sheer arrogance and self-assurance.

Two more doorways opened into other rooms, and Ryan peeked into them as he started down the hallway toward the man. One room was small and plain, similar to the one he had been in, while the other was larger and looked familiar. It was just as stark as the other rooms, only slightly larger and with an attached bathroom.

He made it to the front room without the man noticing, apparently, because he never looked up from the table as he stared out of the window in front of him. Ryan looked to his right and saw a couch with a tangled blanket on it. Both looked vaguely familiar.

"Excuse me, but why am I here?"

The man looked up as though he didn't hear Ryan and he put the radio down.

"It's about time you woke up."

"Did you bring me here?"

"You don't remember? That was hours ago."

"No." Ryan looked out of the window. It was dark outside, exceptionally so. Why weren't the streetlights on? "I'm sorry, but do I know you?"

The man stared at him, hard, then chuckled to himself. "I think you fried your brain, kid. You must have been in the backwash of whatever stunt you pulled. Give it some time."

"I'm sorry, but I don't understand." Ryan looked around again and whatever it was that left him drowsy and detached suddenly fled. His heart leapt forward without warning. It pounded out a beat, growing faster by the second. None of this made any sense.

Ryan took a step back and shot a furtive glance behind him. "Where's my family? Who are you? What'd you do to them?"

"Kid, slow down. You're overloading."

Ryan continued to speak, though the strange-yet-familiar man spoke to him and was clearly trying to calm him.

"Did you kidnap them? Did you kill them? Where

are they? What am I doing here? Where am I?" His voice grew louder and more panicked with each thought. "Who are you? What's going on? Why is my arm bleeding? Why—" The lantern fell from his slack fingers and Ryan's eyes rolled up in his head. He collapsed on the floor.

"Hey, you need to reboot that brain of yours. If you don't, you're fucked."

Words. Meaning somewhere. Reboot brain?

"Get the gears turning, kid. Wake up. Follow me here. You have to focus."

Focus. Okay. Focus on what?

"Okay, you see me now. Your name is Ryan Sutter. You used to work for the County Library until it was attacked. Bad things happened. I rescued you. My name is Malone and I work for the shadow government."

So much information. How to process and follow it?

"Stick with me. That's right, keep looking at me. Don't look around, just at me."

Friendly enough face in a brusque sort of way, but such an odd story.

"There's big things happening now. This city is under attack and my friends and I are trying to save it. Sikes brought hell down and we're going to fix things."

Sikes. Heard that name before. Where?

"Hey, follow along. You picked out Fisher, told me he sold us out."

"Fisher. Oh, fuck."

"Hey, you're back."

Malone leaned back and smiled. He remembered Malone. It all seemed like some sort of crazy, drug-induced dream, but it wasn't. The house was real, the couch he sat upon was real, and the guy in front of him was real. The lantern with the piercing light was real. Just accepting that this was reality opened the dam on the memories.

Fisher, that guy with the glasses and pointy nose and that sore on his head. Sikes, dark hair, flat top like something out of the eighties. Malone, sitting in front of him, able to do some pretty freaky shit. Ryan, himself, able to…

"What the hell is going on?"

"You overloaded your brain. I think it's been going on for a couple of days now, but just hit you about eight hours ago. It would explain certain things."

The memories continued to surge. Pressure built in his head with each recollection, until at last they stopped and left Ryan with an intense headache that settled in right over his eyes. He remembered his friends at work being killed. He remembered the bombs. He remembered trying to run away only to find himself entangled in some mess he didn't understand. He remembered his family and that he hadn't been in contact with them in days.

"My parents. Where are they? Are they okay?"

"Hey, slow down, I don't want to lose you again. I can't keep bringing you back."

Ryan put out a hand to steady himself as he sat up. "No, it's okay, but I'm worried. Do they know what's going on?"

"I'm sure they're fine if they stayed inside."

"But they had to have heard the library was destroyed. They must think…"

"We'll pay a visit, okay?"

Ryan looked up. "Really?"

"Yeah, tomorrow, but for now, I need you here with me." Malone leaned forward in the chair. "You have to tell me what happened back at city hall."

Ryan thought back and the sudden pain in his arm reminded him. He remembered them going to city hall and running into a police officer who was, apparently, just a police officer. Then they found a man who was moving equipment from city hall into the back of a truck.

"I remember a guy putting stuff in a truck. He was responsible for something, something bad. He hurt people I knew and I didn't think we should just leave him there, then something hit me."

"Yeah, you were shot in the arm. You were lucky the bullet only grazed you, but I bet it stings. Do you remember anything after that?"

"I was overwhelmed." Ryan closed his eyes and took a deep breath. His heart started to beat faster with the scattered memory and he felt it all coming back again. "Emotions. Like a levy broke and they flooded in." A hand grabbed his arm, firm yet supportive. He looked up to see Malone watching him, steadying him.

"Calm. You're fine now. Tell me what happened, but don't relive it."

Ryan nodded and took another deep breath. "I was worried and scared. And angry. He was one of the men who," Ryan paused and took a deep breath, "killed my friends. The sight of him made me angry beyond anything I've ever experienced and something stirred in me, some feeling." Ryan shook his head. "I can't describe it other than to say it was like a power, a building pressure maybe."

Malone slowly nodded his head. "What did you think about after that?"

"I could only think about how hurt I was by their loss and how much their families must be suffering. I was hurt and angry for them. I wanted this guy to die." Ryan shuddered involuntarily with the admission.

"And what did you think, specifically?"

"I wanted him to know how much damage he'd done. I wanted him to feel what I was feeling."

"That explains it."

"Explains what?"

Malone shook his head and a touch of a smile came to his lips. "I'm sorry to find humor in this, but what you did is unheard of for a novice. Absolutely unheard of."

Panic began to surface again and Ryan rushed the words out. "What did I do?"

"I'm not sure you want to know. But that guy won't be shooting anyone any time soon."

"Did I kill him?" Just spitting out the words made him feel ill.

"No, but he's sufficiently incapacitated."

"How can you be so sure?"

"I'm sure, kid. I've seen psychic assaults before and the one you laid on that guy was like Mike Tyson hitting a four-year old. You almost knocked me out, too, but I know a psychic assault when I feel one. The attack was focused just enough that I could stay conscious and keep a shield up to stop bullets. A lot of unfocused energy went out with that attack and anyone even nearby was knocked on their ass."

Ryan shuddered. "So I did that?"

"I said as much."

"How?"

"That's the question. How do you feel now?"

Though it held no answers, Ryan looked at the window. With the lantern inside and no light outside, he couldn't see anything except the glare of the lantern on the glass. Was it still chaos out there? It must be.

Ryan put his head in his hands and closed his eyes. "Like I've been dragged over rocks and salted. Everything hurts, I'm worried sick, and I'm beyond confused."

"It'll get better, but it won't ever be the same. When you become innate, something changes in your brain and things aren't the same as they were."

Ryan thought back to the previous day, to how he was able to have a conversation with Malone about what was happening without being overwhelmed by reality. They were even able to drive over to city hall and he hadn't given much thought to the radical changes he'd experienced and the strange power he suddenly found himself wielding.

It wasn't that he had dismissed the thoughts entirely, especially since they were now on his mind again, but it was as though he was able to let go enough to cope with new information and experiences as they came, at least until he was shot by one of the men who murdered his friends.

Thinking of his emotions at that time and those memories reminded him of the headache that seemed to pulse in response. The slow, rhythmic thudding in his head was a clear signal that he had experienced far too much in the last couple of days for his brain to cope.

"It's midnight. I suggest you get some rest if you

can. Things have cooled down enough that we'll go see your folks in the morning. I found another agent tonight and we're going to meet for plans tomorrow. This'll all be over soon."

Ryan took a deep breath and exhaled slowly. "Thanks, Malone. For everything."

"I told you it'd be okay, right?"

"No, really. Thank you."

"Don't mention it."

In the morning, Ryan found the bandages and hydrogen peroxide on the counter in the house's sole bathroom and he promptly changed his dressings. When Ryan walked back into the front room, Malone was seated at the table, radio in hand.

Malone turned the radio off and set it down on the table as he stared out of the window. The morning sunlight was brilliant as it streamed in. Unfortunately, the sunlight glinted off broken glass and highlighted scattered trash that dotted the street and yards.

Ryan tried his phone, but cellular service was still down. Out of habit, he tried turning the television on, but nothing happened.

"Still out, kid."

"At least we have water."

"Nope. Been filling the tank with bottled stuff. You ready to go?"

Ryan provided directions to his home and they drove the bullet-riddled car to a middle-class neighborhood that had fared better in the last couple of days than the hideout's neighborhood. He had expected to find chaos everywhere in the town, but his neighborhood was apparently immune to the disorder that seemed to have swallowed the rest of the town. In his neighborhood, people were outside conversing in the fine Southern California weather.

Ryan thought about that, that people were enjoying their lives without knowing that a war was being tested about them. He was momentarily envious of their ignorance.

A couple of the neighbors had gathered in front of one of the houses and sat in chairs, drinks in hand. It was surreal, like a Sunday morning, except it was Wednesday. Did the world, or at least the town, stop turning once the bombs went off? Didn't people have places to go? Why weren't things fixed, services restored?

They pulled up in front of a light-blue house with a well-manicured yard and a lone mulberry tree in the center of it. Ryan hesitated, his hand on the door handle. For just a moment, he had a feeling that something had happened to his parents, but where that feeling came from, he couldn't say. It vanished almost as immediately as it came, but it left him shaking.

"You okay, kid?"

"Yeah, just a bad thought. I'm fine."

"Good." Malone paused to clear his throat. "Look, this isn't easy for me to say, but I appreciate you helping me out. You didn't have to, but I appreciate it."

Ryan smiled. "Hey, you saved me. I guess that makes us even. Sort of."

"Yeah. Look, I know you probably want this to all just go away, and so do I, but I think I could still use your help, if you're willing."

There it was, laid out before him. Malone asked him

for his help. No longer was he being forced to be a part of this.

He could get out of the car right now, close that door and close this part of his life, but he had so many questions and the only person who had answers was Malone. It seemed to keep coming back to that.

"I'll be back." Ryan got out of the car and he stopped before he closed the door. He ducked and peered back in the car. "You want to come in?"

"No, I'll stay out here. We don't have long."

"I'll be quick."

Ryan walked across the yard and paused at the door. Everything was so quiet in the neighborhood. No cars, no planes flying overhead, no air conditioners whirring away, just birds singing and the occasional laughter of neighbors spending a pleasant morning together. Ryan popped his key in the lock, unlocked the door, and went inside.

The front door opened into a small family room with a small TV on the wall, a floral-patterned couch, and a couple of matching chairs to the left. A small hallway led further into the house straight ahead. Seated on the couch, his mother looked up in surprise.

She practically leapt off the couch and rushed toward him.

Her exclamations and sobs turned into one incoherent string of sounds and Ryan hugged her tightly.

"I'm fine. Really, I'm fine."

"But we heard about the gas leak and the explosion."

"I got out. But..."

His mother frowned and kissed his forehead. "I'm sorry, but I'm so glad you're okay. Your father is at work." Her speech was hurried and jumbled and she took a breath and calmed. "He didn't want to go, but he had to and he wouldn't stop talking about…" She stopped and smiled but it was fleeting. Her look became serious. "Everyone's talking but no one really knows what's going on. What happened at the library?"

"I don't have time to explain, but it's… it's weird. This federal agent was in the area and saved me. Turns out I've been helping him and we're working together to figure out what's going on."

She frowned again but said nothing.

"Tell dad I love him and I'll be home as quickly as I can. I don't know how I got into this, but I'm in it now."

"Stay home, Ryan. I don't know what's going on, but it doesn't sound safe."

"I can't, mom. I owe the guy. He saved my life."

She stared at him with her best I-said-no expression, but it softened and she nodded. "At least be careful. I don't like any of this."

"I will. I promise. I'll tell you about it when it's all over."

He jogged to his room and changed his clothes. He would have loved to get a shower, but he didn't think Malone was willing to wait for as long a shower as he felt he needed, never mind that there was no running water. Still, just getting into fresh clothes was good.

Ryan went back into the living room and found his mother waiting for him. She was wringing her hands as she looked expectantly down the hall.

"Please be careful."

Ryan smiled. "I will. I love you."

He kissed her on the cheek, hugged her again, and ran out. He stopped at the door to exchange waves then jogged to the car.

"Everything okay?"

"Fine, just fine. Thanks."

"Good. Think positively because we're off to discover how bad we're in this."

They pulled into a mostly-vacated strip mall parking lot. A few cars sat in the parking lot, conspicuous in their presence. One car, an old brown sedan, was backed into a spot and two people ran back and forth from a novelty store throwing things in the car. Another car, a white van, was in the middle of the parking lot, apparently abandoned, and one more, a nondescript black sedan, was parked over by a sandwich shop. The windows on most of the stores had been shattered and the stores turned upside down.

Malone pointed at the sandwich shop. "He'll be in there, in the back. I haven't talked to Warner in quite a while, but he's the only contact I could make."

Ryan nodded and studied the car parked in front of the store. It differed from Malone's government issued German sedan. Maybe it was that, maybe it was how Malone said he hadn't spoken with the other agent in a while, but something raised Ryan's suspicions.

"This guy is solid?"

"He's fine." Pause. "Why?"

"I don't know, just a feeling."

"Not another vision?"

"No."

Malone smiled. "Don't sweat it. I said I haven't talked to him in a while but that's because he's been in

New York. He's a good egg."

Ryan nodded and tried to shove the thought away. He had no reason to suspect this guy was trouble, let alone even had any idea what he looked like. His senses must have still been on overload from the other incidents.

Malone pulled up a space away from the other car and cut the engine. Both agents parked between the lines. Ryan wasn't sure why he found it funny, but he did.

"Let's see what's going on."

Ryan got out of the car and started toward the shop but stumbled. The world began to swim and dizziness ambushed him from some dark corner. Ryan fell against the car and placed his hands on it to steady himself.

Buzzing filled his head and water filled his ears. The vision sucker-punched him.

A man, someone he had never seen, stood near several others in a blasé room. Something was off about him, like a piece of a puzzle was missing. Though the man was visible, a light haze hung suspended just in front of him and obscured some details. He wore a dark uniform, maybe BDUs, and boots.

Beige walls, a table made of indistinct light wood, and serviceable dark fabric chairs filled the otherwise stark room. The place looked familiar, like a government building, and the man turned to reveal an assault rifle in his hands. The other men who stood nearby each held similar weapons, but all of their details were lost in an even thicker haze that seemed to encompass them. Two of the men were engaging in a wordless conversation, but they stopped when a sixth person entered the room. Unlike the others, this man was clear and defined, no haze or fog about him at all. The newcomer was definitely James Sikes — flat top hair and an I'll-kick-your-ass expression — and he looked to be issuing orders.

Sound flooded out of the vision — boots crunching on the floor, the squeak of chairs, the tapping of fingers against the stocks of guns. Voices joined the sounds, mostly garbled and indistinct. A few words made it to Ryan, but without context they meant nothing. However, the first man said, "Yes" and saluted Sikes. He motioned to the others and they followed him out of the room. Solidity fell to pieces like so many grains of sand in an hourglass and the vision dissipated.

The tide receded, and with it, the buzzing. Ryan blinked and found himself seated on the asphalt. Malone looked down at him and offered a hand.

"Another vision?"

Ryan nodded while he tried to sort through it and regain his bearings. He leaned over the car and took several steadying breaths.

"I saw Sikes again. He came into a room, some kind of office, and issued orders. This other guy, he was holding a rifle, acknowledged the orders and left. He grabbed the other guys in the room and they went stomping out, all military like."

"Anything else?"

"Yeah, I saw a half-dozen people there, but they were all blurry. I couldn't make out anything. Only the first guy and Sikes had any detail to them."

"Must be related to the wallop you gave yourself. What can you tell me about the first guy?"

"I couldn't see everything, but short blonde hair, no

facial hair I think. Big dude. Six feet and two hundred pounds, maybe two-twenty. He was wearing a dark uniform."

Malone grimaced and turned away. When he looked back at Ryan, his expression returned to neutral. "Did you notice anything? Piercing? Tattoo? Scar?"

Ryan looked into the distance and brought the man back to his mind as much as he could. He could see him, yet he couldn't. Something came to him.

"A scar, I think. Upper lip." Ryan looked over and Malone had a finger on his lip in the same place. Ryan nodded.

"You just described Warner. I gave him that scar in training. Fuck." Malone took a couple of steps away then came back. He looked at the sandwich shop and shook his head. "I sure hope you're wrong, kid. We can't afford to lose any more cleaners."

Ryan remembered what Malone said about the visions being unbiased, only showing what happened or will happen. He felt like he should apologize, but he only nodded.

CHAPTER 6

The front door, a metal frame with two shattered panes of glass, stood open. They walked inside and found the small tables overturned and the chairs strewn about. It looked like a soda fountain once occupied space on a counter, but it was now gone. Plumbing, a rough outline of dust and discoloration, and a small, dried patch of a dark liquid on the counter were testaments of its prior existence. A cash register, or rather the vague outline of one on a counter, showed further signs of looting. Dirty footprints went in every direction and little remained.

A lone door to the side of where the soda fountain had been was slightly ajar. Malone opened it to reveal a hallway with a small assortment of doors.

One of the doors was labeled with the universal blue sign of bathroom, while one looked to lead outside through the back, one to the work area behind the counter, and one more had a few letters on it that read Man fic. The outline of the missing letters made it clear it was the manager's office. They stopped in front of that door.

"Innocent until proven guilty, okay, kid?"

Ryan nodded and Malone opened the door. An office of microscopic proportions, it was large enough to hold a narrow desk at the not-so-far side and a chair on either side of it. The man Ryan had seen in his vision, Warner, occupied the chair behind the desk. A couple of maps, spread and overlapping each other, covered the desk. Warner leaned over them.

The cleaner looked much like Ryan had seen in the vision. He wore a suit that made him look like Malone's twin, except that it was nowhere near as rumpled or dirty. The scar on his lip was also more noticeable without the haze in front of it, a perpendicular shock of white on his upper lip just below his left nostril. When Ryan looked away, he realized that Warner had an aura. He'd become so used to seeing it on Malone that it took him a moment to realize Warner had one, and that it was brighter than Malone's.

Malone walked up to the desk and put his hands on the back of the empty chair. "Warner, what's going on?"

"Bad news. They got—" Warner looked up and narrowed his eyes at Ryan, "who's this?"

"He's with me. I picked him up at the library when the bomb went off."

Warner's intense, unblinking stare was too much for Ryan to meet.

"He's the one we were supposed to pick up," Warner said. "Why is he still with you?"

"He's a latent. He's helping me out."

"This is national security and you have some kid tagging along?"

Ryan didn't like how Warner said "kid." It lacked the endearing quality that Malone's "kid" had and replaced it with sizable portion of contempt.

Malone took his hands off the chair and held them up. "Hey, he's cool, okay? He's provided us intel."

"You should have left him at the base."

"And you know what happened to the base."

Warner turned his stare from Ryan to Malone. Ryan let out a breath he didn't realize he was holding. Malone straightened up but didn't back away.

"This isn't happening with him here," Warner said.

Malone turned around and gave an apologetic look. "Give us a minute?"

Ryan looked from Malone to Warner, who openly glared at him, and walked away. He heard the door close behind him and he stopped to listen, but he could only hear an exaggerated "s" whenever Warner spoke. He walked to the kitchen side of the shop and found a few pieces of bread still in the oven. He helped himself to one of them. The bread was stale, but it didn't have tuna slathered on it. In the moment, it could be considered gourmet.

He fished out a bottle of mystery juice—the wrapper was missing—from under the counter and took a bite of the bread and let his eyes and mind wander.

He took another bite and nearly choked on it when a dozen cars pulled into the parking lot, all police vehicles. They pulled in without their lights spinning or sirens wailing and he damn near missed them in his daytime reverie. Food and drink fell from his hands. Ryan quickly swallowed and ran to the office and opened the door.

He blurted the words out as quickly as he could. "Company's coming. Those assholes found us here."

Warner looked from Ryan to Malone. "What sort of amateur hour shit is this, Malone?"

Malone raised a finger. "Fuck you!"

The two looked ready to come to blows.

"Hey!" Ryan had to shout to get their attention. "Let's get out of here and you two can have a pissing contest later, okay?"

They looked at Ryan then traded glances with each other. Malone turned away first and left the office. "Keep your head down, kid."

Warner picked up a small black duffel bag from the floor then stomped by while muttering something about, "fixing his problems."

Ryan fell back against the wall as they passed by then followed them to the lobby. The agents went outside and stopped on the sidewalk as the police vehicles pulled up. Warner opened the black bag, took its contents out, and threw the bag behind him. Ryan couldn't see what the agent held, but he had a good guess.

The car doors opened and men and women scrambled out of the cars and ducked behind the doors, guns drawn. Warner threw something, then another, and the familiar pop and hiss of smoke, complete with billowing clouds, engulfed the front of the store. Nothing happened for a tense moment as the grenades continued to cough out smoke, and then someone ordered they open fire.

Gunfire chattered and drowned out everything. Ryan stared in disbelief then realized how vulnerable he was and threw himself down behind an overturned table. He slammed into it with his injured arm and grunted. What the hell was he doing just standing there in the lobby?

Gunshots rang out one after another, but no bullets zipped by. Ryan peeked his head around the side of the table. Both Warner and Malone stood with their hands out. Malone was on the left and Warner was on the right, slowly making his way forward. They must have been stopping everything that came at them.

With smoke flowing all around him, Warner, barely visible, threw his arm forward. Gunshots continued to fill the air, and after a few seconds, a brilliant flash of light and a thunderous bang filled the smoky area inhabited by the police.

The two agents now had both of their hands out in front of them as they took another step forward. The smoke circled around them, its long tendrils reaching upward. The hazy cloud pulled the agents into its mass. Ryan lost sight of them, but the gunfire continued, only with less enthusiasm.

Ryan came out a little further from the table in an attempt to see, but a few bullets whizzed by through the store and slammed into the wall behind him. Ryan ducked behind the table and another bullet ripped through it only a few feet away from his face, sending splinters and shards into the air. Ryan sucked in a surprised breath.

"No!" It sounded like Malone.

Ryan peeked out again. Malone backed up a step and threw one arm forward. The smoke swirled away just enough with the motion and invisible force to reveal the outline of a body on the ground next to Malone. Malone yelled again and thrust both of his arms forward. The smoke leapt again, this time revealing the identity of the body. A crash and scrape of metal tore through the sound of gunfire, and cries of retreat filled the air. Malone put his arms out wide, as though collecting something, and then swept them forward.

Some wind or power, completely unseen, followed those arms and sent the smoke dancing in the air as it ripped through the parking lot. Gunfire completely ceased, replaced with the sound of metal, rubber, and people being swept away as though they were little more than straw in a tornado.

The smoke swirled away with the passing power and left a hazy view of the parking lot. Ryan came out from behind the table and stopped at the windows to look at the carnage. The police vehicles were overturned and bodies lay unmoving about the parking lot. Near Malone, a pool of blood steadily grew in size. He followed its source to Warner and wished he hadn't.

Warner had obviously been shot in the head, and the remains of his head turned Ryan's stomach. Blood poured out of it, and maybe it was Ryan's imagination, but he thought he saw some skull and brain matter nearby. He looked away and choked back bile.

"There's nothing we can do for him now. I don't even know if you were right."

"I'm sorry, Malone."

"It's not your fault, kid."

Malone knelt, careful to stay out of the blood, and fished through Warner's pockets and pulled out his keys. He nodded at the corpse then unlocked Warner's car. "Let's get out of here."

"I don't even know why I'm here."

"I told you before. Look, you helped. You picked out Fisher, and even if Warner wasn't a turncoat, you gave us warning before the posse arrived. We might not have made it out otherwise."

"You don't need me for that. You would have heard the cars pull up."

"But sometimes those extra seconds count."

Ryan stared out of the window and tried not to bring to mind Warner's bloody head. The agent's head was so mangled it could no longer be called a face.

"Why do you even need me to find your traitors? There must be other agents."

Malone said nothing for several seconds.

"Oh. Right." Ryan sighed. "I was wrong. I shouldn't be here. I don't know why I thought I could help you."

"That's not why. You can say it, though. I've thought it before."

Ryan thought of Warner, thought of his parents, thought of his coworkers. His voice was little more than a whisper. "I don't want to die." The silence that filled the car was oppressive, made him feel small and insignificant. He slouched down in the car seat.

"When I ask someone for their help, which isn't often, you can bet your ass I do everything I can to make sure they're safe."

It was comforting, but it only reinforced that this was real. He had somehow gotten himself involved in something that was absolutely beyond him. This wasn't a video game. People lived and died in games, maybe even had strange powers. Though he tried to convince himself that this wasn't real, that he would wake up in bed from a dream, he knew that was a lie. A quick flick of a power button wouldn't end this story, wouldn't return him to a world where everyone he knew was still alive and where the most dangerous part of his day was the drive to and from work. No, this was real, and he was in danger. This was his life and he was making decisions he was going to have to live with. Assuming he lived long enough to see the results of those decisions.

They drove in silence for another minute.

"Look, kid, let's start over. What I'm asking of you isn't right, and I recognize that. This isn't your fight and you don't belong in the middle of it, let alone with all sorts of craziness going on that you're still trying to figure out. I'll take you home right now, no questions asked, no hard feelings. I won't put you in a position you're not willing to be in. You just say the words."

Ryan studied the agent. Little trenches ran around Malone's eyes, and his eyes could have been glass. His clenched jaw compressed his lips. He turned, briefly, and met Ryan's eyes. Malone was definitely exhausted, but he looked sincere.

Ryan nodded and looked out of the window again. Why was he here? Malone was right: it wasn't his fight. Everything that happened, that was happening, that was going to happen, none of it involved him in the slightest. What sort of macho bullshit made him think he had any business thrusting his nose in the middle of a gigantic beehive?

But there was Fisher and that attack at the base, never mind what happened at the library. Ryan wasn't sure that Malone's conspiracy theory about Sikes was correct. Malone believed it, Ryan could see that, but perhaps because he was an outsider and had a different set of data to draw from, Ryan wasn't convinced of the same conclusions. Even though it was more outrageous, he found the idea he tossed at Malone to be more compelling. Though Malone tried to brush it off, he was sure that Malone considered the idea and might have even moved to do some investigation.

How would Malone know who to trust if Ryan was right? Look at Warner: What was with the vision and him taking orders from Sikes? Those cops, or whoever they were, sure did show up conveniently when both he and Malone were certain they hadn't been tailed. Maybe Warner was pretending to put up a fight when all along he meant to take down Malone, and by association, Ryan, but something went wrong. With gigantic clouds of smoke rolling around through the parking lot, it wasn't a stretch that a bullet could have been accidentally fired at Warner instead of Malone. If so, in the confusion, maybe it somehow bested the agent's defenses.

The outcome of that confrontation could have been different if Malone went in unprepared. Ryan gave Malone warning, and Malone saved both of their asses again. If Malone hadn't been on guard, it could have been Malone or Ryan or both of them lying on the ground instead of Warner.

Yeah, maybe he didn't belong in the middle of it, but it was a little late for that. Besides, in some small way, he was enjoying it. Not so much that it was fun, but it was gratifying to play a small part in not only helping his town out, but his country.

"No, I'm good. Thanks, but I'm in."

"You're sure? No hard feelings or anything if you're not. I don't have to insult you and tell you how serious this is because you've seen it for yourself, but if you're with me, I need to know you're committed."

"I'm with you, Malone. I'm not sure what all I can do just yet, but I owe you this much."

Malone turned and scrutinized him. The agent nodded. "Okay. Let's go figure out what to do."

ॐ

The city rolled by. Houses, businesses, dead traffic lights. Malone turned down this street and that, seemingly without purpose. The minutes passed and Ryan could finally take no more. "Why are we just driving around?"

"You're not getting anything?"

"You mean a vision? Nothing."

"Damn it." Malone chewed on his bottom lip. "Then we've got nothing to go on. Only person I could get on the radio is Warner."

"There's got to be someone else who knows what's going on, or at least has a clue."

Malone's expression suddenly changed to one that suggested he smelled something he didn't like. "I can think of one, but we've had a sour history. It might not be pleasant, assuming he's even there."

"Well I sure as hell got nothing."

Malone drove them into a wealthy neighborhood that Ryan was completely unfamiliar with. The homes, while not mansions by any stretch, were still large and lavish. Tall roofs that would tower over his own and large covered patios greeted them from all sides. Decks large enough to be rooms looked out over precision-manicured lawns. Trees and flowers bloomed, explosions of color that brightened the already welcoming neighborhood. Not a single dead, old clunker of a car rusted in a driveway. It almost too surreal to be true, like one of those movie neighborhoods you'd see, a Stepford thing.

They stopped in front of a house with a Mercedes parked in the driveway and a small fountain of a lion roaring water. They exited their car and walked along the curving flagstone walkway to the large, double front doors. Ryan expected to see brass knockers on the door to complete the ridiculous image, but they were rather plain wooden doors, intricate carvings of mythical creatures aside.

Malone sighed and lifted a hand to the door. He gave it a solid rap. They waited for some time, and after no response, he knocked again, this time more insistently. Again they waited to no avail.

Ryan looked back to the car. "Where to now?"

Malone pulled a small pouch out of the inside pocket of his jacket and extracted a couple of small, thin pieces of metal.

"We don't have anywhere else to go, so this is it. If he's in there and something's happened, we need to know." Malone inserted both metal strips into the lock and only then did Ryan realize he was witnessing real life lock picking.

Ryan expected it would take a while to pick the lock, as it always does in the movies and on television, but Malone popped the lock in less than three seconds and slowly opened the door. He replaced everything into his jacket and took a step inside.

They walked into a large foyer with light marble floors and lots of green houseplants. Paintings, expensive looking abstract things, hung on the walls while a large circular rug of earth tones broke up the marble flooring. A staircase gently turned a large half-circle up to the second floor while hallways opened to the left and right.

They went right and turned a short corner that dumped them into a large family room where a man in Bahamas shorts and a flower-print shirt sat in a chair with a clipboard and a sheaf of papers. More papers and several folders that contained stacks of documents were piled on an oversized coffee table with carved legs that stood in front of him. A closed laptop sat next to one of the folders, its power cable draped across the table and plugged into a large box Ryan guessed was a backup battery. The rest of the room consisted of a variety of plush furniture in warm colors — sofa, love seat, chairs — that looked expensive and gaudy. They were all arranged around the coffee table.

The man looked up from the clipboard he held, his eyes large. "Malone? What are you doing here?"

"I need your help."

"How did —"

"There's problems in the agency. Warner didn't make it."

"What?" The clipboard sagged in the man's grip.

Was that a gun hidden under the papers? Ryan looked away.

"Warner, they got him." Malone sat on the couch and suddenly looked older. He slouched over and looked every bit as tired as he likely was. "I was there. I don't even know what happened, but there was shit I could do about it." He shook his head.

The man narrowed his eyes as he looked at Ryan then at Malone. "Why are you bringing this to me?"

Ryan looked from Malone to the unknown man and was surprised, he wasn't sure why, to find the man had no more aura than the computer in his lap.

"I don't know what to do, Hansen. I can't find anyone else. I don't know where to go."

"What happened?" Hansen said.

"I found Warner on HAM after the attack. We met to figure out what was going on, but they showed up. He was gunned down. I don't know how something got past him, but one bullet hit him and that was all it took." Malone stared at his feet. Silence filled the space.

"What aren't you telling me?"

Malone ran a hand through his hair and looked at Hansen.

"Fisher is a traitor."

Hansen shook his head and placed the clipboard on the coffee table. He moved slowly and deliberately. He looked as though he was getting ready to stand but he stopped with his forearms flat on the chair's arms.

"You're talking about treachery in front of some stranger? Are you insane? Do you want me to bring you up on charges for this, too?"

"I have no choice, Hansen. Everyone else is either dead or in hiding. Hell, I'm surprised you're still here."

Hansen squinted, a little, and flared his nostrils. "Who is this guy?"

"He's helping me track down the traitors. He's a latent."

Ryan waved but said nothing.

Hansen glared at Ryan then turned an incredulous gaze on Malone.

"He's the latent? You do realize you were asked to bring him in, not involve him in everything that's happening."

Ryan looked to Hansen and leaned forward. He was getting tired of people saying he was supposed to be "brought in," yet no one had bothered to go into any detail. Malone had only touched upon it, and that was the extent of his knowledge. Ryan opened his mouth to ask, but Malone spoke up before he could.

"I know, but I was going to take him home when the base fell apart. What else could I do?"

"Yet he is here."

"Like I said, he's helping. He volunteered."

"And you trust him?"

Ryan sat back and looked at Malone.

Malone pointed at Ryan, his eyes still locked on Hansen. "He picked out Fisher before I ever said a word about him."

Hansen slammed a fist on the chair's arm. "Not this shit again. And I suppose he picked out Warner, too."

"Maybe. It doesn't matter now."

Hansen did stand now and he stopped to straighten his shirt. "Why are you really here, Malone?"

"I need the case file."

"Impossible, and you know that."

Malone stood, straight and calm. "You're damning us, Hansen. Sikes is in town and you know it. He has fingers in us that not even the council knows about, assuming they made it through the attack."

"I don't know why you're here, but the information in that file is strictly confidential and you don't have clearance for it. You know damn well there's already a team working on tracking him and his minions down. You need to leave," he turned to face Ryan, "and you had better watch what you see and say. The agents were given specific orders to deal with you and I can see that Malone has failed in that endeavor as well." He turned back to Malone. "You can let yourself out. Now."

Malone sighed and looked at Ryan. "Can't do that, Hansen. Not without that file."

"Even if I could, the battery is almost dead. You don't have enough time to figure out the password, let alone nose around to find the information."

"Sorry, Hansen. Really."

Malone thrust a hand out and Hansen flew back into the chair. Man and chair collided and both crashed to the ground. Papers on the table rustled with the invisible passing energy and a couple of them drifted to the floor.

Ryan stood and looked from Malone, to Hansen, and back again. "What did you do?"

Malone turned to him. "He gave me no choice, kid."

"But he was just standing there!"

"Hey! Do you want this city to fall to shit because of bureaucracy?" Malone turned away and walked to where Hansen lay.

Stunned, Ryan stood there for a breath then shook it off. He hurried over to check on Hansen. He was scared to learn if Malone had just knocked Hansen out or done worse.

It must have been one hell of a sucker punch. Hansen's arms and legs were splayed across the floor and chair, but his chest rose and fell evenly. His hair was a mess, but Ryan figured that would be the least of the man's worries when he awoke.

"I hate that I had to do that, but I'm out of ideas."

Ryan watched Hansen for another moment then looked at Malone. It was a little frightening what the agent could do, but Ryan had to admit that he had no better ideas, even if this one wasn't particularly good.

Malone pulled a USB stick out of his jacket. He plugged the stick into the laptop and turned on the computer on. Ryan watched with interest as it booted.

"What is that? What's it doing?"

"It's a customized Linux distro. Watch."

The computer booted and the operating system came up. It immediately opened a program and windows appeared on the screen showing folders of user files alongside a warning dialogue that the battery was low.

Malone quickly clicked through the folders and, not finding what he wanted, opened another window and typed something into a box that looked like Jaguar. Ryan wasn't sure why Malone would be looking for a car or a cat, so he just watched. Malone was moving quickly and it was all foreign to Ryan. The box vanished and was replaced by a couple of empty panes; a continuously changing line of text flashed by too quickly to read.

A groan sounded from behind them and Ryan turned around. Hansen moved, but he was still out of it. Something about the way Hansen groaned and moved worried Ryan. "I think he may be waking up. Hurry up with whatever you're doing."

Ryan looked back to the computer and Malone was in the middle of opening a document. The first page practically screamed classified with its various warnings and logos he'd never seen. Malone scrolled through the document and then stopped. There it was, a list of names, and three of them were highlighted in red, with short blurbs that Ryan thought looked like possible locations.

"Remember these names, kid: Barajas, Fredriksson, and Rainier. Those are the ones we need to find to give us a chance to take this city back." Malone turned the laptop off and grabbed his memory stick.

"I'm sorry, Hansen, but you gave me no choice."

They left the house and got back into the car.

"So who was that guy?"

Malone buckled his belt then looked over at Ryan. "Head of the agency in these parts."

Ryan looked up from his own buckle. "Shit, and you just broke into his house and computer, not to mention you sucker punched him. That can't be good."

"You're telling me. But what choice do we have?"

Ryan popped the buckle in and nodded. "What was that on his computer? Some kind of report?"

"Exactly. He knows there's possible leaks in the agency and has people looking into it, but look how much good it's done. First Sikes shows up here and blows the library to hell, then our base gets creamed, and now we've lost another cleaner and I don't even know if he was in on it, too, but it sure smells like it. Hell, his name isn't even on the list."

"Was Fisher's?"

"Yeah, prime suspect. But we know about him, thanks to you."

"So how do we start tracking these guys down? Are they at a hideout? Another base?"

"That's the problem. I have no idea. They might still be under, or they might have taken off when the attack came." Malone pulled the car out and looked aimless as he navigated the neighborhood.

"Maybe I can help find them. You know about this stuff. How can I get another vision?"

Malone's face went a shade lighter and he made an effort to stare straight ahead.

"I can throw things with the best of them, but I don't get what you're doing."

"You're withholding something."

"It was a bad time in my life, kid. A bad time."

CHAPTER 7

Malone took them out of the neighborhood and started to drive across town.

"I went in for training years ago, and I don't remember what happened."

"How so?"

"You know how you felt the other day, like you didn't know where you were or who anyone was or anything? I was like that, only worse. For three weeks, or so they tell me."

"What happened?"

"I don't know." Malone threw his hands into the air then grabbed the wheel again. "I tried to do some mind trick, then wham," he slammed a fist against the wheel, "it's three weeks later."

"You blacked out for three weeks?"

"I wish. I don't know the truth of everything that happened, but what I do know wasn't good."

"So what do you remember?"

Malone shook his head and said nothing for several seconds. "No, it wasn't good. I'm not proud of it." Malone squinted, as though he was seeing or reliving something painful. Ryan decided to drop it.

"If you don't know how to trigger the visions, maybe you can tell me about the guys we're looking for. Maybe it'll do something, maybe it won't, but at least it'll get another perspective on this."

Malone nodded and took a deep breath.

"Barajas is another agent, but she's a norm. You don't get to be an agent in this organization as a norm unless you're good. She's worked this area and several nearby for years. Young, ambitious, and a crack shot with a rifle. She was involved in a bust years ago, before we knew what Sikes was up to. Took some of Sikes's thugs down and opened our eyes to what was really going on.

"I don't think she turned right away, I mean no one does that, but she got to know a few people right there. She's been doing recon in LA recently." Malone turned, his head going side to side as he drove. "I heard she was back in town last week, but I've been in the field. She may have come and gone for all I know."

"Curious timing, wouldn't you say?"

"Yeah, curious."

"Okay, that's Barajas, what about Frederickson?"

"No, it's Fredriksson. Say it like a Swede." Malone said it with a bad accent and Ryan snickered. "He's another agent. Not a norm, not a cleaner, but something in between. Limited powers, but enough that they aid him in getting around and into places he's not welcomed. I don't know a lot about the guy, but he has a nickname in the agency, 'Jaguar.'"

That explained what Malone was searching for. "Which is?"

"What it sounds like: a damn cat. Fancies himself as a super covert ops, but I'm not convinced."

"Rainier?"

Short pause. "Him I know. He's a former cleaner who moved up. He's actually on the council and you saw him, though whether you remember him is another story. He may look old and frail, but he's one wily fuck of a guy. The boys at the agency have a lot of respect for his powers. Dangerous doesn't even begin to describe him."

Ryan nodded, slowly. "I think he can wait until last."

They passed an abandoned car in the middle of the street and Ryan considered what little information Malone had for him. He asked Malone for a physical description of each of them, but he wasn't sure what he was supposed to do with the information, even if there was something he could do.

Whatever triggered his psychic episodes was beyond his control, but at least the next time one happened, since it seemed likely, he'd know who he was looking at.

Ryan's mind began to drift, was no longer focused on the suspected traitors and their individual appearances and jobs. He wasn't focused on anything specifically, just had a general sense of being, as though he existed without interfering with the world.

Several seconds passed before he realized that his perspective looked different. The change was gradual, subtle. His vision was expanding beyond his normal sight, as though he were hovering somewhere above the car and slowly gaining altitude and speed as he moved off. He wasn't thinking of doing it, but was just kind of there, in the moment, looking around as though it were perfectly normal that he could see the top of the car from the passenger seat.

He felt a tap on his shoulder and looked over and found Malone staring at him.

"You okay? You looked like you were gone."

"Yeah, no, I think so." Ryan took a breath and looked around.

"Well I was telling you what the plan is but it didn't look like anybody was home."

"Sorry. I just have no control over this thing."

"Time, kid. Just takes time. I figure we should stick to the known agency holes while we're here. At least one of them is in town so we start looking for them. I caught word on the radio earlier that the military will be rolling in soon, and I don't know what to expect when they show up."

"So they are coming. Okay." Ryan thought about the military taking over the town and the idea of guns and heavy artillery ripping up his home came to him. Tanks rolling through the streets, smashing everything in their path, their cannons punching massive holes in buildings. He shoved the thought away. "And if these people aren't at any places you know, then what?"

"We hope something hits you, because they have the intel necessary to put this city down before long."

"Shit, you're serious about all of this."

"You think I've been fucking with you for days now?"

"No, it's just the implications." Maybe he had been thinking Malone was messing with him. "It couldn't last long, right? Sikes can't have fingers into the military. They'd just declare martial law until everything is restored."

"Maybe, maybe not. Either way, this is bad. Look, I've given some thought to what you said earlier, about this going higher up the chain." Malone paused. "I'm still not sure I buy it, but the more I see now, the more I'm inclined to think you might be on to something."

Ryan looked at Malone before he turned his gaze outward. On the one hand, he was glad that Malone was considering his idea, but if he was right, then that likely meant this was a lot worse than either of them had initially thought. Despite everything that had happened, there was still a part of him that thought it was nothing more than some big game, that it would end and everything would be reset and lives would go on just as they had before. But the weird visions, the power, that alone was a reminder that nothing was as it had been, never mind everything else.

And here they were, looking for leaks in the shadow government trying to prevent this extreme terrorist act from succeeding, and they had little more to go on than what Malone had learned over the years from working with the same people he was now trying to bring down. Ryan looked over at Malone again, the agent impassive behind the wheel, and realized that it must pain the man to have friends and coworkers turn on him. And to bring them down? Awful.

Considering the secrecy of the agency, it must almost be like family turning on you. Ryan couldn't imagine it and didn't want to.

Buzzing and the sound of water came to his ears without warning. He blinked and his vision blurred before he looked upon a concrete floor.

He tried to find some details, something, anything, but it was just a grey floor and a wall. Whatever it was supposed to mean, it meant nothing. He tried again to look around, but it was still just concrete and a nondescript wall. Ryan forced himself to relax and took a deep breath. He stopped focusing on the experience of the vision, the sound in his ears and the buzzing in his head and placed himself there, in the actual situation.

Ryan didn't try to force it; he just looked around. The view zoomed out, lazy and uneven as though a drunken cameraman controlled it, and he realized he was looking at a rooftop, and that the wall was roughly chest height and ran the edge of the building. The fog was still there, but it was lighter, less significant. The building top was somewhat old-fashioned, with a big door and angled roof that led into the building. A small greenhouse sat off to the side of the door, with plants and flowers inside and a few chairs arranged around a small circular table.

Ryan turned his head. A woman, average height, maybe a few inches over five feet with straight dark hair in a ponytail, looked over the wall with binoculars in her hand. She wore a dark suit and held a radio in her other hand. Her head moved as she followed something in the binoculars. She put the radio to her mouth and said something, but it was nothing more than noise whatever she said. The radio screeched back, a shrill, harsh sound.

The view zoomed out even more and Ryan realized the building was the hospital. This woman, he couldn't make out exact details, was on the hospital roof, watching someone or something. Her shadow stretched out behind her several feet.

The vision passed and Ryan relaxed. He drew a deep breath as he sat back in the seat and rubbed his eyes. It was clearly the hospital, but the fog was mostly gone. Perhaps the effect of the psychic feedback, or whatever it was, was finally wearing off.

Maybe it was because he was already sitting, but the usual weakness and dizziness seemed less severe, and it was only after a few moments of thinking about it that he realized he felt better than he expected.

"Give me good news, kid."

"I think I found Barajas. She is, or was, or will be on the hospital rooftop. I still don't have a feeling for how to tell time with this, but I think it was late afternoon or early evening. She was following something with binoculars and talking into a radio."

Malone said nothing, but he made a sudden turn at an intersection to change their direction.

"So? Good? Bad? Neither?"

"A little of both. Good that we know where to find her. Bad that she's at the hospital."

Ryan thought about it and it didn't seem particularly bad, except the hospital being a seven-story building. Seven flights of stairs wouldn't be that bad to climb, and if they knew she was on the roof, it wouldn't be difficult to find her.

"I don't get it."

"Cops. They'll have the place surrounded until order is restored. Hell, it'll be the only place doing any sort of business.

Malone was right. It didn't take them long to cut through town and get to the hospital. They stopped a block away. Emergency vehicles of all kinds dotted the parking lot, and a small triage center had been raised near the front of the building. They likely had generators, but those didn't last forever, thus the hospital's services would likely be limited.

Something caught Ryan's eye in the distance, a black chopper, and he noticed that the sky was slowly turning a deep orange. On a hunch, he looked outside the car and saw the shadow left by a light pole and had a feeling.

Ryan pointed up at the chopper. "I think she was watching that, maybe even talking to someone on board. Think she's directing traffic from upstairs?"

Malone looked around and Ryan did the same. There weren't many other large buildings in the area — the hospital trumped them for a good couple of miles.

"It'd make sense. Good height, clear line of sight. Let's go find out."

Malone put the car back in gear and they slowly approached the hospital. He drove around the parking lot at its outer perimeter and kept throwing glances to the hospital proper. The slow tour took a minute, but he pointed out a side entrance that had fewer people stationed around it. He turned the car that direction and navigated the lot.

Although there were many cars in the parking lot, Malone had little trouble finding a space within fifty yards of the side entrance.

They stopped the car but didn't get out. The side entrance was clearly a delivery entrance. The door was larger than normal and had a loading bay in front of it. One police car was partially backed into the delivery spot while another was parked in front of the door.

"Okay, it's time for your first official lesson. I can't guarantee what's going to happen, but my gut says you'll be fine. You're a hell of a lot better at this mind stuff than I ever was. You okay with this?"

"What do I have to do?"

"We don't know if those guys are legit or not, so you're going to make them forget that they've seen us. It's like we were never here."

"Oh, you mean like a Jed—"

"Yeah." Malone sighed. "Look, it's not too difficult. Focus on those guys. Think about them, but look past them. Don't see them, don't see me, don't see yourself, don't even think about us or hear our footsteps. Cars in the parking lot, other cops, that's fine, but not us."

"So I have to think of two things at the same time without actually thinking about anything?"

"Yeah. Not so hard, right?"

Ryan was shaking his head before Malone finished the question. "This isn't going to work. I can't even control my own visions and you want me to control what someone else sees and hears?"

"Just try it, okay? The worst that happens is we have to go to Plan B."

"What's Plan B?"

"Guess."

Ryan nodded. "Right."

"Ready?"

"No, give me just a minute."

Ryan considered the cops and thought about Malone's instructions. If he could make them not see or hear things that were actually there, then he should be capable of making them see and hear things that weren't there. It was simple deduction, right?

Ryan studied the scene closer. Three cops stood by the doors playing cards on the back of one of the police cruisers. They hardly paid any attention to their surroundings, though one did occasionally look their way, as if to say he hadn't forgotten that he saw a car pull up.

Ryan focused on that officer, pulled the man into his mind, noticed the few details the distance allowed him.

In the middle of putting those details together with the man, Ryan realized he could hear something. Words. Whispers. He blocked it out but still focused on the officer and on the weird banging sound that came from just around the corner. It sounded as though someone was hitting a pipe against a trashcan: a brash sound, one that was hard to miss.

The officer looked up, turned his head, and started toward the sound. He had one hand at his waist while he scanned the area. He turned the corner, vanished for a few seconds, and then reappeared with a shrug and calm body language.

Ryan couldn't suppress a smile.

"Okay. Let's go."

They got out of the car, but Ryan faltered and nearly fell. He braced himself against the car. He was dizzy, tired, and sweat dripped into his eyes.

"What'd you do, kid?"

"I think I may have tried a little too hard."

"Keep it simple. See nothing, hear nothing."

Ryan nodded but he was tired. He hoped it would pass quickly.

"Do we need to go to Plan B?"

"No, just go slowly."

"Okay, but I'm ready if this goes to shit."

They started toward the delivery entrance, slowly. Ryan thought that if the cops decided to look their way, it might be to their advantage that he looked as if he might be ill. Convenient, if nothing else.

The same cop that Ryan had messed with looked up once or twice as they slowly approached, but the others seemed more interested in the game. When they were sixty feet away, Malone elbowed Ryan.

Ryan nodded and focused on the cops. It was difficult to think of them all at once, to notice their features and see them and keep it all in mind, while also thinking of nothing else. The cops looked up as a single unit and stared at each other.

His mind was being stretched a dozen different directions while simultaneously being pressed in. Control, tenuous as it was, began to slip. The police offcers' heads started to shake, slow and twitchy, but rapidly gained speed, like a bobblehead doll on a car's dash. Ryan forced himself to be calm and to focus on them yet think of nothing. Their heads settled back to their normal positions.

Cops. Step. Cops. Step. Cops. Step.

They made it to the door. Cops. Click. Cops. The door opened. Cops. Walk inside. Cops. Click. Slam.

Malone elbowed him.

"Stop, kid. You did good."

Ryan put his back to the nearest wall and slid down it. His breath came fast and shallow. He put his head between his knees and forced himself to be calm and slow his breathing.

It had to have been minutes, but they passed in silence and Ryan eventually looked up. Malone was watching a nearby door. He looked back and nodded.

Ryan gave a thumbs up and shoved himself off the floor. Every muscle in his body seemed to argue all at the same time that standing was not a wise option, but he made it to his feet. He rolled his head around to stretch his neck and took a deep breath. Though he was exhausted, he could continue on now.

Malone quickly looked him up and down. "You okay?"

"Yeah. Lead the way."

Malone tossed him some scrubs and instructed him to put them on. Ryan looked at the blue scrubs and looked up at Malone. Malone was already wearing some. Why hadn't he noticed before?

Ryan shook his head and put the scrubs on over his clothes, since it looked like Malone had done the same. They were big, but sufficiently covered his clothing. He put the mask on last and decided he didn't like the confined feeling it left him with. His breathing started to come faster and he had to stop and remind himself that he was fine, that it was just a mask, that he could still breathe.

For the first time since entering the room, Ryan took in their surroundings. Emergency lights cast a dim glow on the wide room and didn't reach far enough to illuminate the far corners. Carts and dollies lined the walls for deliveries while a stack of boxes occupied one corner. A side door led to what Ryan guessed was a storage room, while Malone waited at the far end at another door.

Ryan started toward the door and Malone held out a hand.

"Stay back, kid. You're obviously not feeling well and you've done your part."

"I said no in the car and I'm saying it now. What if I get another vision and something changes? Then what?"

"Then I roll with the punches."

"And what if the punches happens to be twelve angry guys with machine guns, and they're all shooting from different angles? How long can you keep a shield up?"

"I'll figure something out. I always do."

"That's bullshit, Malone, and you know it. I saw Warner's aura and I know he had more juice than you do, but look at what happened to him."

Malone frowned but said nothing and eventually nodded.

"But leave the heavy lifting to me, alright?"

CHAPTER 8

Emergency lights cast everything in an orange glow while managing to look like oversized night lights. Had he not known otherwise, Ryan would have thought it was Halloween lighting. Not all of the lighting in the building was holiday themed as clearer lights shone in some rooms, but in the common area Halloween was the plan.

Occupied gurneys lined the outside of rooms and sat in clusters in the middle of the lobby. Orderlies and office staff moved from one room or area to another, their faces haggard, their movements slow. Groans, cries, wails, the sounds bounced around the hallways. Surely Sikes and his followers were responsible for putting many, if not most, of those people in the hospital, be it directly or indirectly thanks to the breakdown in society.

A couple of police officers occupied the lobby as well, though whether they were legit Ryan couldn't tell. They did look alert, however, as they scanned the room and slowly made their rounds.

The doctors and nurses ignored Ryan and Malone as they went about their business, but many had a look in their eyes that belied their otherwise calm appearance. Their eyes darted about quickly and they moved from one person to the next, doing what they could, though it was clear they were overwhelmed.

Panic, sudden and harsh, materialized and Ryan wondered what he would do if someone stopped him and wanted his assistance since he looked like a nurse or maybe even a doctor. He knew nothing about medicine, hadn't dedicated his life to saving others' lives.

It was a baseless worry. They moved through the lobby and reached the stairs. Seven floors hadn't seemed like much in the car, but Ryan eyed the staircase with suspicion. Malone took to the steps first, Ryan close behind. Several others passed them along the way as they made their way up, but they looked hurried and moved with purpose. The other people didn't so much as look at them.

After two floors, Ryan had to stop and rest. He sat on the landing and wondered if Malone was right, if he should have stayed back. He could hardly believe how winded he was. It wasn't as though he'd done anything physically demanding, but somehow that trick he pulled in the parking lot sure felt like the equivalent of running a marathon, not that he'd ever run one.

"It's like soccer. You don't just go out there and play an entire game without conditioning first. You have to build up to it."

Ryan looked up and stared at Malone. He narrowed his eyes then turned his gaze to the stairs in front of him. "You would like soccer."

"I would have said football, but I know you would have assumed I meant the terrible game with fat oafs and prima donnas."

Ryan smiled. Malone was right, on both accounts. Or at least he assumed Malone was right about having to build these muscles up, or whatever it was that controlled the strange power. If it were like other things, then it required practice, dedication, learning, and patience. Those were things that Ryan didn't have a surplus of at the moment.

He forced himself back up to his feet and indicated Malone should continue to lead the way up the stairs. They didn't stop until they reached the seventh floor, though Ryan's pace slowed considerably in the last few stories.

Ryan took the last step and held onto the railing at the landing. A few steps beyond, more stairs led up to and stopped at a worn metal door that proclaimed Roof Access.

This was far enough. Ryan sat and watched Malone with his peripheral vision. Malone's aura glowed vibrantly and Ryan reminded himself that he was with a guy who could stop explosions with his sheer will. It gave him some confidence to get out of any potential conflict, if nothing else. They had, after all, made it through bombs and lots of bullets, so why should this be any different?

And then panic hit him without warning again.

"What the hell am I supposed to do up there?"

"Has the information changed?"

Ryan had to stop and think, but he was sure he hadn't had another vision. He shook his head.

"Then maybe you can wait this one out. She's a norm, anyway."

"You're not going to see if she's a traitor first?"

Malone gave him a look that could have been translated as a pat on the head. "Of course, but I don't doubt Hansen's intel. I don't like him, but he's seldom wrong. Still, there's always a chance."

Ryan nodded. He could understand, at least he thought he could, that Malone was going in suspicious.

He'd already found one traitor, possibly another, and he didn't intend to be surprised. Ryan had to admit he'd likely do the same if their roles were reversed.

Though he knew he could get up and make it up the stairs to the roof, Ryan worried about getting in the way should it come to a fight, which certainly seemed inevitable. He didn't want to admit it, but he'd become a total liability.

Ryan waved Malone on. "I'll hang back here. I'll figure something out if I get anything different."

"Sit tight, kid."

Ryan nodded and leaned back against the wall. Malone watched him for a second then turned and put his foot on the first of the stairs that led to the roof.

The omnipresent buzzing and flow of water came to his ears and his eyes flickered out of control. The more it happened, the more he was getting used to the experience, and the less intrusive the sounds and sensations were becoming. The buzzing was still present, but it had taken on a different quality, as though it was softer, kinder somehow. And the sound of water no longer left him with the feeling he was drowning, but perhaps just swimming in the ocean or maybe even a pool.

The sounds washed past him and his vision showed him the top of the hospital again. Ryan immediately recognized the woman looking over the building top. A scoped rifle leaned against the retaining wall within her reach. She held black binoculars up to her eyes and watched the northern sky. Something black came into view. A haze hovered around her, but it never completely obscured her from view.

Time seemed to speed up and the small black thing in the sky quickly grew into a helicopter that approached the roof. The woman, Barajas, put the binoculars down and raised her arm against the incoming wind. She picked up the rifle and continued to shield her face as the chopper landed.

A door opened and a man dressed in black stepped out, but his features were imprecise like so many other little things. He ducked slightly as he walked through the chopper's wake and approached Barajas. They saluted then shook hands and exchanged words, but the sound of the chopper's blades, still spinning, overpowered their conversation. They spoke for what felt like several minutes, then the man returned to the chopper and it lifted back into the air and flew off.

Barajas returned to the wall. She grabbed the rifle and braced it against her shoulder, put her eye to the scope. Time seemed to move into fast forward again as the angle of the shadows gradually changed, then it seemed to stop and Ryan could only focus on Barajas. She followed something in the scope, took a breath and held it, and squeezed the trigger. The agent fired off a few more rounds in rapid succession before she released her breath. She stared through the scope for several seconds then put the rifle down with a smile.

Ryan's vision took a turn that left him lurching but able to see over the side of the hospital. The parking lot rushed toward him while a car careened into a parked van.

The car was familiar, and as Ryan flew in closer to see it, he realized it was Warner's car, only Warner wasn't in it. There were two people in the car, but both were slumped forward. Blood and carnage covered the interior of the car. Several large holes left spiderwebs of glass in the windshield. At first Ryan couldn't make out the occupants, but as he flew down and came up to the side of the car, he recognized both of them and his heart jumped.

Ryan jerked back and looked around, the vision suddenly ended.

Malone had stopped on the stairs and was staring at him. His grip on the rail was tight, but he said nothing to give away his tension.

Ryan sucked down a few breaths before he could manage to speak.

"I just saw Barajas, on the roof, meeting with someone in a black chopper. I couldn't hear anything over the chopper, but when it took off, Barajas picked up a rifle and started shooting over the side of the hospital." Ryan closed his eyes and took a breath. "She shot at a car and it crashed into another vehicle because she killed the occupants."

"Why'd she shoot at the car?"

"I don't know, but I saw who was in it."

Malone's voice was tight. "Who was it?"

"Us."

Malone sucked in a breath, but otherwise appeared calm.

"Obviously that didn't happen. And it's not going to happen."

"But is that what would have happened if we had shown up later? I don't get it, Malone. I saw both of us, dead as can be." A shiver coursed Ryan's spine.

"Maybe you're seeing something, a plan that's since changed. Either way, I think I know what to expect upstairs now."

Ryan nodded. "Be careful up there. That rifle looks like it means business."

"Yeah." Malone released his grip on the rail and straightened his jacket.

The agent nodded and turned around on the stairs. He took the steps slowly, barely made a sound, and stopped at the door. Ryan couldn't tell whether the door was locked, but Malone stood in front of it for several seconds before he finally cracked it open. He turned around and shot Ryan a quick look then opened the door hurriedly and stepped onto the roof. The door held open for a moment then closed itself with a solid clunk of metal on metal.

Ryan rested his head back against the wall and closed his eyes. He was exhausted and it was more than just physical or mental, but an overall, entire body and mind exhaustion. He seemed to recuperate reasonably quickly when he was just having visions, but whatever that stunt was he pulled earlier, twice even, was just too much. It wasn't just that it left him tired and wanting to sleep, but that he still didn't quite understand exactly what he was doing and he wanted to know. He needed to know.

Whatever this power was, Malone seemed to know how to harness it in certain ways, but not how Ryan could. That made Malone a less-than-ideal instructor who seemed almost as baffled at Ryan's abilities as Ryan was, though he tried to hide it behind bravado. It didn't make it any easier to accept, but at this point, what choice did he have?

Maybe he was quick to adjust, or maybe Malone was right and there was a change going on his brain, but Ryan was able to push some of the questions aside, at least in part, for a while. Answers would come eventually, but for now, being alive was enough.

He could do little more than sit there and wait. He hoped that Malone knew what he was getting himself into. Sure, Barajas might not be a cleaner or have any powers, but a rifle like the one she was shooting in his vision would pack a hell of a lot stronger punch than a pistol. Then again, Malone did stand in the middle of an explosion and come out little more than pissed off and sweaty.

Still, what if Barajas had a trick up her sleeve, a trap, or maybe another person on the roof? What if Fredriksson's powers were greatly understated? And what about Rainier? The way Malone spoke about Rainier, the man could be a walking army unto himself.

Sleep, a quiet siren that lulled him into darkness with promises of peace and freedom from worries, drew him to the edge, but Ryan became cognizant that he was seeing and hearing things even though his eyes were closed. Similar to his vision, distortion clouded his sight, but it was different, as though it were a television channel getting poor reception. Snow obscured the picture and the sound buzzed with static. For fractions of a second, everything would come through with clarity, but it was fleeting.

He wasn't sure, but he thought he was seeing the rooftop, perhaps seeing it in the present. Malone and a woman, Barajas obviously, talked on the roof. No, argued, he corrected himself as he noticed their animated body language and caught the slightest raised voice in a brief window of clear reception. In that moment everything became clear. Barajas had her hair in a ponytail, only a lock of it had broken free and was blowing by the left side of her face in the breeze. The clarity was stunning and gave Ryan pause. The static returned and Ryan changed his perspective.

Ryan focused on the room his body occupied and realized that he couldn't hear anything through the door. The agents were either being quiet, or there was so much ambient noise that their arguing wasn't enough to override it.

Back on the roof, the argument continued for another few seconds then Barajas reached into her jacket. Something unseen slammed into Ryan and his eyes flew open in surprise. His breath caught in his chest, but whatever had slammed into him was entirely insubstantial. White filled his vision and static filled his ears entirely. He blinked and tried to look around the room, but all was white.

A sound, something harsh, broke through the static. Then just as suddenly as it came, the blindness and the static were gone. Ryan blinked for the shock of it and grabbed the rail even as he sat. Though he was tired, beyond exhausted, his eyes were large and he looked around in the room in sudden alertness. What the hell just happened?

Silence replaced the buzzing, just as disturbing in its own way for the unexpected change. Where up until moments ago there had been a fairly constant stream of noise coming from the stairwell, now there was none.

A loud bang, unmistakable, broke through the wall of silence and Ryan jerked in surprise. His eyes went to the door, but it offered no answers. He needed to know what was happening on the roof, but body and mind wouldn't comply, He tried to take himself out of his body, to look around and see, but his heart was beating too fast, his blood pumping loudly in his ears, his mind racing. Silence fell on the stairwell again, but Ryan only became tenser with each passing second.

He forced himself to his feet and stumbled with the sudden clumsy action. Legs that were weaker than he last remembered threatened to give out on him. Ryan steadied himself against the rail. A deep breath, then two, and he looked down the open stairwell, but there was still no one around. Besides, the sound had come from above, not below. No use thinking it could have been a door being slammed.

The roof door opened and Ryan turned to face it. Someone appeared in the doorway, but in his disorientated state he had no way of knowing who it was. Fear prodded him, vicious and sudden, and Ryan dug deep within his brain and threw his will against the person in an attempt to keep them away.

The person grunted in pain and surprise, but Ryan expended almost all of his energy with that attack without realizing it. Ryan stumbled down to one knee, still holding the railing, and breathed heavily as he looked at the metal landing. Lifting his head was too much. If the angel of death were bearing down on him, so be it. He was tired. Beyond tired, even.

Footsteps echoed down to him a few seconds later, though he was still too tired to even look up.

"What the hell, kid? What was that?"

It was Malone. Ryan shook his head and felt his heart start to slow. He almost fell over as he turned and put his back against the wall again. His breathing was loud and raspy and his head started to swim as he could feel himself start to faint. Everything took on a weird fast-yet-slow feel as though time was constantly being sped up and slowed down. Everything moved quickly in front of his eyes, yet he felt as though he were swimming through molasses.

Hands steadied him and shook him slightly. Ryan struggled to focus on the face in front of him. Sound came to him, something that vaguely resembled words but made no sense. He blinked once, twice, three times and could finally feel everything start to return to a normal speed.

"Don't go out on me, kid. I don't want to carry you. Hey, good, look at me."

Ryan managed a smile and pushed Malone's hands away. "I'm alright." His face grew warm with embarrassment. How many times had he fainted or almost fainted in the last few days?

"I don't know what you did, but it felt like you hit me with a psychic truck."

"You're still standing."

"It was a truck that was coasting and out of gas, but still a damn truck." Malone's eyes were large and he even had a slightly raised eyebrow, a distinct difference from his usual impassive expression that spoke volumes.

"I thought Barajas was coming down those stairs ready to shoot. I don't know what happened after that."

"What? Why would you think that?"

"I saw you and her arguing. Then she reached into her jacket and I blacked out. Or whited out. There was nothing. Just white noise and white everywhere. It faded and I heard a gunshot, though I don't think it was the only one." He looked to the side and tried to recall what he felt and saw at precisely that moment, but he at last shook his head. "I'm not sure what happened, I just know I was scared shitless when I saw that door open."

Malone nodded and looked grim. "Hansen's intel was right." He shook his head and looked away. "Barajas won't be giving anything to Sikes or his grunts anytime soon."

Ryan nodded and looked down. "I'm not sure how much I have left now."

"I don't know what that whiteout was, but it may be something left over from the feedback. You've been really reaching today and might have just spent yourself. You need rest."

Ryan was shaking his head before Malone finished. "No time. We need to find these guys."

"Then I'll go looking. I didn't make it this far without learning how to investigate a case."

The idea of rest, even if it were only for a few hours, was damn inviting. The mere thought of sleep seemed to send his body and mind into a downward spiral.

Ryan let out a sour chuckle. "You're right. I can't keep doing this."

Malone extended him a hand and pulled Ryan up to his feet. He wasn't sure how he was supposed to make it down seven flights of stairs, but at least they were going down instead of up. Ryan grabbed the handrail and started down.

Down turned out to be better than up, but not by much. Tired beyond anything he had ever felt, they had to stop a couple of times for Ryan to catch his breath. When they reached the bottom floor, they found it much as they had left it before. The faces on the gurneys lining the hall could have been the same, but it seemed that at least one or two had moved.

Even in the middle of a terrorist attack, the hospital had to remain open and would be busy, perhaps especially so. Ryan felt bad for the people on the gurneys, unable to receive a standard level of care.

At some point Ryan realized he was paying more attention than strictly needed to the faces on the gurneys. He realized he was looking for friends and family and he dragged his eyes away and shuffled to catch up to Malone.

It took some snaking around the building, but they walked out the front door without being stopped or questioned and made their way around the parking lot to the car. Once in the car, Ryan took the mask off and threw it in the back.

He caught a momentary glance of his face and didn't recognize himself. A few days' growth of hair covered his chin and cheeks and his skin had a grey tint to it. He didn't like how tired he looked. It made him appear much older than he was, though he supposed he had aged a fair amount in the last few days, at least as far as naivety was concerned.

Dusk had fallen and sunlight was quickly fading. Malone started the car and they left the hospital and rejoined the city streets. It was more difficult to navigate the streets since it looked like additional law enforcement had been called in to block off the roads, but they still managed to make their way through town back to the hideout.

Ryan was almost asleep by the time they pulled up, and a rough shake of his shoulder roused him from his near-dreaming.

"Just a few minutes, kid. Open the door, will you?"

Ryan blinked several times and waited for his eyes to settle. They were back at the house. With some effort, Ryan got out of the car and managed to raise the garage door, though just doing so worked up a good sweat. He waited by the inside door and Malone unlocked it shortly thereafter. With barely a conscious thought, Ryan staggered to the couch and collapsed upon it.

CHAPTER 9

It wasn't a lucid dream, exactly, but Ryan knew he wasn't awake either. That he could sort of see and hear things that were happening around him—though he ought to be sleeping—was a disturbing realization. The problem wasn't that he could see and hear, but that he couldn't see or hear well enough to make out the details.

It was like sitting too far from the TV with the volume turned down. Only vague shapes and sounds came to him, but he knew he saw Malone sitting on a bed with the rugged HAM radio. Malone hardly moved as he spoke. He appeared to be having a conversation, but Ryan couldn't tell what about. Malone continued to speak quietly off and on for several more minutes, then he dropped the radio, removed his jacket and shoes, and lay down on the bed.

For some time Ryan watched the room, could see the subtle shifts in the shadows as he presumed clouds passed by overhead and obscured the moon and stars. All the while he watched Malone sleep. It was a boring way to pass the time, especially if it could be considered a dream. What sort of loser dreams about watching someone sleep? Shouldn't one be a superhero in their dreams, or at least do something slightly more exciting than watch someone sleep?

His gaze eventually drifted out of the bedroom and to the front room where he saw himself asleep on the couch. It was odd to see himself lying there, perfectly still except for the rise and fall of his chest, or at least he assumed it was since he couldn't quite see it happening. Still, it was an odd, surreal experience, but when combined with the idea of seeing the world around him despite him being asleep, it seemed perfectly natural.

The experience reminded him of a documentary he had seen about a man who had surgery. The man, completely incapacitated thanks to anesthesia, actually witnessed his operation as it took place. He later recalled details about the surgery, such as where the surgeon operated or what the surgeon looked like. The odd thing was that he was spot-on with the details of the surgeon, even down to the doctor's bald spot on the back of his head, yet the man had never seen the surgeon before.

Even more interesting, the details of the surgery he recalled were also correct, even if he didn't quite nail everything to the most minute point. Had the man awoken during the surgery—though video of the surgery confirmed he was asleep the entire time—there was a tall screen set up on his chest that would have prevented him from viewing the surgery as it took place.

At the time, Ryan remembered laughing at the documentary and its clearly exploitative nature. People wanted to believe in impossible things and this documentary was just trying to take advantage of that, complete with some guy who'd been paid off to act as if he saw and knew things even though there was no way for him to have that knowledge.

Of course, Ryan had a different perspective now, and he reflected on that even as he realized that he shouldn't be capable of any heavy thinking or extreme memory recall while he was supposedly sleeping. Perhaps the full realization of what he was doing in his sleep triggered something, but he fell back into a deep sleep shortly thereafter and awoke some hours later when he heard voices, though not ones in his sleep.

Ryan opened his eyes. The house was dark, and aside from the voices, still. He wondered how many days he had slept when he looked over at the source of the voices and just made out Malone's silhouette at the table. The voices clearly came from the radio.

Ryan focused on the sound and one of the voices, a monotone one that droned on about some problem or another. When its owner finally paused for breath, another voice chimed in.

"It doesn't matter because the army is setting up now. I saw them drive past my house. They already have roadblocks up that make the police ones look like toys."

Silence for several seconds then Mr. Monotone, as Ryan dubbed him, replied. "We're not being told the truth. I saw a newspaper from LA and they say its terrorists. They can't even get into town, but they have contacts. If it was only a gas leak, why would the town be cordoned off?"

"And if it is, the army is moving in now and will take care of them." The other man's tone was that of a parent speaking to a child. "Just stay inside and they'll have it figured out in a day or two."

"We'll see."

Ryan got off the couch and went to the front window. He wasn't sure if he was expecting to see a tank drive through the neighborhood, but he felt as though he needed to see the military for himself to believe this attack had spiraled so far out of control.

All was quiet outside and no tanks or Humvees drove by. Soldiers didn't march across lawns and down sidewalks. Aside from the lack of power and traffic, it looked like what must have been most any other night in the neighborhood.

Without the two men speaking, the only sound was the radio's slight hiss. A buzz sounded from behind Ryan and he turned to see Malone suddenly look up. It looked as though Malone had fallen asleep with his chin on his chest.

Malone put a hand to his ear and moved it around. Ryan started to ask what was going on, but Malone put a finger to his lips and waited.

Ryan could no longer hear whatever the buzzing was.

"Malone here. Copy that."

Malone still had his finger to his lips then he finally put it down.

"That was base. They've restored power and need backup."

"Are they under attack?"

"No, but they're in danger."

"What? You just said they're not under attack."

"They're not." Malone stood and turned the radio off. "But Rainier has been left in charge after attrition and there may be other insurgents inside still."

Ryan sucked in a breath. If Hansen's intel was correct, and so far it seemed to be, then what was the agency looking at with Rainier left in charge? A shudder coursed Ryan's spine, then he remembered another possible traitor was still unaccounted for. "What about Fredriksson?"

Malone put his jacket on. "This is priority. If Rainier is left in charge, there's no telling what may happen." Malone paused in mid-button and looked at Ryan. "This could be a trap."

"Who was on the radio from the base? Did you recognize the voice?"

Malone resumed buttoning his jacket up. "I'm not sure. There's static in the line and there's several who work in communications."

"Like police dispatch?"

"Yeah."

"The military is in town, Malone. What does that mean?"

"I'm not sure, but it may mean that we're going to have a hell of a time getting out of here."

Ryan grabbed the last two bottles of water from the refrigerator—long since gone warm—and met Malone in the driveway. If they meant to come back to the hideout, they were going to have to bring supplies or fix whatever was happening first.

Ryan hopped in the car after closing the garage door and passed one of the bottles over. He looked at the fuel gauge as he did so and wondered if they had enough gas to make it to the base. He realized he wasn't even sure how far the drive was. Perhaps it didn't matter because they had to get out of town before they could get to the base.

"Okay, kid. I'm not sure which way this is going if we hit the military, but we're going to try the diplomatic approach first. I may be able to stop most firearms, but we're talking about a completely different caliber of weaponry here."

"I thought you've seen assault rifles before."

Malone grunted. "Yeah, I have. But not tanks."

"No way. They wouldn't."

"Don't worry, kid. We'll get through this."

Malone backed the car out of the driveway and made it to the end of the street. They still had another couple of turns before they could get out of the neighborhood, and when they made that last turn, a new roadblock cut off exit from the neighborhood.

The car's clock read just after two in the morning. They'd made it back to the house not long after dusk, so the military must have come in some time after and wasted little time in setting up barricades about town. Where the police used long saw horses, the military used big ugly masses of wood with barbed wire wrapped around it that gleamed in the headlights. Soldiers stood on either side of the barricades, their attention and their assault rifles trained on the car.

Malone slowed as he approached and two soldiers moved to intercept from the sides while two stayed up front and continued to aim at the car. Malone rolled his window down and waited.

"This area is under control of the United States Army. Turn around and go home, citizen."

Ryan looked at Malone. The soldier had said Army, not National Guard. Malone didn't seem to notice, however.

Malone pulled a small case out of his jacket and presented his badge to the soldier. The soldier took the badge and turned it to catch the moonlight. He stared at it for several seconds then consulted a clipboard. He passed the badge back to Malone and shook his head.

"I'm sorry, sir, but your name isn't on the list of agents granted access. Return home and you will be notified at the appropriate time."

"Son, I'm under strict orders to get back to my base and you're going to make me go AWOL."

"Not my concern, sir. You don't have the required clearance."

"I'm fighting the assholes responsible for this and you're hindering my progress."

The soldier narrowed his eyes but said nothing. He pointed back the way they'd come.

"Fine."

Malone put the car in reverse then turned it around and started back. Once he turned the corner, he turned it around again and took his seatbelt off.

They'd done this once before and Ryan swallowed a lump in his throat. "Hold the wheel?"

"You know the drill."

Malone started the car forward and turned the corner then stomped on the gas. Foot still on the gas, he leaned out of his window and pulled an arm back. Ryan grabbed the wheel and stopped watching Malone and instead looked forward.

The soldiers gathered behind the barricade and pointed their guns toward them. It would only be another couple of seconds before they hit the barricade.

The barricade and soldiers leaped off the ground and spun away. They landed several feet away from their original locations and the soldiers hit the ground hard. Malone slid back into the car. He took the wheel back and maneuvered them past the barricade.

Ryan turned back to see one of the soldiers just getting to his feet. He held something other than his gun in his hand, perhaps a radio. Ryan quickly lost sight of the man as they started to crisscross through town.

Perhaps the Army wasn't finished, or maybe they didn't have the manpower and supplies, but they hadn't covered the entire town yet. The major intersections were all blocked, but Malone was able to pick their way through town using smaller streets and alleys.

It wasn't long before the two-lane highway that led to the freeway on-ramp came into view. Blazing lights made it visible from miles away.

The army must have had generators and put them to use on a large portable light system. Flood lamps blasted light over the area, a stark contrast to the darkness that covered the rest of the town. Bathed in light, two Humvees were parked broadside to the road. Their mounted machineguns on top glinted in the harsh light.

"I don't suppose you traded cars earlier because this one has thicker metal and glass."

"No, but it had gas."

"That's what I was afraid of."

"Grab the wheel."

Malone slipped out of the seatbelt again and leaned out of the window. Ryan grabbed the wheel and had a moment to reflect on how he both enjoyed and dreaded the moments when Malone would lean out of the car like that.

Ryan could almost feel the air abuzz with tension. It was as if they were recreating some wild stunt out of a movie: Malone leaning out of the window and preparing to attack, the unbelievable devastating power that he would direct toward anything in their path. But this wasn't a movie, and there was a significant threat in front of them. That part, at least, was getting old.

Perhaps these soldiers were less forgiving, or perhaps they'd heard something from the others, but they opened fire from three hundred yards away.

Ryan held his breath and waited for the inevitable, be it a bullet lodged in the windshield or lodged in his forehead, but nothing seemed to hit. Warning shots, he reasoned.

Two hundred yards away and still more shots, but nothing hit.

One hundred yards away and now the distinct sound of something hitting the front of the car came to him. They were moving fast, exceptionally fast. Another shot ripped through the windshield and left a spider web around the hole. Ryan glanced back. The bullet passed through the rear windshield.

Ryan looked back to Malone for a second. "Hurry up!"

Thirty yards and several shots rattled the front of the car.

Twenty yards and Malone did his trick.

The Humvees bucked and turned outward and Malone scrambled back into the car. One of the lights wobbled and pitched over sideways, casting long shadows that stretched out along the road.

The vehicles stopped moving and Ryan knew there was no way they were getting through without touching them, but Malone didn't slow.

The car hit the front tires of each Humvee and split them like a four-thousand pound linebacker. Their car shuddered with the impact and slowed, but it kept thundering forward and they were on the highway. Ryan looked back to see if the Army was following them, but only shadows tailed them. The highway was clear and they were able to jump onto the freeway without further trouble.

They merged into light traffic, though only a few cars were headed the same direction. It comforted Ryan to see humanity still existed outside of his besieged town.

Ryan settled back to watching the road in front of them and focused on the sound of wind whistling through the numerous bullet holes. Even though what those holes portended was frightening, he'd gotten used to the sound of it in the other cars, like a battle wound he could proudly display to others, never mind it wasn't even his car.

Neither spoke as the minutes passed. Ryan watched the clock as it incremented and threw the occasional sidelong glance at Malone or the outside world. The darkness of the outside world, complete with the relative silence in the car, left Ryan with the feeling that he was alone, even though he knew it was ridiculous. Malone was right there next to him, but Malone was so utterly focused on driving, his thoughts obviously elsewhere, that he could have just as easily been elsewhere for as little as he was mentally present.

They'd been through quite a bit in their few days together, but Ryan thought that this was the most intense he'd ever seen Malone. If they were only driving now, he wasn't sure what to expect once they reached the base. Would Malone be able to control himself? Well, no reason to think he couldn't, but Ryan risked another glance over and watched for some time as Malone looked straight ahead without so much as blinking.

As personally as he'd taken the actions of the other traitors, Malone seemed especially bothered by the idea of confronting Rainier, but also made it clear it was important. Maybe it was because Malone made the man sound like a tank packed into a human's frame, or maybe there was also some history there, but Ryan wasn't so sure he'd readily jump into the fray for this battle.

If the last encounter with Barajas hadn't truly made its impact, then it was time to admit his limitations. He was good for recon, but he was no soldier. He knew it was true, but there was some thought somewhere, some hope that he had something else to contribute. Malone wasn't the only one with power, after all, but Malone had training and skill and knew when and how to best put that power to use.

Ryan knew that he didn't, that he had a lot to learn, and that it was time he stop acting like his contribution was more than it really was. Ryan bit back a chuckle as he realized how ridiculous he'd been acting. Sure, Malone asked his opinion and even seemed to consider what he had to say, but what did Ryan know about any of what was happening?

Maybe it was the age difference and Ryan reminded Malone of one of his kids, if he even had any, but he realized that Malone had been hearing him out in the same way a parent might guide a child. But this time the child was out of his league, and it was time to realize that they each had their purpose in this struggle, even if it wasn't glorious or exciting, Ryan's part was still important, but it ended at giving Malone information. Malone was sage enough to know how to handle things.

"You okay, kid?"

Ryan looked up in surprise and his thoughts scattered. "What? Yeah, I'm good."

"That so? You were spacing out."

"Just thinking. I'm sorry for being a know-it-all ass, Malone."

Malone smiled, briefly, then pointed toward the off-ramp. "We're almost there. Just ahead."

"I haven't had anything hit me."

"We still have time."

Ryan stared at the off-ramp and imagined the base somewhere down the road beyond it. He had an uneasy feeling, one he couldn't quite label.

"I don't have a good feeling about this. What if I don't see anything?"

"I always have a backup plan."

They hit the off-ramp and joined the canyon road. It looked different in the darkness, the turns in unfamiliar locations, but Ryan remembered the mountainside that housed the hidden door when they pulled up to a stop in front of it.

"So they have power out here?"

"Yeah. Been up for a couple hours now. Just a second."

Malone snickered and pressed a bunch of buttons on the center console until the door opened. "Been so long since I've driven one of these I forgot what the trick is."

Ryan looked back out of habit and couldn't see anyone nearby. They drove into the mountain and Malone hit more buttons until the door closed.

The lights in the tunnels flickered as they started toward the base at a slow pace.

"If nothing has hit you by now, then don't think about this guy. Nothing. Okay, kid?"

Ryan scrunched his eyebrows together but nodded. Was just thinking about Rainier dangerous?

The shift was so subtle he almost missed it. It seemed natural for the view to slowly dissolve into one of the offices in the base, as though he'd been there all along.

A man with a horseshoe of hair sat in front of a desk, his face hidden behind a computer monitor. The rest of the office was a blur, just a dark room with functional but inelegant furniture, the only light that which the monitor supplied. Ryan became more aware of where he was and forced the view to turn around.

It was like something out of a movie, when the camera was on a rail and would turn a circle, his view did the same. The man's face was familiar and he could almost remember seeing him seated at the table with the rest of the council earlier, but couldn't. Regardless, the man fit Rainier's description and Ryan had no doubt it was him. Malone's warnings about Rainier registered and Ryan wanted to leave.

But he also wanted to see what was on the monitor, perhaps gain some insight into what the man was planning. The view shifted around and eventually stopped at an angle that allowed Ryan to look past the man's face to see the monitor beyond.

He didn't recognize what Rainier was doing, perhaps using proprietary software, but information filled the screen, including what looked like a map of the town. Most things on the screen were blurry, but he recognized the top-down view of the town having seen the maps in the library before, and he recognized where there were red dots on the map. One looked to be roughly where the sandwich shop was, another the hospital, and another looked to be somewhat near one of the major industrial complexes. Other dots were on the screen, different colors and in places he didn't immediately recognize.

Ryan started to inch forward, but he stopped. Rainier paused in studying the monitor and looked around. Ryan had the distinct impression that Rainier realized someone was nearby. Ryan panicked and thought to end the vision. He blinked his eyes and looked around at the inside of the car.

"Some timing you have, kid."

Ryan tried to laugh, but his breath came in adrenaline-assisted bursts. It was all he could do to just breathe. He closed his eyes and forced himself to slow down, to breathe normally.

"I think he sensed my presence somehow."

"What?" Was that worry in Malone's voice?

"I saw," Ryan was about to say the man's name, "you know, and he was looking at a monitor, studying something. There were dots on it, and I recognized some places, like the store where Warner was and the hospital. He was looking at the monitor, then he stopped and started to look around the room. I panicked and I somehow managed to end the vision."

Malone stared ahead and narrowed his eyes. "Okay, let's think this through. He might know someone is coming, but he doesn't know you. He only saw you once." Malone turned to face him and his words came out in a hurry. "You need to blank your mind."

"What?"

"Blank it. Nothing. You have to clear it. This guy is dangerous and he might track you down. He needs to think it was nothing, that he's just nervous."

Ryan's breathing had just stabilized when his heart started to pound again. He forced himself to remain calm and closed his eyes and thought of nothing. Nothing. Then his mind would start to wander and he had to come back and stop himself and focus on nothing. Ryan was beginning to understand that thinking of nothing was a lot more difficult than most people realized.

This differed from the parking lot at the hospital, because he had someone to focus on there. Here, he had to ignore everyone.

Damn it, nothing. Focus on nothing, he told himself.

It went on for some time as they drove, and after a while, Ryan could no longer think of nothing, but he could force himself to not think of someone or something. He just looked ahead and started to count flickering lights in the ceiling.

He was at thirty-seven flickering lights, fourteen dead lights, and eighteen functional ones when Malone stopped the car.

Ryan looked over at Malone then looked to where there had been a door that led to hallways and more interior doors. It'd been replaced by a large, burned-out hole.

"I can't keep focusing on nothing. I can't do it."

"It's okay, kid. Just stick to surface thoughts, nothing more. You're doing fine."

They exited the car and entered the burned-out hallway. Instead of doors along the way, there were just scorch marks until they reached the final door. Someone had put up another door there, as the original one hadn't been wood with a metal sliding plate in it.

Malone knocked on the door and announced his arrival. The plate slid open a fraction of an inch and a moment later the door opened.

The large, open office area that had contained computers and people galore before looked completely different now. Rubble filled the room, and only a few desks stood upright and had computer equipment on them. What was there looked old, like something that had been dragged out of storage in the wake of a bomb shaking the entire room.

Ryan snorted at the thought and realized he was likely right. Surface, he reminded himself.

Malone looked around the room, a mixture of disgust and pity in his expression.

"What's the damage?"

The man who answered the door closed it as they walked in and made a sweep of the room with his arm. He was thin and his clothes looked severely rumpled and dirty.

"Bad. We lost a lot." His voice trailed off.

"The council?" Malone still looked around the room.

"Everyone but Rainier is missing."

Malone looked over at the man and shook his head.

"Shit. He's in charge?"

"Last man standing."

Malone put a hand on the man's shoulder then started forward.

"This is it, kid. This is the big one. I know we're still not done, but this is the one that counts."

"Yeah." Surface.

"We tackle this one and we're on the path to cleaning this up. Then we can go after the guys who're really behind this shit."

"Looks like you took a big hit, though."

"Yeah." A long pause. "It hurts, kid. It does. But you push forward. You know that. We'll call in the big guns from the east and we'll get payback."

They reached the formerly-glass wall and door and found a pile of shards that'd been pushed aside to clear a path. The door was still in its frame, but it was nothing more than twisted metal.

Malone walked in and took a left. He turned around and met Ryan's eyes.

"Okay, I need you to dig for a second and give me any other details you can. Take yourself back and tell me everything you saw."

Ryan nodded and shook himself from his self-inflicted daze. He thought about the vision, thought of the man at the table. He closed his eyes and blocked out the sights and sounds around him and remembered Rainier at the desk, studying a map.

The room was dark, the only light coming from the computer's monitor. It lit Rainier's blurry face in a particularly scary way that he hadn't noticed before. And the map, what was on the map? The red dots he recognized, but the others? What were they?

Blue dots were placed on the map in places that seemed familiar somehow, but he couldn't figure out why. One of those dots, somewhat near the middle but a little east, was one that he knew he should know. It was like forgetting the name to a song and it was on the tip of his mind, just out of reach, when he suddenly felt a psychic blast the likes he'd never experienced.

He didn't think it was directed at him, but it was like a wave that washed over him and pulled at his ankles. It frightened him and shook him out of his reverie but did no real damage, at least that he could tell. He opened his eyes to see that he was alone in the room. Malone was gone.

Ryan's heart jumped and he looked around again, but Malone was nowhere to be seen. The walls that were once glass and now nothing allowed a perfect view of what remained of the bombed structure. The few people still in the base continued to work as though nothing was amiss.

Another wave hit him, though weaker than the first, and Ryan oriented himself in the direction he thought it came from. It was difficult to tell because the mere nature of being hit by it disoriented him. The blast forced him to think and remember who he was and where he was, yet it seemed like it was coming from the direction of the office that the council had met in before.

Ryan took a step in that direction before he even realized it but he stopped when another wave hit him. It was nothing more than a weak breaker that came in after the tide.

Ryan looked around again, but people were still ignorant of what was happening, so he ran forward. He stopped as he found the office the council had met in, but it was full of rubble. The hallway continued and

Ryan slowed as he looked into another room, this one empty, and he kept going.

He looked in another as he passed and thought he saw someone, so he stopped, backed up, and could clearly see a silhouette in the room.

It was dark inside the room, the only light shining off to the side from a monitor, and Ryan took a step inside. He thought he recognized the silhouette, that it looked like someone he knew standing over someone.

Clear, sharp pain stabbed his mind. Ryan closed his eyes to it and tumbled to the ground.

CHAPTER 10

Pain. Significant pain. Hurt to open eyes. Couldn't think.

Ryan tried one eye, then the other. They eventually made it open far enough to see, but it was extremely dark. A dim area of light was somewhere before him and just to his left, but it was all blurry. Why couldn't he see? And what was with that pain in the back of his head?

He blinked a few times and only succeeded in shifting the blur around, but it was still too dark to make out details. He tried to rub his eyes and realized his arms weren't working. Panic was too complicated a thought for the moment and instead he wondered with a dull curiosity why his arms weren't working. That certainly wasn't normal, and he didn't remember having any problems with them in the past.

The minutes passed as he slowly wondered what was wrong with him, why his vision was so poor, why his arms—and legs, he realized—weren't responding, and why everything seemed to move in horrible, slow motion. Not so much as a groan escaped his lips as he—was he sitting? Ryan couldn't tell. He waited and hoped that whatever it was would pass.

More minutes ticked away and the fog that shrouded his brain seemed to burn away. As it did, he found himself thinking and feeling better, except for the part where he couldn't move.

Ryan realized that it wasn't that his arms and legs weren't responding, but that they couldn't. He was bound, in a chair, with his arms behind his back and his legs tied to the chair legs. Fantastic.

His vision started to clear and he remembered where he was and where he'd been going. Something weird had happened, a wave of psychic energy had hit him a few times and he feared that Malone might have been in trouble. He was running down the hall, looking into the various offices, and he thought he had found someone in one of the rooms, only it was so dark he wasn't certain who it was or that he even knew them, and then there was nothing. Just emptiness.

The surrealism of it started to slip away and fear began to creep in.

His head slowly cleared and Ryan realized someone sat at a desk in front of him— definitely a man. The monitor was the uneven source of light and this person was clearly focused on whatever was happening on that screen. Ryan had a sudden memory of someone— Rainier?—staring at a screen and looking at a map.

The person at the desk was familiar, but in the darkness and with the harsh light and fuzzy brain, he wasn't sure who it was.

"Malone? Is that you?"

"You're awake, kid."

So it was Malone. What the hell was going on? Ryan looked around the room again, convinced he had missed something, that there was some reason Malone was sitting at the computer while he was bound to a chair. Was someone standing at the door with a gun, ordering Malone to do something on the computer? Send false information? Retrieve information for their conspiracy? But no one was at the door. He looked back at Malone and found the agent staring at him.

Ryan opened his mouth to speak, but stopped when he caught sight of motion at the door. A man walked in that Ryan certainly recognized—the sore on his head was unmistakable—and he only had a second, maybe two to warn Malone.

"Malone! It's Fisher!"

Malone turned around in the chair and stood, waited a moment, and shook hands with Fisher.

"What?" Ryan looked from one to the other. He couldn't manage any other words.

"You haven't figured it out by now? I'm disappointed, kid. I thought you were smarter than that." He turned to face Fisher briefly. "Works in a fucking library, too."

Fisher laughed, a wheezy sort of chuckling sound, and slapped Malone on the shoulder.

"Malone? What's going on?"

"Must I explain everything to you? Come on, you've got a brain in that head of yours. Use it."

Ryan blinked and looked at the two men. He just couldn't figure out what was happening, refused to figure it out. Malone turned back to the computer and paid him no further attention. Fisher glanced his way a couple of times, but he seemed just as disinterested.

It made no sense. Fisher had turned on them, had sold them out, had joined Sikes and was, somehow, responsible for the crazy shit going on around them. Ryan and Malone had taken down Warner and Barajas, so they couldn't do any further damage. So why was Malone just sitting there, shaking hands, even, with a traitor?

Was Fisher a double agent—or would that be a triple agent? It would certainly make some sense, but why hadn't they received any intel from him? Why did he vanish after the attack only to surface now? Did he have to hide to make it look as if he died in the attack? But if Fisher was a triple agent, what was with the bindings?

Ryan shook his head—the only real movement he could make—and he looked around the room again for something, anything. Now that his eyes had adjusted to the dimness, he could make out more details, but nothing made sense. Wait, what was that just beyond the desk? Something was sticking out.

Without realizing it, Ryan stepped outside of his consciousness and walked through the room to inspect what was on the ground. Both men looked up at his body and it looked like Fisher made a sharp movement, but Malone restrained the man's hand. What were they worried about?

Ryan looked past them and to the edge of the desk and looked down. It was a shoe. It had once been on the man lying near it as it matched the other still on his foot. A dark trail of blood started at his throat and ran down to disappear under his clothing. Ryan looked closer, and though he had never met the man, he looked like the blurry image of Rainier, only he was much more defined in person.

But if Rainier was dead, and he was primary to the traitor triangle, then what in the hell was happening?

Ryan closed his eyes and felt himself return to his body. He kept his eyes closed as he processed the conflicting information.

He'd helped Malone finger a traitor, helped him track down two more, and now that they were out of the picture, it should have been that much easier for the shadow government to find Sikes and put an end to things. Right?

Shit.

Before Ryan could open his eyes, he heard the water and felt the buzzing and was looking at an expensive office suite. The furniture was immaculate; a lot of glass and stainless steel filled the space, a meeting room with a door that opened into the rest of the office. Several men and women were gathered around a large glass table, all seated in expensive looking leather chairs. Almost all of them wore suits and jackets and they all looked like business professionals of the Nth degree. They conversed quietly and Ryan heard each word, though it was clear that it was little more than small talk. He looked around and realized that everyone gathered there was clearly visible despite the vision, that the furniture and building itself were startling in their details. It wasn't just one or two of the people or objects, but everything, as though he were actually, physically there in that room.

He didn't recognize some of the people, but he recognized the man at the end of the table with the scar under his eye as Sikes, only he didn't have a crew cut, but short and shaggy dirty blonde hair that looked perfectly styled to appear as though it was naturally messy that way. It could have been the hair, but he looked younger than Ryan had remembered, maybe in his thirties instead of forties.

Next to him was another man Ryan didn't know, but beside him sat Fisher, wearing what looked like a well-worn dark suit. The sore on the man's head looked to be bleeding, just slightly, as there was a faint crimson trail just below it.

A woman sat on the other side of Sikes. She looked to be in her early forties and had blonde hair and an intoxicating smile as she laughed at something Fisher said. If it hadn't been for the crooked nose that would make Owen Wilson blush, she would have been extremely attractive.

The four spoke easily, as though longtime friends, and stopped when another man entered the room.

He was tall, strong, had dark hair with grey at the temples and a silver Van Dyke with a touch of black remaining. Though still in good physical condition, he had deep frown lines in his forehead and crow's feet at his eyes. Malone was unmistakable.

Malone closed the door and took a seat near the far end of the table.

"Gentlemen." Ryan turned to Sikes. "Meet our newest comrade, Mr. Malone. He is going to be a valuable asset in the coming operations, and if he handles his first assignment well, it will be my suggestion that he becomes a full-fledged member of the board."

Murmurs came from all sides of the table, but they quickly hushed as Fisher stood.

"Mr. Malone's skills are not to be underestimated." Fisher turned to Malone. "If you don't mind."

Malone looked to Fisher, nodded, and lifted his hands, palms up. Every seat around the table, those with people in them and those without, lifted and hovered several feet off the ground. Several people let out cries of surprise, a few even mingled with cheers, and when Malone put them back down, several of them looked at Sikes and exclaimed their agreement.

"Thank you, Mr. Malone. I think your acceptance

onto the board will be trivial compared to the task set before you. Might I suggest that the sooner you partake of that assignment, the sooner you may join us here? Do keep in mind, however, that this operation is entirely under the sheets and you will receive no assistance."

One of the men stood up and straightened his suit before he spoke. "While I recognize the need for secrecy, I don't believe you should keep the entire board in the dark, Mr. Sikes. This is the first we've heard of this man and his participation with this organization."

Sikes looked at the man, no expression on his face, then smiled. "A fair statement, Mr. O'Neil."

O'Neil nodded and sat back down. Sikes stood up and paced before he turned around and looked at O'Neil first, then took in the rest of the board as he spoke.

"Mr. Malone has been specially chosen by Mr. Fisher," Sikes nodded at Fisher, "to remove the board as well as the team investigating our organization."

"You have one man to do what dozens couldn't?" There was a slight murmur that joined O'Neil's disbelief.

Sikes raised his hands and smiled. "Please, patience. You just had a taste of the power Mr. Malone wields. In addition to that, he is a high ranking agent within their organization with access to all of the classified documents, as well as the board members and other high-ranking officials."

Ryan knew that was bullshit, but the board members looked mollified.

"Further," Sikes said, "if he fails in this operation, his

life will be his price, so this can only be seen as a positive for the organization."

"So how is he going to do this?"

Sikes turned to face the woman who spoke and smiled. "Ah, but you know I can't reveal specifics about operations. That would be ill-advised." Sikes smiled as he looked over the board. No one else spoke up and he turned to Malone. "Mr. Malone, I believe you have work to do."

Malone nodded at Sikes. "Keep a seat warm for me."

Malone turned, opened the door, and walked out.

Ryan blinked and his vision returned to find Malone and Fisher staring at him. Fisher had a smirk while Malone looked impassive as usual.

"You finally had the vision, huh, kid?"

Ryan looked at Malone and couldn't muster any words. He couldn't look at Malone any longer and he lowered his gaze.

"Oh, don't give me the disappointed look. You fooled yourself."

"How could you, Malone?"

"I'm guessing you know the answer to that."

"Those men you killed. You used me to murder them."

"You utilize resources as you come across them."

"Mr. Malone, this is not the time for exposition. Finish your task and be done here."

Ryan looked up and noticed, for the first time, that Fisher's aura was blinding. Ryan had to close his eyes against the sight of Fisher leaving the room.

"He read 'How to be an evil overlord' on the web and takes this stuff way too seriously."

Ryan looked back at Malone and just stared.

"Not funny?" Malone looked to the computer, tapped out some command, then stood and walked over to Ryan. He stopped ten feet short of him.

"Look, kid, I'll level with you. You're not a bad egg. I mean that, but this is business. You can appreciate that things happen in business, can't you?"

"I thought I was helping you save people, and you were just murdering them. What's next? Dropping bombs? Spreading disease?"

Malone shrugged.

Ryan shook his head and looked away. He couldn't believe it. This wasn't happening. Couldn't be happening. That would make him responsible for so many deaths, and worse, more deaths or other things that might happen in the future thanks to his help.

"I told Fisher that we could use someone with your talents, but he said we already have a seer. I even tried to kill you before you woke up, but he wouldn't have any of it. He gets some perverse pleasure out of watching people realize they've been double-crossed and used like a cheap rubber. I tried to show you some measure of mercy, I really did."

Ryan looked back to Malone and looked him straight in the eye. "You killed the people looking for the real traitors."

Malone didn't blink. "We knew they were around, but we couldn't get to them. So, you stage an attack which calls in the big guns, and," Malone opened his hands and shrugged.

"Hansen?"

Malone chuckled. "Stupid asshole had confidential documents on his home computer, not that they helped. At least they'll know now what kind of idiot they had running things."

"'Was?' 'Had?'"

"You don't think I'd just walk in, knock him out, then leave do you?" Malone didn't so much as move a single muscle to smile. He just continued to look Ryan in the eye.

"So you work for Sikes, and he works for what, another government? China? Russia?"

Malone barked out a laugh. "That's good. I should remember that. Sikes, he works for himself. They say you shouldn't mix business with pleasure, but this is a little of both for him. He didn't like being kicked out of the agency, and they're in the way of him doing some things he wants to do because they know about him."

"Sounds like he should have been killed, not kicked out."

"Don't think they didn't try."

Ryan stared at Malone.

"You had a plan all along. You didn't need me."

"I didn't."

"So why take me?"

"Do you hand over weapons to your enemies?"

"So that's it? I'm a cheap rubber and a water gun?"

Malone shrugged. "This is an exclusive club. Don't feel bad about it. Others have tried to join and weren't admitted. It was fun while it lasted, right? You got to watch me crush the mercenaries a couple times at least."

Ryan wanted to laugh, but there was nothing funny about it. He'd helped Malone murder a bunch of innocent people, good people at that. They were trying to find the ones who were really threats, and Ryan was responsible for their deaths.

Ryan snapped his head up. "Fuck you!" He didn't realize it, but he directed a massive wave of psychic energy at Malone, but Malone didn't flinch.

Fisher appeared in the doorway again and looked at Ryan. "There'll be no more of that, young man." He turned his head. "Mr. Malone, I said to finish and come along."

Ryan squinted his eyes against Fisher's aura, and then Fisher disappeared around the corner again and Ryan could reopen his eyes.

"Was ready for that one, kid. If it's any consolation, I'll make sure your obituary says you died trying to save your friends at the library. It's the least I can do for you."

"Fuck you, Malone. Fuck you."

"Sorry, kid. Gotta' go. It wasn't all bad, you know. I didn't plan it this way, but Rainier was unprotected and you gotta' change your plans sometimes. But hey, I appreciate the assist. You really did make it easier for me. Would have been a lot more legwork without you."

Malone reached into his jacket and pulled out a pistol that gleamed in the dim light. He pulled the hammer back with his thumb and Ryan looked down the barrel.

"Places to go, things to take, people to shoot."

Ryan's breath caught in his throat. He'd been betrayed. His friends had been murdered and he in turn murdered a bunch of others. And now he was about to join them in death. At least he wouldn't have to live with the agonizing shame of his failure and the guilt of what he'd help cause.

"Any last words? You've already suggested I fuck myself multiple times, so that's old hat."

Unbelievable. Just fucking unbelievable. Ryan looked Malone in the eye.

"Pull the trigger, asshole."

"As you wish."

CHAPTER 11

The base was completely razed. Furniture and papers burned as fires greedily consumed them. Bodies lay on the ground, some blackened, some not, but all exhibited bullet holes in their heads.

He stepped over the fallen body of one of his comrades, the heel of his polished shoe crunching on something, and stopped and looked around. How could it have come to this? How did they let everything fall apart? But he knew the answer wasn't that they let things get bad, but that someone, or some ones, had sabotaged them. And they knew who was behind it.

Even the other arms out on the East Coast knew about it now. Did they have insurgents there like they did out here? It was a disconcerting thought. He loosened his tie and took a deep breath.

Jaguar had seen a fair amount in his years at the agency, but nothing like this. He heard about what happened at a couple of the other bases, but he didn't witness the carnage himself. He shook his head.

He looked to be in his thirties, average height and an athletic build with blonde hair, blue eyes, and fair skin. He looked the part of a Swede, but that was about where it ended.

Jaguar stopped to inspect a pile of partially burned papers. He flipped through them, but they were nothing important, just weeks old reports that had proven inaccurate. The real information had been on the computers, and they were stolen.

He had tried to say before that they shouldn't store

any local information, and that doing so was just asking for trouble, but had the council listened? "Where would we store it?" He shook his head and started forward again.

The lights flickered off, and for a couple of breaths the only light came from the small fires still burning. When the lights came back on he was still moving forward.

The glass hallway, Wonderland as it was sometimes called, was nothing more than rubble and shards. The door had been twisted and warped like it was little more than aluminum foil, and it was somehow still on the hinges, though the frame itself had fared slightly better. The door stood wide open and he stepped in, looked left, and went right. He stopped to inspect each room, but there was little to find in most.

A body covered with rubble lay on the floor in one of the offices. Jaguar managed to find an arm to check for a pulse, but it was cold. He couldn't even see the face, but he thought it might have been Clarkson, one of the council members. She was one of the ones who laughed at his so-called paranoia about their data. He felt no pleasure at finding her so.

Jaguar left the office and continued to inspect the others. The damage was less severe the further he went down the hallway, and as he turned into one, he stopped. A computer and monitor sat on a desk, and they even looked to be working.

Jaguar narrowed his eyes and stepped up to it. The screen was almost entirely black, except for bright red text in the center that read, "Thanks, M."

They didn't need to take the other computers if they had everything from Rainier's, but it still stung. The thought of the council member made Jaguar look around, and he noticed the body just to side of the desk. He knelt and, despite the poor light, knew it was Rainier. His throat had been cut. That was low. Cutting throats was reserved for the lowest scum, and Rainier was not scum.

The agency's base was a lost cause, and possibly the entire West Coast operation. This was worse than he thought.

About to leave, Jaguar scanned the room and nearly jumped when he saw an aura about a body bound to a chair. He rushed over. Jaguar didn't recognize the young man, but he was clearly alive. That didn't make sense, because blood had rolled down his forehead from a bullet hole.

Jaguar put a finger to the man's neck and felt a pulse. It was weak.

"Shit."

Jaguar pulled a flashlight out of a pocket and shined it into the bullet hole. Light reflected back off of something in that hole. He lifted the man's chin and focused on the shiny object. He pulled it with his will, slowly, aware that he may be damning the man to death, or worse, should he accidentally shove it forward any. But it came out, and when it finally peeked out, Jaguar grabbed it with his fingers and a rush of blood followed it out.

"Shit!"

Jaguar flailed as he struggled to take his jacket off, but he persevered. He pressed the jacket against the man's head, flipped the jacket over the top of his head, and tied its arms together like a makeshift bandana.

He closed his eyes and saw Lion.

I have a survivor, but I need a medic. Meet me at the usual place.

He hoped that Lion wasn't in the field and in the middle of something. He thought of Tiger and sent the same message and hoped that he could get the message through.

Jaguar looked down and wondered if the young man would make it that far.

Jaguar carried him out of the base and put him on the ground near the exit of the long hallway. His bike was nearby and he hopped on, turned the key, and zipped down the tunnel and turned and followed it into the garage.

The flickering light and scattered debris only added to the reality that the base had been attacked and that nothing had escaped uninjured. Cars were riddled with bullet holes and dented from cement that had fallen from the tunnel's ceiling. Even the secret exit was wide open because the door was blown in half.

However, it looked like some vehicles were still drivable, and Jaguar pulled up next to an SUV with a dented hood and roof, but that otherwise appeared serviceable. He got off the bike, opened the driver's door, and hopped in the seat.

The previous agent hadn't left the keys in the ignition, but they dropped out of the sun visor when he lowered it. The SUV started and Jaguar couldn't suppress a smile. Getting that guy out on the bike wasn't going to happen.

He hopped back out, cut the engine on the bike, and moved it around to the back of the SUV and managed to muscle it in, though sideways. At least the back of the SUV was carpeted and wouldn't give the bike road rash.

Jaguar left tire marks as he stormed back to the tunnel and stopped where he left the young man. He got out and put a finger to the man's neck. His pulse was even weaker, and certainly the aura was dimmer.

"Going to be bumpy!"

Jaguar went to the SUV and opened the door behind the passenger seat. There was no way to avoid moving the guy, so Jaguar hefted him and slid the man in the SUV across the seats. It was going to be close, perhaps too close.

On the freeway, Jaguar did his best impression of a crazy asshole driver. He exceeded the speed limit and weaved in and out of lanes whenever possible and necessary. The sun was just coming up and the rest of the world was making its commute, and this was a freeway known for its commuters.

The off-ramp into town was still guarded by the army, but Jaguar knew of another way in and took a different exit and doubled back on a seldom-used old interstate road. He left the road after several miles for the desert where he was able to cross into town well past the roadblock that had been established on the road.

He watched the rear-view mirror every few seconds for a minute and darted around streets where possible. It looked like someone had seen him cut across the desert to get into town and was following him, but he had a good head start on them.

After several minutes of changing directions, he was convinced he lost his tail and he continued to make his way through town. None of it was easy going as the police and army had set up shop, but Jaguar knew the streets better than most, even if it had been years since he spent any meaningful time in town. Certain knowledge was permanent.

Jaguar took a path that sent him down alleys and back roads, some unfinished and dirt, and wound his way into the back of an industrial complex. The parking lot was deserted with the town still in chaos and he pulled into a double-level parking complex near a large warehouse.

He made a complete pass of the ground floor then turned and drove up to the second floor and made a complete circle of it as well. Satisfied, Jaguar came back around to one of the corners and stopped by the elevator. A nearby door led into a tunnel that connected to the warehouse, and he went and pounded on it three times.

The door opened and a tall woman wearing all black—cargo pants, combat boots and a black muscle shirt that showed off toned arms—emerged from the dark tunnel carrying a large duffel bag. She had short, almost spiky black hair and pale skin that appeared that much more translucent with all of the black clothing. Her blue eyes quickly looked to Jaguar then the SUV as she set the bag down.

"Who is it?" she said.

"Never seen him. He was in Rainier's office."

"Lion's busy, but I'll do what I can."

"Hurry."

Jaguar opened the driver-side back door and pulled the man out as gently as he could. He placed him on the ground.

Tiger knelt and looked the man over and looked

back up at Jaguar. She furrowed her brows.

"They shot him in the face? And he's alive?"

"He's gifted, Tiger."

"I'll say."

Tiger opened the bag and pulled out a variety of medical equipment. She cleaned the wound first and wrapped a large bandage around it.

"How much blood was on the ground?"

"He'll need to drink."

"Check his pockets for a medical card."

Jaguar fished a wallet out of the man's pocket as Tiger went about setting up a portable IV and performing what limited tests she could in the field.

"Name's Ryan Sutter. Born in '85. Hair, blonde, height—"

"I didn't ask for a biography. Medical card."

Jaguar flipped through the cards and found what Tiger requested, but it only listed insurance information.

"Nothing."

"Then hope he makes it. I've done everything I can do."

"And?"

Tiger looked up, shrugged, and stuffed supplies into the bag. "I tried."

Jaguar chewed on his bottom lip and looked around. Where the hell was Lion, anyway?

"His pulse is weak but stable," Tiger said. "He needs a hospital or Lion if you want him to get better. And soon."

"Thanks. I just want to know what the hell this guy was doing in the base because he sure as hell doesn't belong there."

"One of theirs they left behind? A form of punishment?"

"Maybe."

"Anything else there that might give a clue?"

"Just Rainier's cut throat and computer. Malone left it there with a lovely parting note. Bloody traitor."

Tiger clenched her jaw. "No one else around? I said, no one else around?"

"Shh, I heard you." Jaguar looked around. Someone was coming; he could hear cars approaching. "I think I was followed. Damn it. Help me get him in."

"You want to hole up in the warehouse?"

"No. I have a bad feeling about this. We need to leave."

Tiger looked at Jaguar and nodded. People who wanted to continue to live had long since learned to trust Jaguar's gut.

Jaguar picked Ryan up and put him into the back seat again. "Get your bike. Mine's in the back."

"There's room?"

"This thing is like a moving truck."

Tiger disappeared into the hallway, and a few moments later, the roar of a motorcycle echoed forth. Tiger rode out and cut the engine as Jaguar opened the back of the SUV. They had to move Jaguar's bike, but they managed to cram it in. Tiger ran to the passenger side and they hopped into the SUV.

"Steamboat Willy's?" Tiger said.

"Yeah, but we have to get out of here, first."

Jaguar started the SUV up and tore across the parking lot and shot down the ramp. He thought his tail was getting closer.

They left the parking garage and hit the larger

parking lot and could see the vehicles headed their direction. Several police cars sans lights and sirens followed a nondescript European sedan. They were only half a mile away as Jaguar and Tiger left the parking lot in the other direction.

"Move faster, you donkey!" Jaguar pounded on the steering wheel and willed the SUV forward. However, a look into the rear-view mirror told him that it was inevitable their pursuers would catch up.

Tiger punched him in the arm. "Can't you make this shitbox go faster?"

"My foot is all the way down."

Jaguar looked into the rear view mirror again. The sedan and police cruisers were closer still. He turned them onto a main street and then cut back onto a side street that ran behind the industrial complex.

"Take the wheel."

Jaguar blinked himself in and out and appeared in the back of the SUV.

"Jesus, Jag!"

Jaguar looked back to see Tiger scrambling to get out of her seat and into the driver's seat. "Get to Willy's. I'll meet you when I can."

"Where are you going?"

"To say hello."

He moved, bent over the bike nearest the door and muscled it over.

"Hey!" Tiger said. "Take yours!"

"Yours is in the way."

"No way! You're not taking mine!"

Jaguar couldn't suppress a smile and he flipped the top half of the back door open and was greeted with a view of the sedan closing on them quickly. He popped open the lower door and moved the bike out onto it. With the top door opened high, he could stand the bike up, but it was still too cramped to sit on it. Instead, he held it up straight, took a breath, and then pushed it forward.

The bike sailed out of the back of the SUV and landed hard on the ground. Jaguar blinked himself out once the bike left the SUV and blinked back in just in time to right the bike on the ground as it threatened to roll. He turned the key, popped a wheelie, and shot off down the road. He probably shouldn't have just done that in public, but it was too late for shouldn'ts.

The sedan was still in the lead and Jaguar stayed wide of it. He took a quick glance as he passed it and thought he recognized the driver. The police cars moved to intercept, but he was far more agile on the bike and cut across lanes faster than they could anticipate. He passed all five police cruisers coming his way and came to a sliding stop and turned back around.

Tiger, I'm about to get their attention. Get the hell out.

Jaguar opened the bike's saddlebag. He pulled out two machine pistols and chambered each gun. He closed the bag, put the bike into first, put the guns in the side holsters on his belt, and twisted hard on the gas.

The bike took off so fast that within a couple of seconds Jaguar had tears in his eyes from the stinging wind, but he didn't care. He grinned as the adrenaline rushed through his veins. It only took a matter of seconds, but accompanied by the whine of the turbo, he caught up to the rear car in the police convoy. The police car tried to move to block him, but it may as well have been a net trying to stop the flow of the ocean.

Jaguar swerved to the side and pulled up with the rear tire, grabbed a gun, and shot. The tire cracked with a bang as it popped and the bullet pinged off the rim. The police car swerved in response, but Jaguar was already moving forward again, gun pointed at the front tire. The front tire popped and the car swerved again, but he was already ahead of the car and darting to the other side, never driving straight, never giving them a good target.

He proceeded to shoot out tires, sometimes on the left, sometimes on the right, but every time they tried to get a shot on him, he was too quick, too agile on the bike. He pulled up to the final police car, intent upon shooting out its tires as well, but had to brake and swing around to the other side as the passenger leaned out with a shotgun in hand.

"Shit!"

The shotgun blast was loud and harsh even over the roars of the engines and the crunch of asphalt underneath their tires. Though he could never say for certain, he could have sworn he dove the bike left just in time for the buckshot to pass right by him.

Jaguar pulled up behind the police car and grabbed both guns. He emptied each magazine into the rear windshield. The guns barked in rapid succession as fire and bullets blazed out of the barrels. Where just a moment before it had been a perfectly clean rear windshield, it was now nothing but a mess of holes and spider-webbed glass.

He dumped the magazines out off to either side and holstered the guns. One of his bursts had opened a melon-sized hold in the windshield and that gave him an idea.

Jaguar reached back into the saddlebag. He pulled out a grenade and thumbed the pin out, his hand wrapped around the body and lever. Jaguar twisted on the bike's accelerator and pulled up to the car. Though he had to stretch, he dropped the grenade in the large hole in the rear windshield. He quickly fell back and then pulled around far to the opposite side of the street.

The explosion was muffled with the bike's engine spinning high RPMs, but he couldn't miss the police car in his mirror as it swerved off to the side, hit the curb, and careened into a utility pole.

"Asshole."

The sedan was dangerously close to the SUV now and Jaguar hurried to catch them. He was a couple hundred feet away when the driver leaned out of the window.

"Shit!"

Jaguar reached behind his back and pulled one of his own handguns out from its holster on the back of his belt and fired a shot toward the sedan. The driver looked back and he fired again. The driver pulled his arm back and Jaguar cut across the lanes as the man threw his arm forward.

An invisible wave of energy went past him, but it still sent the tail of the bike into a dangerous frenzy and he had to slow to catch the back end and right the bike. The gun almost slipped out of his hand, but he caught it at the last moment and looked up to see how far back he'd fallen. The distance he had made up was lost and he accelerated again and fired a couple more shots at the sedan. He was too far away to be accurate with the pistol, but the sedan still swerved even as it continued to move forward.

Jaguar caught up to the sedan and fired another couple rounds as he came up on the driver's side. Holes bloomed on the side of the car, but he knew they didn't penetrate the reinforced steel. No sooner than the last bullet pinged off the car, the driver emerged from the window again and turned to face him.

A sudden psychic blast hit Jaguar and he nearly toppled from the bike, but he kept himself upright and steeled his nerve, but this time he did lose his gun. It flew from his hand and bounced away toward the side of the road. The sedan pulled away again while Jaguar slowed to steady the bike.

"So both of you are in there."

Jaguar reached back into the bag and grabbed another grenade. He pulled the pin out but again held the grenade and lever tight. The driver managed to right himself and was now looking back in his direction.

Jaguar accelerated hard and pulled up behind the sedan and blinked himself into the back seat.

One moment he had been on the bike, and in less time than it took to bat an eye, he was sitting in the back seat of the sedan, air whistling through the cabin around him. He reached behind him and grabbed his other handgun.

"Merry Christmas!"

He shot the gun into both front seats, but he could feel the wall in front of him. The bullets slammed into the invisible shield and stopped as if they had been swallowed by quicksand. It may have stopped the bullets, but he dropped the grenade behind the driver's seat, using the sound of the gun to mask its sound, and he blinked himself back to the bike. He hoped that the wall would be taken down in time for the grenade to explode.

The bike was wobbling by the time he was back on it, but he gave it a little gas and it steadied right out. Almost immediately after catching the back of the bike, he braked and cut to the side.

The driver in the sedan leaned back out of the window, but there was a sudden flash and burst of smoke as the grenade went off. Shrapnel flew out of the car and it swerved hard, too hard, and the left tires couldn't keep it straight. The car slid entirely sideways, but it was going too fast and physics took over.

The car rolled, once, twice, three times and came to a stop upside down. Jaguar stopped short of the car and hopped off of the bike, machine pistols in hand. He quickly reloaded them from the saddlebag and emptied both pistols at the car. Another psychic blast slammed into him and sent him stumbling. He ground his teeth and dumped the magazines and put a couple more in but stumbled again as another wave of energy pressed on him, this time accompanied by a physical blast that sent him to his knees.

Jaguar hauled himself to his feet and heard cars approaching from behind. The damaged police cars were closing. He ignored them and emptied the guns into the sedan again. He jumped back on the bike and holstered the guns. Return gunfire from the sedan skipped past him and he rolled on the throttle, middle finger in the air as he passed the car.

CHAPTER 12

Steamboat Willy wasn't a steamboat captain, certainly not in the middle of California, but he did own a large yacht many years ago that had been jokingly called a steamboat for its penchant to constantly break down and spew smoke out of the engines. The name had stuck since.

A former CIA agent who had retired and made his money on Wall Street, William Avery still had contacts within various government agencies.

Jaguar always thought about a particular outing on the "steamboat" whenever he rode up the long driveway that led to Willy's house. At the time, it was hardly an incident. He and Willy had been fishing out in the Pacific and Willy made a catch so big he couldn't reel it in. Jaguar went to help, but by the time he arrived at starboard, Willy had already gone over. While most sensible people would have let go of the rod, Willy held on, refusing to let his catch go.

With a little muscle, and quite a bit of help from another agent, the two managed to pull Willy, and his catch, back onto the yacht. It turned out that Willy's catch had actually been a massive length of thick chain, and when he felt the tug he started to reel it in, but slipped on the deck and tumbled over.

Over the years, the story evolved until, in its most recent form, it involved Willy catching an orca whale and being swallowed where he lived inside for thirty-nine days and thirty-nine nights. He just couldn't hang for forty.

Jaguar laughed to himself as the small mansion come into view beyond the sloped driveway. The black SUV was already parked near the front door. Tiger had likely been there for some time since Jaguar had to make sure the disabled police cruisers were actually disabled. That, of course, led him to a couple of other cruisers that were in perfect operating condition with aggravated officers inside.

After leading them in circles for several minutes, Jaguar rolled the accelerator back and lost them in the span of a couple of breaths. As a bonus, he had managed to recover his lost pistol.

He pulled up behind the SUV, killed the engine and put the kickstand down. Previously hidden from his sight, Jaguar noticed that Lion was there as well, because a white convertible Porsche was parked on the other side of the SUV.

A cobblestone path lined with immaculate rose bushes of a variety of colors and scents led to the giant double front doors of Willy's mansion. The porch looked something like a smaller version of the Parthenon, complete with pillars and bas-relief.

Jaguar knocked on the solid mahogany door and Tiger answered a few moments later with a smile on her face.

"Do you have any idea who that guy is?" Tiger said.

"Ryan Sutter. I read it off his ID earlier, remember?"

"You have no idea how big this is."

They were gathered in a large receiving room replete with plush couches and velvet drapes, thick rugs, and bright landscape paintings tastefully arranged on the walls. A table with gilded edges sat in the middle of three couches arranged in a rough triangle on one of the many expensive looking rugs that covered the marble floor. Frosted skylights and sheer curtains placed in front of open drapes invited natural light to suffuse the room.

A middle-aged man with dark skin and a shaved head hovered near Ryan with a blood pressure monitor in hand. His pinstriped suit fit him in a way that bespoke money. He looked up from Ryan, briefly, and nodded at Jaguar before he pushed his wire-frame glasses back up his nose.

Jaguar nodded in return to Lion and looked over at Ryan. The young man appeared dazed as he sat on the couch sipping a bottle of water.

Steamboat Willy, ever the perfect host, entered the room. With unnaturally blonde hair and a slightly bulging stomach that suggested retirement was treating him well, he was dressed casually in slacks and a shirt that likely cost three times more than any sane person would pay. He bore a tray of snacks, and upon seeing Jaguar, smiled and held it out.

"Thanks, Willy." Jaguar grabbed a finger sandwich off the tray and stuffed the entire thing into his mouth. "So what's the deal, mate?"

Lion looked up. "What?"

Jaguar chewed and swallowed. "What's the deal?"

Tiger joined Lion behind the couch and tried to look at what Lion was doing, but he shooed her away. She gave Lion a dirty look but moved without complaint.

Ryan looked up and focused on Jaguar. He narrowed his eyes. "Hey, aren't you supposed to be Swedish?"

"I am."

"Then why do you sound like a Brit?"

Jaguar laughed and sat on one of the empty couches.

"I was born in Sweden but moved to Birmingham at four. Schools are nasty places when you sound different than everyone else, so I adapted. Would it make you feel better if I said 'bork'?"

Ryan stared at him. "You know you're being hunted, right?"

"You know you were shot in the head, right?" Ryan frowned and looked down. Jaguar cleared his throat. "So what happened with that?"

Ryan looked away and his eyes glimmered. "Malone. Fisher."

Jaguar turned to Lion. "How is he, Lion?"

"I patched him up best I could."

Jaguar studied Ryan more carefully and realized that the bullet hole in his forehead was healed over. A scar remained, but where there was once a hole slowly oozing blood, there was now skin, though it was red and scarred.

"So he's good?"

"Mostly." Lion unwrapped the blood pressure strap and walked around to the front of the couch and looked at Ryan. "You've been through major trauma. Time is the only thing that'll help now."

Ryan nodded but continued to look away. Lion placed the blood pressure monitor in an even larger duffel bag than the one Tiger had and zipped it up. The bag was large enough to hold a body once all of the equipment was removed from it. Jaguar knew that because they'd done it before. Lion picked up the bag and moved to leave the room.

Tiger, mostly forgotten at this point but shifting from foot to foot behind the couch, practically raced the words out. "Tell him what you found!"

Lion paused and turned around. "I caught a glimpse of what happened. He's a seer."

Jaguar straightened and looked at Ryan again. "But his aura doesn't indicate that."

"You could talk to him. He's right there."

Jaguar flipped off Lion and stared at Ryan again. The man's aura looked like any other latent's aura, except that it was stronger than normal. Raw power bristled about him like light beams in a plasma globe. It was dangerously unfocused.

Lion left the room and an uncomfortable quiet filled it. Steamboat Willy shuffled his feet and at set the tray on the table and sat, legs crossed European style. Tiger still hovered around Ryan as Jaguar watched him.

Ryan closed his eyes and rubbed his left arm before he wrapped the back of his neck with his left hand. Eyes still closed, he laughed, a hollow sound, and opened his eyes and looked at Jaguar. He stared at him and shook his head. Lion came back into the room and silently sat on a couch and listened.

"I've never been betrayed. Nothing like that." Ryan hung his head. "They used me to murder people. They murdered my friends, a bunch of your friends." He stopped to put a finger to the fresh scar on his forehead. "Hell, maybe even my family. I wouldn't be surprised if Malone did that and called it 'collateral.'" Tears fell unchecked from his eyes.

Jaguar leaned forward. "I'm sorry, mate. I didn't know. Will you tell us what happened?"

Ryan shrugged and wiped the tears away. "I have

nothing better to do."

He proceeded to tell them everything, from the library and bombs and Malone showing up with his weird powers, to Fisher walking in and Malone admitting he double-crossed him and everything between.

It took some time to retell the story, and by the time he finished, Jaguar looked around and saw that all four of them were staring at Ryan in rapt attention from the other couches. The room was darker, the sun having shifted positions and no longer shining directly through the windows.

No one spoke for a solid minute until Steamboat Willy cleared his throat and announced he would go bring them all a drink since he could certainly use one.

Tiger, who had been leaning forward, sat back against the couch and blew out a sigh while she ran a hand through her hair. "Jesus, that's rough."

Jaguar stood and walked over to the couch Ryan sat upon and took a seat next to him. "Malone shot you in the head. How are you still here?"

Ryan winced. "I don't know. I told him to shoot me and I just remember thinking that if the bullet hits my brain, it's over. I felt like shit, but I didn't really want to die. I'm not so sure about that now."

Jaguar looked to Lion and raised an eyebrow.

"It's unusual, but not unheard of," Lion said. "Seers tend to stick to scrying, but they do sometimes cross into other areas like the others, just not as frequently. He has already mentioned accessing other powers, after all."

"But he stopped a bullet at close range," Jaguar said.

"He was also panicked. Endorphins, adrenaline,

amplified mental activity."

Jaguar nodded and looked at Ryan again.

Ryan looked from Lion to Jaguar and shook his head. "I know you're saying something important, but you know, I don't care right now. Is there somewhere I can just sleep and not wake up?"

"Follow me." Steamboat Willy walked back into the room and placed several bottles of water on the table. He led Ryan out of the room.

"Are you shitting me?" Tiger said. "You found a seer? Do you know how big this is?"

"It's big, I know," Jaguar said. "I'm just not sure what it means, yet. He was emotionally murdered. That trauma, combined with his burgeoning powers, he may not even recover. That's a lot at once."

"He'll be fine." Jaguar turned to Lion and Lion had that authoritative look about him that irritated people because they knew that he was right whenever he adopted that smug look. "His powers are being nurtured and they'll dull his trauma soon."

"He's not fully innate and has gone through hell the last few days. It may be too much."

"But he's a strong latent. He may turn out to be an omni, though I have my doubts."

Jaguar blew out a low whistle. It'd been a long time since they had a seer, but it'd been even longer since they had an omni, especially since they burnt out so quickly. He backtracked and reminded himself they had nothing but a damaged man who was in dire need of recuperation. Even though he thought Ryan could help them, and they could help him in return, unless Ryan healed first, this was a fruitless idea.

Jaguar banged a fist on the couch and stood. "We'll

look after him, make sure he recovers."

"That would be advisable because there was a note from Chameleon to find him."

Jaguar turned to Lion. "Chameleon is looking for him?"

"Yes. The order went out several days ago, shortly before all of this began. I would suggest we do not allow him to leave our presence."

"Blimey. Right." Jaguar scratched his chin and wondered what that meant. Within the agency, the nameless and faceless "Chameleon" called the shots. It'd been years since Chameleon alerted them to a new latent. "Right, we keep an eye on him. But let me tell you what I found earlier today."

Tiger looked like someone about to bite into an onion. "This isn't going to be good, is it?"

"Let's play 'What Malone Told You Was a Lie.'"

Ryan stared at Jaguar blankly.

"Okay. First, we're not a shadow government, rather just an agency that's a last resort when no one else can get the job done. Hell, we don't even have an official name since we don't really exist, but some folks call us The Debate Team."

"I haven't seen you guys argue that much."

"Yeah, well it's been known to happen." Jaguar put a finger up then retracted it. "There's so much distortion in the shit he fed you it could take weeks to clear everything up, and we don't have that kind of time, so it's time to play synopsis."

"Why are you even bothering?"

"Call it professional courtesy with the hope that you'll consider our request."

"You're up front, at least."

"Yes, we'd be interested in having you join our ranks."

"You speak for the agency?"

"No, but I do speak for the motley crew assembled here. But I have reason to believe you'd be asked to join."

"A few people said they were looking for me."

"Yeah, Chameleon's been trying to find you."

Ryan raised an eyebrow. "Chameleon? A lizard? Like the insurance commercials?"

Jaguar laughed. "No. A person, or persons. No one knows who Chameleon is because a chameleon blends in."

"Someone has to know."

"Well we don't, and I'm willing to bet only one or two aside from Chameleon even know."

Ryan shrugged. "So you're not a shadow government. Are you really an agency that was formed out of secret research and cows?"

Jaguar looked to Lion.

"Yes," Lion said. "This agency was officially eliminated over six decades ago, but continues today. There are a few within the government who know of its existence, but most have no idea and wouldn't believe it possible."

"I see things and apparently stopped a bullet with my mind and I still don't know what to believe."

"It'll get better." Jaguar offered him a smile. "It just takes time. Besides, no one is better prepared to help than the agency."

"So you want me to help you out?" Ryan looked from Jaguar to Lion to Tiger and back, and they nodded at him.

"What's with the names?" Ryan looked at Jaguar, "I know your last name," his gaze flicked over Tiger and Lion, "but have never heard about you two."

"You know my last name because Malone is a dick, and you don't know them because few people know they're involved with this team. In the field, we go by other names, which I'm guessing you've figured out are cat related, because in the wild, it's the cats that rule, not dogs. Stupid things."

Tiger leaned in and spoke with a loud whisper, her hand covering the side of her face that Jaguar could see. "He had a bad experience with a dog years ago and doesn't like them."

Ryan stared at her then looked back to Jaguar and shrugged. "I've never been a fan of cats, but go on."

"Here's the deal: the shit he told you about them taking over the world, well, half-truths as far as we can tell. Sikes is a serious player who's been ramping up his organization in the last several months, but we're thinking he's looking for monetary power before he makes any overt moves, if at all. This shit the last few days may be a test of their reach, but we think it was more about taking us out."

"And now Sikes has two of your former goons working for him, one of whom is a major enforcer."

"And that other guy is the reason you were sucker punched. Malone is Mike Tyson to Fisher's Don King. Fisher is the guy with the smarts, and his powers all revolve around the mind. I'm not sure what his limits are, but he's a rocket launcher with the mental guns."

Ryan leaned back and rubbed his temples. "Do visions lie?"

"Only when they've been altered." Jaguar shot a look at Lion and Lion raised an eyebrow but said nothing. That wasn't something they were aware Fisher could do. And if it wasn't Fisher, then that meant that Sikes had someone else working for him with powers. The implications were worrisome.

"Son of a bitch."

"Here's the important part: they're coming after me because they have my name and know that I've been investigating them." Ryan winced. "No worries mate, they only know about me. Sure, they saw the SUV but don't know who was in it since I was able to detour them."

"But if Fisher was doing mind tricks, he could see into the SUV."

"Not exactly. He can do things to people's minds, but seeing things, that's different. Not everyone can do that."

Ryan shrugged.

"Anyway, we can handle them, but I'm more interested in learning what their plans are that'll lead them to dreams of global domination and universal conquest and whatever other shit they told you. We've heard similar rumblings but haven't figured out if there's anything to it yet."

Ryan stood and paced the far end of the room. "Were Warner and Barajas part of your crew?"

"No, but we've worked with them before."

Ryan stopped pacing. "Did you know Sikes's crew was going to hit this town and knock everything out?"

"Specifically? No, but it makes sense since one of our bases is nearby." Jaguar sighed. "We had one in Washington state, but it's gone. So's Nevada. The next closest base is Colorado, then the Midwest and East Coast. Local law enforcement is woefully unprepared for this sort of thing, so this gives them one hell of a foothold. As soon as we heard what was happening we got here as quickly as possible."

"Which is exactly what they wanted because they're trying to get rid of you."

"What else could we do?"

Ryan nodded. "So what about Hansen?"

"Hansen is the head of this location's agency. Or was. No one's heard from him in quite a while."

"So what do you want from me?"

"Everything you're willing to give."

"Gee, that's all? What do you need me for? You have these others here." Ryan looked from Lion to Tiger then stopped. "Hey, why aren't you glowing?"

"I'm not innate. I'm just your average can of Soylent Green."

"She may not be innate, but she's no more average than you or I."

Ryan nodded and walked a small circle then shrugged. "Yeah, okay, whatever. Let's go break heads."

Tiger shot Ryan a thumbs up and looked to Lion and Jaguar. "I like this guy."

CHAPTER 13

They were gathered about the coffee table making plans and Ryan paid scant attention. They were speaking of things that made little sense to him and apparently didn't notice that he'd been quiet for some time. Instead, he sat back and watched them.

Lion was the one who interested him the most, because while Tiger and Jaguar were both outspoken and animated in their own way, Lion appeared outwardly passive and said little. When he did speak, however, Ryan noticed that the others showed considerable respect and listened carefully to what he had to say. Whoever the man was, he was apparently intelligent and highly regarded. It made him think of Lion as a sage or a prophet, and he thought the man should be old with white hair and a long beard and colorful robes. Instead, Lion looked to be in his late forties with a shaved head and a clean shaven face. Only the glasses, wire-framed and smart looking, seemed to fit Ryan's expectations. He gave up the line of thinking and leaned back on the couch.

Ryan felt a little better with each passing hour, and at some point, he realized that his arm was no longer bothering him. A quick check of it revealed that the wound had closed itself, much like the one on his head.

Clarity came with time as well, and Ryan was finally starting to see that each person's aura looked a little different. He caught a glimpse of his own in a mirror, and where before it seemed like nothing more than a blinding radiance, there was now a certain order to it, a pattern of colors. It shifted, however, and it was difficult to say what color, or colors, it was exactly. At any second it could be green or yellow or blue or red.

Lion, however, had a distinct orange to his aura, and it was bright. Ryan wasn't sure if it was just the vibrancy of the color or that the aura itself was so strong, but he was convinced that Lion, whatever his power may be, was formidable. Ryan had an incomplete memory of Lion doing something to him, but everything after Malone's gunshot and prior to him waking up in a strange bed in a strange house was full of holes. He was growing tired of the repetition.

He turned his focus on Tiger and noticed, again, that the woman had no aura. No, that wasn't quite true. Tiger didn't have an aura, exactly, but there was something about her that didn't appear wholly normal, as though there was a slight distortion in the air about her. It was subtle and not always present, but at just the right angle, Ryan sometimes found that Tiger seemed less distinct, almost slightly translucent. That confused and intrigued him since Jaguar and Tiger had confirmed that Tiger was not "innate."

That left Jaguar, and Ryan saw that Jaguar had something in common with himself, namely that he had multiple colors to his aura. Where Ryan's seemed to shift with no sense of order, Jaguar's glowed with a calm duality. Yellow and green, that he thought should form chartreuse where they met but didn't, glowed about Jaguar.

Ryan focused on Lion, confused. Was Lion's aura orange because it was a combination of yellow and red, or was it orange because it was orange? He shook his head and returned to studying Jaguar's aura.

The yellow was clearly the dominant of the two colors. For a reason he couldn't quite define, Ryan was convinced that Jaguar had a power different from what he'd seen from Malone and Warner.

As he considered the thought, Ryan recalled that Malone seemed to have a certain hostility in his voice toward Jaguar. He mocked the Swedish accent—which in itself was wrong since Jaguar had a British accent— and had a dismissive tone about Jaguar's so-called "self-described super covert ops" status.

Ryan studied Jaguar a little more. The agent had blonde hair and an average build. He certainly looked Scandinavian. The suit he wore looked better than Malone's, but looked cheap next to Lion's, perhaps because in part the jacket had been used as a bandage. He was clearly confident and respected by the others, though they all seemed to share a slightly antagonistic relationship.

Ryan leaned back to watch them all again. They were engrossed in their discussion and traced fingers about on the map and generally argued, albeit civilly. As Ryan watched and listened, with a little focus, he realized he could hear more than what they were saying. He couldn't quite read their thoughts, but he received vague impressions from them, or some of them, at least.

Lion's mind was just as unreadable as his face and body language. The man may as well have been a statue that spoke when one pressed a button for all the emotion he showed. Tiger, however, bristled with energy, and Ryan thought that she was somehow irritated, but he couldn't state why.

Jaguar, however, seemed excited, which seemed a

little odd considering the circumstances, but without knowing them, Ryan couldn't say why he saw those impressions or what they really meant.

Jaguar suddenly turned to him and Ryan blinked and realized that though they had all stopped speaking, he clearly heard Jaguar's voice in his head.

"I said, are you getting this, mate?"

"You didn't say that."

"You heard me, didn't you?"

Ryan looked from Lion to Tiger and back to Jaguar and just shrugged. "Yeah, I'm getting it."

"I hope so, because you said you wanted in on this."

Ryan leaned forward and paid attention to the conversation and realized they were arguing over strategy. Jaguar was of the mind that they should find somewhere on the west side of town to stage an ambush while Tiger was vocal that the warehouse, wherever that was, was the perfect location.

Ryan started to drift as he watched them argue all the while Lion watched and listened and generally looked contemplative. Something about how Jaguar and Tiger went at each other made Ryan wonder, just for a second, if they were related. However, they didn't look like one another, but he still wondered. Cousins, perhaps?

Ryan continued to watch them and decided that, while the name The Debate Team might not have been applicable to the agency as a whole, it certainly seemed appropriate to this crew. The way that Jaguar and Tiger argued gave Ryan the impression that this was something that had happened on more than one occasion.

"Lady and gentlemen." Ryan looked over to see

William, as he had introduced himself, enter the room. He was carrying what looked like a regular terrestrial radio. He walked to the coffee table, set it down, and turned it on.

The radio was tuned to a local channel and the radio announcer said that the town was in the process of getting its services back and that it was all the result of construction gone awry. A large conduit had apparently been cut that contained not only power lines, but telephone and cable as well. Because the new water plant that had been built years ago relied on computers to operate properly, water service was terminated when the power went out and caused a spike that overloaded their servers. The power spike also overloaded cellular towers and caused them to malfunction, which without a connection back to the main servers, led to a massive network collapse in the area.

Additionally, but unrelated to the construction, a gas leak had been found near city hall, which unfortunately had destroyed the library.

Ryan harrumphed.

The announcer then welcomed a guest onto the air, a sergeant in the United States Army, who confirmed these statements but had little extra to say on the matter.

William turned the radio down and tried to turn on a light in the room, but the light didn't respond.

"Well we know that's a crock of shit." Tiger turned the radio off entirely. "Is anything back, Willy?"

"We have water, and I anticipate power soon. Landlines are also up, but they're sketchy at best."

Ryan pulled his phone out of his pocket and waited

for it to boot. He looked up when he realized it had become quiet in the room and they looked at him expectantly. A few seconds later the phone finished loading.

"Still nothing."

Jaguar nodded and looked at each of them. "That's not a bad thing because that means that there's still a little chaos and they may still be around."

Ryan put the phone away. "I think I mentioned at some point they were hunting you down, right?"

"Precisely."

"What?"

"If everything was back to normal, they may as well just move on to their next plan. But if things are still wonky, then maybe they're still in town, hoping I'll poke my head out."

Ryan snickered. The way Jaguar said "wonky" like it was two distinct words, was funny to him.

William adjusted the collar on his Hawaiian shirt and looked up. "I've spoken with a former colleague. There's an abandoned grocery store on the south side of town that he believes them to be in."

Tiger stood and started to speak before Jaguar cut her short.

"We're not going into the wolf's lair."

"I agree that is a dangerous course."

Jaguar and Tiger looked at Lion who met Tiger's gaze with an unblinking one of his own. Tiger sat and sighed.

Jaguar looked as though he had to contain laughter, but his tone was serious. "You're good, but that's insane."

Tiger frowned. "So which is it? West side or

warehouse?"

They started to argue their sides again and Ryan stood and cleared his throat. "What if I gave you an alternative?"

"What, your house?" Tiger said. "And they think I'm nuts."

"No, Tiger. I was thinking of one of the agency's hideouts."

Tiger and Jaguar exchanged looks, but Lion spoke.

"The agency maintains no 'hideouts' within town limits." The way he said "hideout" made it sound like it left a bad taste in his mouth.

"They don't? So Malone took me to his place? Or one that belonged to... them?" Ryan snorted and shook his head.

"Oh, that's perverted." Tiger.

"But it may work." Jaguar.

"I like it. It's vicious."

"It's appropriate."

Ryan looked at Jaguar and Tiger and sat back down.

"Okay, mate, where is this place?"

"It's a house on the southwest side of town." Jaguar shot Tiger a victorious look. "It's small, a few rooms with entrances that go into the same room."

"That's not a bad choke point."

"I thought you might like that."

"But it is a house," Lion said.

Ryan turned a suspicious eye toward Lion. "Yes."

"Then it has windows. There are numerous entrances."

"Well, I suppose."

"This house, can you vouch for it not having any traps or alarms or other inconvenient and dangerous components left there by its owner?"

"Well, no, but I didn't see anything and I was there a lot. Look, I'm just throwing out options. Are you always a buzz kill?"

"I am merely pointing out the fallacies in your plan."

"Who said I had a plan?"

"You would not present such an idea if you did not have one."

Ryan glared at Lion then looked away. Of course, Lion was right. Ryan had been formulating a plan that would see the doors completely covered, be it with standard or nonstandard munitions. However, he had to admit that it was something of a Swiss cheese plan.

"Fine, you're right. You guys figure out a plan and let me know." Ryan turned to William. "William, can I use your restroom? Preferably one on the other side of the house."

Jaguar and Tiger started their arguments again and William led Ryan out of the room. Ryan paused at the threshold and shook his head. With all the shit going on, how could they sit there and just argue?

Then he remembered that they were, after all, a government agency.

Small houses had likely sold for less than what William's bathroom must have cost. Ryan stepped foot outside of it and into the master bedroom. For such an opulent house, the bedroom was surprisingly stark. A sleek bed with a black duvet sat with a red accent wall behind it. A black and white rug covered a solid twenty square feet of open floor, and an equally sleek though barebones table sat next to the bed. The room hardly looked lived in, though he supposed others would say it was modern and minimal. It was, however, in direct opposition to the styling in the rest of the house. Maybe William was in the middle of renovations.

What was he doing? Ryan laughed at himself. Watching home renovation shows with his folks must have given him something of an eye toward interior design.

Ryan pushed the furnishings out of his mind and made to find his way back through the house, but he caught sight of a telephone, an old-fashioned one with an oversized receiver sitting on the nightstand. William's words played back: landlines worked, but were sketchy.

How long had it been since he saw his mom? Wouldn't they be worried about him? He was certainly worried about them. Ryan grabbed the received and dialed. He tapped a foot as he listened to the phone ring. His pulse raced, but after a couple of tense seconds someone picked up on the other end.

"Hello?"

"Dad!"

"Ryan? Where are you?"

"I'm, well I don't know where I am, but I'm fine."

"Your mom mentioned you were with some government agent and that something weird was going on."

"Yeah, I don't think I can explain it right now, but I'm okay. As good as I can be."

"Are you? You don't sound like yourself."

Ryan sighed and stared at the wall. What could he say? That'd he been helping out some government agent who duped him and turned out to be a super soldier who sold himself to the highest bidder and was now working for a terrorist organization with unspecified plans of world domination?

"It's complicated, dad."

"But you're okay?"

"Yeah, I guess. How are you, and how's mom?"

"She's worried sick about you, but hearing you're okay helps."

"I'm ready for this to be over, but I still have something I need to do before I come home and I don't know how long it'll take."

"Be careful. Work is calling me away for a few days and your mom is coming with me. We might not be home by the time you're done, but be safe until then, okay?"

"Of course. You too, dad."

They resolved to meet shortly — Ryan did live with them, after all — then ended the call.

Ryan left the bedroom and wandered down the hallway. He hadn't been paying much attention when William led him through the house and it took some trial and error to find everyone else. At length he followed their voices and oriented himself in the right direction. He entered the sitting room to a scene that he thought looked strikingly similar to the one he had left.

Jaguar and Tiger appeared to be locked into the same argument, both still advocating their sides without either backing down.

"Really? You're still fighting about this?" Ryan looked to Lion and gestured toward the two, but Lion only shrugged.

Tiger threw up her hands. "He thinks the warehouse is a bad idea and is still against the idea of hunting them down at their... hey, what is it?"

Ryan felt his focus shift and he was suddenly looking at himself and the rest of the room as though from a third-person camera. The shift in perspective was entirely unconscious and he pulled the view back until he was looking around outside.

The sudden shift gave him reason to believe that something was amiss, but he couldn't find it if so. Everything outside looked normal, so Ryan pulled back even farther and panned around. Again, everything looked normal, but he noticed that the speck of black he had mistaken as a distant plane was growing larger and moving toward his view.

He shifted his view toward the speck and stopped when he confirmed his worst thoughts. Ryan severed the view and found that they were all staring at him expectantly again.

Ryan took a deep breath. "I think the decision has to wait. They're coming here."

Jaguar stood and looked at him. "How is that even possible? They don't know about Willy."

"I think I may be to blame, guys. I called home. I had to know if my parents were okay."

"Fuck!" Tiger got up and stormed out of the room.

Jaguar cast her a sideways glance then looked at Ryan expectantly. "And?"

"They're okay. My dad said they were heading out of town for a few days."

"Good. I hope they get out of there in a hurry. Come on."

"What did I do?"

"No telling, mate, but it sounds like we need to go greet our company."

"Shit." Ryan ran out of the room and into an office

where he found another phone. He quickly dialed the number and waited. One ring. Two rings. Three rings.

"Hurry up!"

Four rings. Why did they have to insist on setting the ringer so high on the answering machine? Automatic dialers didn't care how long they had to wait for someone to pick up. Five rings. Six rings. Finally, the answering machine picked up. He could only hope that they were busy packing for the weekend and that they would hear his message.

"Hey, it's me. Look, I can't explain, but I think you're in danger. Get out. Now." He hoped that he didn't sound too panicked but also sounded serious. He'd never said or done anything like that and they might not be sure how to respond to it.

The thought suddenly hit him that he might be able to at least look in on the house and make sure they were okay, so he started to pull his vision back. However, a hand shaking his shoulder killed the trance.

"Hey, we have to go. I'm sorry." Jaguar turned and left the room.

Ryan threw his hands up in frustration and followed Jaguar out of the room.

Tiger and Lion were already outside loading things into the SUV. William stood in the open front door of his house.

"Willy, mate, we'll owe you one. Will you be alright?"

"I have a safe room. I'll be fine, though I'll need to move now." He said it as though it was something as insignificant as having to get a new pair of socks.

"Sorry about that." Jaguar threw a look at Ryan.

"Take care, and thanks again."

William and Jaguar shook hands and exchanged a look then Jaguar ran outside.

A car fired up in the driveway, a Porsche, and Ryan saw that Lion was in the driver's seat. He pulled forward a bit and rolled the window down.

"I will be at Location B."

"Go." Jaguar slapped the car's door and Lion took off.

Ryan furrowed his brow as it hit him. "Wait, you're not holding out here?"

Jaguar shot Ryan an incredulous look.

"This is our mate's flat, and you want to hold up here?"

"Oh, yeah. Where to, then?"

"You heard Lion. Location B."

"What the hell is 'Location B'?"

"It's where we're going."

Jaguar hopped on the bike and started it. Ryan knelt to inspect the bike and, despite their predicament, felt his heart pound in excitement.

"No way! You have a 'Busa?"

Tiger jumped out from the SUV and stormed over.

"Hey man, no way. No fucking way! We've been through this already. You get on yours!"

"Yours is already out. Besides, it's fine, right? Not a scratch on it."

Tiger was already waving her hands. "No, you get on your bike! You were lucky last time. I've seen yours."

"And I'll be lucky this time, too."

Jaguar apparently already had the bike in gear because he rolled the throttle back and was out of the driveway before Tiger could say anything else.

"Asshole!" Tiger looked over at Ryan. "What? Come on. Get in." Tiger ran to the SUV. She hopped in and slammed the door.

The driveway had an incline to it and Jaguar caught air as he left it and joined the street. The bike groaned in protest and he thought he heard something scrape, but he continued onward. Cars were on the street, but it was nothing like normal just yet. A chance glance up between buildings as he raced south revealed a black chopper headed his way, and he knew those choppers well.

Tiger, whirlybird coming your way. Take the scenic route east if you can.

Jaguar raced through an intersection where a police officer directed traffic and he split his time between looking up and looking straight ahead. Jaguar sliced through traffic and weaved in and out of lanes and generally didn't blink as he endangered his life and possibly those around him because he knew he needed to draw attention his way.

The chopper passed by overhead, the trailing vehicles not far behind. Once again, a sedan, this time a black one, led a pack of emergency vehicles. With the sedan only a couple hundred meters away, Jaguar turned down a street, careful to stay out of the range of any powers its occupants might throw his way, and circled around the emergency vehicles.

Jaguar reached back to the saddlebag as he rode and pulled out a machine pistol again.

The last vehicle in the line was an ambulance, and as Jaguar pulled up to it, the back doors suddenly opened and gunfire erupted. Jaguar swerved hard and almost lost the bike as it threatened to slide out from under him. A couple of rounds rattled off the bike. Tiger wasn't going to be happy. He hoped they didn't hit anything vital.

He swerved behind another vehicle, seeking safety, but two gunmen opened fire again from the ambulance, heedless of the innocent person caught in the middle. Jaguar rolled the throttle back hard and zipped past the suddenly swerving vehicle and pulled up alongside the ambulance.

Jaguar held the machine pistol out and pulled the trigger. Click. He had forgotten to reload after emptying it at the sedan earlier. He couldn't remember if he had changed magazines after that, but he had his answer. He quickly dumped the empty magazine and struggled to slam a new one in, but before he could shoot, he had to brake and swerve away as the driver leaned out of the window and started firing.

"Asshole!"

Jaguar pulled back and made a sudden turn then another and paralleled the vehicles from a block over.

Tiger, they're ready for me. I'm not buying you any time.

Jaguar raced ahead and looked to the side as he passed through an intersection. He was running in line with the lead emergency vehicle. He kept going and pulled ahead. Jaguar cut over at the next street. He burst back onto the street, now in front of the sedan as it came toward him. Jaguar raised the machine pistol and opened fire.

The sedan swerved hard and Jaguar only managed a couple of shots before he had to stop so that he wouldn't hit a bystander, but he hoped it would be enough to draw their attention. He sped past them and turned around to play catch-up again.

The bike's motor screamed as Jaguar revved it hard and pulled alongside the emergency vehicles. He pulled forward and emptied his magazine into the lead vehicle, a police cruiser, and then charged forward. Careful not to go too fast yet not appear as though he was obviously trying to lead them away, Jaguar turned down a street and looked back. The vehicles kept going straight.

Tiger, they're ignoring me completely.

"Hey, you with me?" Tiger punched his arm.

"I'm watching." Ryan struggled to maintain his concentration as he looked outside of himself and at the city streets despite Tiger's insistence for his attention.

"Jaguar says they're ignoring him, but we may have lost them."

Ryan watched as the cars zipped down a street, then the lead car made a sudden turn that cut off traffic as it angled down a street and turned onto another that, as he zoomed out his view, he understood would put the cars on a course to intercept him and Tiger. It looked as though Lion would be okay, at least.

"They just changed directions. They're trying to cut us off."

"Bullshit. How do they know we're even here?"

Ryan zoomed back in and panned around the sedan. It was like a scene out of a movie as his view swung around from behind the car, along the passenger side, and turned around to stop at the windshield.

"Malone and Fisher are in the lead car."

"Shit. I bet Fisher sniffed us out. If they don't know it was you calling home, they're going to be in for a big surprise."

The sudden thought broke Ryan's concentration. He blinked and looked out of the windshield of the SUV. Tiger was navigating surface streets Ryan wasn't familiar with.

"Do you think he noticed me nosing around?"

"Hard to say, but the chopper sure found us."

"Chopper?" Ryan looked out of the passenger window then peered out windows until he spotted the black chopper overhead. That could explain the sudden change in direction by Malone and Fisher.

The chopper was holding its distance and didn't make any attempt to attack or do anything but provide surveillance. But something felt wrong about the situation.

"Malone said he was after Jaguar, but if so, why are they ignoring him? You said they chased you last time, too. What the hell?"

Tiger snickered and looked into the side mirror; her eyes followed the chopper.

"Dumb fucks don't even know who they're messing with, that's why."

"I don't get it."

"They're chasing ghosts. They know about Jaguar, but they've only now figured out there's more than just him. Unbelievable." Tiger laughed, rolled down the window, and flipped them the bird. She laughed again and kept driving.

Ryan laughed as well, but something still wasn't right. Malone admitted that he didn't know much about Jaguar, other than the guy had powers that aided him with getting into places he didn't belong, but surely they had to know whom he was following and what happened after they were found at the parking structure. It's not every day that someone teleports himself and single-handedly disables half a dozen cars. Surely someone got a good look at the guy.

So why the hell were Malone and Fisher chasing them when the real target was out there on a bike likely filling their cars with holes? Unless they knew he was here, since Ryan knew who was behind the terrorism and who was targeted, that in turn made him a target. But how would they know he was here, physically in this spot?

Lion had taken off right away, and seemed to want nothing to do with any sort of combat, never mind that he had done something that, Ryan thought, saved his life. Jaguar looked eager to jump into a fight, and there were bullet holes in the cars when Ryan saw them. That left Tiger. Shit.

"Hey, pull over for a second." Ryan's voice was even.

"What? Are you kidding? You just said they're heading our way."

"Pull over. I know a trick that Malone taught me that can make them turn around, but I can't do it in here. I need to be somewhere quiet and stable."

"No way, can't do it."

Ryan looked at Tiger and glared at her. "Pull over."

Tiger's expression went suddenly blank and her pupils dilated but she brought the SUV to a stop on the side of the road.

They had been running around the outer perimeter of town and it was nothing but old houses and dirt around them.

Ryan hopped out of the car and took off at a run toward the nearest house that didn't look entirely dilapidated.

He had gotten maybe a dozen steps away before he heard Tiger. "Hey! What the fuck!"

Tiger's voice fell away as Ryan continued to run, but he heard the SUV come up behind him. Ryan dashed over a half-broken wooden fence and into the dirt and weeds that made up the backyard of the house. He changed directions and started running back the way they came and cut across the yard and hopped the fence into the next one. Sirens pierced the air and he heard the SUV as it started to turn around.

He ran from yard to yard, and by the time he was in the sixth, the sirens were loud enough that he thought he'd see the vehicles when he looked up. Ryan stopped and looked over a fence. The SUV took, off, dirt and dust flying into the air. A line of emergency vehicles, led by a plain sedan, zoomed by a few moments later, bringing with them a cloud of dust that would do the Sahara proud.

Breathing heavily, Ryan watched for several more seconds then hopped the fence and started down the street. He wasn't going to be turned on a second time.

CHAPTER 14

Ryan checked his phone—still no cellular network—and found he'd been walking for a couple of hours. He cut across the street and moved closer to the city proper. He was near a commercial district on the east side of town. A large shopping center with an electronics store, three kinds of clothing stores, a home and garden store, and half a dozen fast-food restaurants was just on the other side of the street.

The light changed and Ryan walked across the street and angled for the first restaurant that looked open, and there was surprisingly more than one. It was amazing how different the town was now that everything seemed normal again. Though it had only been a handful of days, he had gotten used to the quiet chaos of the sleeping town, and now to have most services restored and see the day-to-day chaos returned, he wasn't sure it was a good thing, at least not entirely.

The violence and crime aside, there was a certain serenity the town had for a few days that was now gone. It was a surreal experience to be out in the town when technology had failed and left it little more than a concrete wasteland. It was akin to a return to more primal days, when one's concerns lingered more on survival than how large a television one could put on a credit card. Of course, he had also been an accomplice in multiple murders and was running for his life, so he didn't really get to experience the change, but he imagined what it must have been like for others.

He entered the store, and only after a moment's thought that San Vincente had been plunged into chaos for the last few days, was he surprised to realize that the store looked unscathed. He placed his order, dropped a few bills on the counter, then sat and waited for his sandwich to be made. Ryan realized it was probably ridiculous that he was stopping to eat with all sorts of hostile, and potentially hostile, people looking for him, but he needed a moment to stop and feel normal. And what was more normal than eating a sandwich?

His sandwich ready, Ryan picked it up and sat back down and started to eat. For a moment, that promise of normalcy was reality. For a moment, he was just in a store eating a sandwich and the outside world progressed just as it always had. For a moment, he was Ryan Sutter, employee of the county library, just a regular guy with a regular job and friends and family.

The feeling faded when he saw the bike pull up in front of the store. He debated running, but he was tired. If this was it, so be it.

The door opened and Jaguar walked in and straight to his tiny table. He didn't say a word, just pulled out a chair and sat. He pointed to the open bag of chips on the table and Ryan shrugged.

Jaguar popped a chip in his mouth, crunched, and fixed Ryan with a stare that left him uncomfortable.

"You've pissed off Tiger something awful and scared the shit out of me and Lion. You know that, right?"

Ryan put his sandwich down and gave Jaguar an exasperated smile.

"It's not happening again. And if it is happening

now, then just finish it. I'm sick of this shit. I didn't sign up for any of it and I don't want anything more to do with it. Just do something or leave me alone."

"What? What in the bloody blue bumblefuck are you on about, mate?"

"Jesus, you assholes." Ryan looked around—he hadn't meant to raise his voice. He took a deep breath and shoved his sandwich away. "I trusted Malone and he stabbed me in the back. I got out of Tiger's SUV before she could do the same. If you're involved too, which wouldn't surprise me considering how blind I am to it, then just end it now. Make it quick, that's all I ask."

"Are you high, mate? Tiger is not Malone and neither am I and neither is Lion. Where did you ever get that idea from?"

"I'm not stupid, okay? Malone said he's looking for you, so why was he chasing Tiger? She was obviously delivering me, just making it look like she wasn't."

Jaguar stared at Ryan then looked away and said something under his breath Ryan couldn't hear.

"You stupid wanker. She saved your life. She was the one who drove you to Willy's house. Don't you think if she were going to turn you over that would have been the perfect opportunity?"

"You guys said you wrecked all their cars. Too obvious."

Jaguar ran a hand over his face and stared again. "Then what the hell did you think she was going to do now?"

"You went in different directions. I saw the cars change direction to follow us with no warning."

"The chopper found you."

"Or it was supposed to look that way. And then all this driving along the old back roads while you and Lion were in completely different areas."

"And where did she go when you got out of the car?"

"She tried to follow me then took off."

"Because she was followed."

"Yeah."

"And where did they go?"

"Away."

"And did they come back?"

Ryan looked at Jaguar then looked past him. He considered everything Jaguar said, that Tiger had driven him when he was unconscious, that the chopper found them, that Tiger led Malone and Fisher away and didn't come back.

"Stupid asshole."

"Yeah, you stupid asshole. Stop thinking with your ass and start using that brain of yours. It's occasionally good for something, or so I'm led to believe."

"I can't believe I did that. She's really pissed, isn't she?"

"You have no idea. You messed with her head, and she hates that."

Ryan leaned back and stared out of the window. He really messed up and put Tiger in danger.

"I suppose I owe you guys, Tiger especially, an apology."

"Yeah, you do. Come on."

"You mean this isn't over? Almost everything is back to normal."

"Malone and Fisher are still out there, and even then, there's Sikes. I think we can worry about him later, but you're not safe while Malone and Fisher are around."

"Can I finish my sandwich?"

Jaguar laughed as he stood and pushed his chair in. He started to walk away then stopped at the door. "Five minutes."

Ryan grabbed his sandwich. He hurriedly ate the rest and washed it down with his soda. At least the simple pleasure of food wasn't entirely ruined by his arrogance and stupidity.

Jaguar was waiting on the bike outside, and he pulled a black helmet out of one of the saddlebags.

Something was still bothering Ryan. "So if they are after you, then why were they chasing Tiger?"

"That's a good question, but I don't have the answer. Hop on. We need to get back and figure out what to do."

Ryan got on the back and Jaguar passed the helmet back to him.

"I'll risk the ticket, but you need to protect that head of yours, though I can't imagine why if you don't use it."

Ryan glared but said nothing and popped the helmet on. It was too small, but he squeezed it on with only minor chafing of his ears. It was better than nothing.

"You know bikes?"

"Yeah." Ryan's voice was muffled under the full chin guard. "Used to race off-road but never quite got into street. Wanted to, just never did."

"Well hold on."

Ryan wrapped his arms around Jaguar's stomach and put his feet on the pegs. Jaguar stepped the bike back then shot off.

The guy apparently had no fear and didn't mind that

he occasionally, technically, broke some traffic laws because he zipped in and out of traffic and ran several yellow lights just as they turned to red. With unnerving speed and wild movements, they made good time. Jaguar made a particularly bold move to cut off a large SUV. Ryan shook his head in disbelief. Jaguar was what other, safer riders commonly called a squid.

They were cutting across town to the west—the direction Jaguar had argued for earlier—and turned into an average looking neighborhood and down a couple of streets before they stopped at a house that looked just like any other on the street. Jaguar honked the horn once, and several seconds later, the garage door opened and he pulled the bike in. The SUV and Porsche were already parked inside and it was a tight squeeze to fit the bike between the two, but he did.

Tiger, standing near the door that led inside, hit a button and the garage door rolled down. She shot him a particularly nasty look before she went inside.

Ryan left the helmet on the bike and followed Jaguar in. A short hallway went a couple of directions and they took the one that led to the kitchen and larger entertaining rooms.

Sparse, serviceable furniture filled out most of the house, while a similarly plain table and several chairs were in the dining room adjacent to the kitchen. A couple of maps were spread on the table, complete with what looked like Monopoly houses and figurines used to denote specific locations. Lion was at the head of the table, pencil in hand and tapping against a finger, as he looked over a map. Tiger was seated to his right and she looked up, briefly, but only at Jaguar before she returned her attention to the same map.

For a group saying they didn't have any hideouts, this certainly looked like one. Ryan made a mental note to inquire about that later.

"You two figure it out yet?" Jaguar said. He pulled a chair out and looked from one to the other. "Well?"

"Possibly. We believe we might have an option, but it relies on certain questionable tactics." Lion held a pencil by the butt end of it and pointed it at a Monopoly hotel then tapped it on the map just south of the location. "They are gathered here, we believe, and while an approach from the south would be unwise, the store faces the west and has an alley behind it that could serve as an acceptable entry point."

"Wait, didn't you guys say it was a bad idea to be assaulting them at their base?" Ryan looked from one to the other, but they paid him no mind.

"There are multiple delivery entrances in the back, and it should be possible through certain means to gain entry into one" Lion said.

Jaguar tapped on the map next to the house. "I can walk right in, you know that."

Lion took on a sudden wise, fatherly appearance.

"You could, yes. Have you forgotten that it is entirely possible, if not probable, that there are at least two exceptionally dangerous innate inside?"

"Well of course there are."

"And one of those is a master of mental manipulation, and now that they know us, will know to expect you."

Jaguar leaned back and frowned.

"I could just get in and gas them. We can sort it out later. Innate or not, tear gas is going to suck."

"Except that Malone could neutralize a gas attack."

Omni

Jaguar looked back at Ryan for confirmation. What
Lion said made sense, even if it was yet another buzz
kill. Ryan nodded in agreement.

"Why are we even talking about this if getting inside
is too dangerous, let alone doing something assuming
we do get in?"

Lion looked to Tiger who crossed her arms and
looked away, and then he turned to face Jaguar. "Ryan
is the questionable tactic."

Ryan looked up in surprise. "Me?"

"You. You have demonstrated that you have some
access to and control of minds, and you could greatly
ease the infiltration of their base. It should be possible
for you to create a mobile stealth device, so to speak."

"Wait, you're giving me too much credit. I just know
a couple of tricks. I don't even know what the hell
you're talking about let alone know how to do it."

"Yeah, like you didn't know how to take over my
mind and damn near get me killed when all I'm trying
to do is save your ass."

Tiger pushed her chair back and left the room
without another word. Ryan looked down, at a wall,
just somewhere away.

"I believe you may need some focus, but a lack of
power is not your problem. What I am asking of you is
not easy and not without some hesitation, but our
intelligence indicates that we have limited time to
strike. If we do not move soon, they will leave town
and we won't have an opportunity to remove these
terrorists until they surface for another attack. If we
wait, their next attack could be even worse."

"This is dangerous, Lion. You're asking me to put
my life in the hands of an untrained innate. What does

Tiger think?" Jaguar looked out to the family room.

"She has certain issues with the plan, but is otherwise supportive."

Jaguar turned and stared Ryan in the eye. "Can you do it, mate?"

Ryan looked from one to the other and shrugged. "I'm not sure what I'm supposed to do, but I can try. What do you mean by 'mobile stealth device'?"

"A simple trick, yet one that requires great focus and energy to maintain," Lion said. "Through means I don't quite understand, you project an aura of nothingness, as though your existence is not actually there."

"Wait, Malone taught me this. We walked right past a few guards at the hospital when we…" The memory of the murder stopped him with a shudder. "At least, I think I did, though now I don't know if the police were in on it."

"Let's find out. Sit down." Jaguar pointed to a chair and waited for Ryan to sit. "Do whatever you did back then, but wait until I leave the room."

Jaguar pushed his chair out and walked out to the living room. Ryan looked at Lion and felt his face redden under the man's calm but unrelenting gaze.

Okay, mate, block me out. I'm going to keep talking to you until you block me, so it's to your benefit that you do it sooner rather than later, because I can put together one hell of a string of words that can… you getting this? Hey, Ryan? You there?

Jaguar spoke to him, and he tried to focus on nothing. It was a little difficult when being talked to—a lifetime habit of trying to pay attention to others and be polite had to be ditched in a matter of seconds, because his ability to block out the rest of the world determined their safety. About to focus completely on nothing, Ryan found that he was still able, though he couldn't quite say how, to hear what Jaguar was saying, and to process it, without bringing his wall of nothing down. It was odd, and Jaguar's voice changed in his head to something lighter, more whispery, but he could definitely still hear Jaguar's. He wondered if he could respond.

I still hear you.

What in the blue hell? I can't find you.

Then it's working?

Mate, I think we're going to be fine.

Ryan ended his focus and was surprised to find that he didn't feel the same exhaustion as he had before. He realized that he was focusing on himself, not on others, and decided that must have been the reason for the difference. It was a bit like running multiple lights on a battery: many would drain the battery quickly, but a single light could shine for hours and hours. He wasn't sure the logic was correct, but it made sense to him.

Voices in the living room came to him as he rejoined the real world, but he couldn't make out the specifics. After a few seconds, Jaguar reentered the room, Tiger behind him. She scowled as she walked into the room.

"Lion, this guy's a kick," Jaguar said and thumbed toward Ryan. "He could still hear me talking to him even when I lost his presence, and then he started talking to me. It was like the voice of god because it came from someone that didn't exist."

Lion turned a contemplative look on Jaguar. "Are you satisfied with the performance?"

"Bloody amazing, mate."

Lion nodded and looked back to Ryan. "So, Mr.

Sutter, are you in?"

Ryan shrugged. "Sure."

"Very well. Here is the plan."

It was a simple plan: get in, get Malone and Fisher—and if he was there, get Sikes—and get out, all without dying. Though it sounded easy enough, Ryan knew, or thought he knew, just how dangerous this really was.

What was being requested of him was still somewhat baffling, but Lion insisted there were ways of manipulating the nothing bubble that would reduce the strain required to maintain it. Jaguar only shrugged when asked about it and insisted he only knew how to talk to people and could perform no other mental tricks.

The biggest—and most troublesome—unknown was whether Fisher, or even Malone, would be able to detect their presence, standard means aside, because Ryan was going to be pumping out large doses of energy. It was Lion who reminded them that this was their only opportunity in the foreseeable future to get the targets and the decision was made.

The drive to the grocery store was quiet, with all of them except Lion in the SUV. Ryan sat in the back and debated how to apologize to Tiger, but he wasn't sure what to say. After several minutes of silently berating himself, he at last decided he had to say something. The tension was too thick and might cause a problem otherwise. Besides, he had messed up and needed to make it right, or at least try to.

"Tiger, look, I'm sorry about what I did back there. I was freaking out and not thinking clearly. After Malone—"

"About what you did?" Tiger turned around in the passenger seat and practically spat the words out. "Say it. You took over my mind and put me in danger."

"I'm sorry. It's just that I thought I was being set up again and I couldn't handle it."

"If you're apologizing, you're supposed to say you're sorry and that's it. Don't give me any bullshit excuses." She turned around without waiting for anything further from him.

Ryan sat back, surprised at the anger in Tiger's voice. He had thought she was mad at the house, but that had been calm in comparison. Her tone was a whip, and each word cracked and stung, not just because of her anger, but because she was right. It didn't matter why he did it, just that he was wrong and he needed to apologize. Perhaps at another time it would matter, but now. Sitting in the back of the SUV on the way to endanger themselves for a job no one even knew about, it meant even less than the squashed bugs on the windshield.

"Tiger, I'm sorry I took over your mind. It won't happen again."

She turned around in her seat again and looked him in the eye. "You're fucking right it won't."

Ryan heard the unspoken promise clearly.

Jaguar cleared his throat. "If you two are done, you might want to pay attention. We're almost at the drop point."

Through the tinted window, a dimmed residential neighborhood a mile east of the abandoned store came into view. As they turned into the neighborhood, Ryan found himself questioning his agreement to help. Obviously, they, even Tiger, seemed convinced that his participation was a necessity, but he was a damn library employee, not a government agent. He wasn't trained to storm buildings and have a shoot-out with terrorists.

It was the same argument he had with himself several times while he was helping Malone, and now, just as then, he had to convince himself that he had to do it because people were relying on him. It was important that these terrorists be caught, and he admitted to himself that he wanted to be there to see Malone be brought down. He wasn't sure if it'd make him feel any better or even close the wound of betrayal and assuage his guilt over the murders, but he needed to see Malone brought down. It wasn't a want; it was a need.

That, more than their reliance on him to keep them all unnoticed and allow them to do their job, was what convinced him that he needed to ignore the questions in his head. Besides, it wasn't as though he had a job to get up to in the morning, so why not?

"Okay, we're here," Jaguar said. "Ryan, just like we talked about. Okay?"

Ryan looked up from his mental deliberations and found Jaguar and Tiger both looking at him. He nodded. "I'll do my best."

"Good."

They exited the vehicle, which was parked on the street in front of a random house, and Ryan took a moment to look at the other two as they pulled equipment out of the back of the SUV. They both wore black BDUs that looked to contain lots of armor. He hoped he wouldn't need any.

Though the nearby shopping center had fallen into

ill repair thanks to difficult economic times, this neighborhood retained most of its charm. It was quiet, but a pair of completely dark houses with signs in the yard indicated the neighborhood hadn't entirely escaped the economic troubles.

Ryan closed his eyes and slowed his mind. All of his worries, all of his questions, all the pain, the doubt, he rolled it into a ball and pushed it into a dark recess in his mind. To do this, he needed every bit of his focus, every bit of his will. They needed a way to move quietly and without being seen, and he was the only one who could do it. With a deep breath, he pictured the bubble in his mind and began to pour his will into it, to remove thought and sound, sight and smell. It was all coming together, would only take a few seconds, then Jaguar tapped his shoulder and shoved something into him. Ryan lost his concentration.

"Put this on. Just in case."

Ryan opened his eyes and stared without understanding at the vest Jaguar held out to him, then it registered. A bulletproof vest.

"Thanks." Ryan took the vest and opened the straps.

Jaguar helped get the vest situated, but the extra weight was bothersome It didn't look anywhere near as heavy as it actually was. He could think of nothing else for several seconds as it pulled his shoulders down and made normal movements awkward, but he eventually found a good place for it to sit and tightened the straps enough that he could stop thinking about it.

"Calm, smooth, in and out and in thirty minutes. Okay?"

"In and out." Tiger nodded as she shoved a small armory of knives into sewn-in sheaths on her black

235

vest.

Ryan closed his eyes, and after calming his mind again, thought of a bubble thirty feet in diameter, invisible and undetectable. He extended his will to form this invisible barrier of nothing, but then he decided that nothing was the wrong way to go about it. A barrier of nothing was wrong, like a void in the world. It should be something, but nothing important. It was an odd distinction, one he prevented himself from doting on, and instead focused on his bubble of nothing important.

Ryan opened his eyes to find Jaguar and Tiger watching him, both with eyebrows raised.

"Go. Stay close."

Jaguar led the way, Ryan in the middle, Tiger behind him. They moved through the quiet neighborhood and made their way back to the main thoroughfare. A car entered the neighborhood from the other end, but it stopped at a house before it ever came close to them. Though cars passed by on the cross street, no others came their way. They moved in silence until they neared the thoroughfare.

"I don't feel anything," Tiger said.

"That's the point. He's extended a bubble of nothing."

"But wouldn't a bubble of nothing be noticeable? Or rather, wouldn't things disappearing into it be noticeable?"

Jaguar stopped and turned around. "Ryan?"

"Bubble of nothing important. I modified it. Please go."

Jaguar gave him a blank stare then grinned. "How about that? A bubble of nothing important." He started off again with a shake of his head. Ryan imagined him grinning again. He wondered if Tiger was smiling, then remembered he needed to focus.

"How big is this bubble of nothing important?" Tiger said. Ryan thought there was some derision, albeit slight, in Tiger's question.

"Fifteen foot radius."

"Every direction?"

"Yes."

"But no one is looking for us underground."

Ryan thought about that and realized that Tiger was right. He was focusing his energy on creating an entire bubble, and though it was still easier than forcing others to think of nothing, he was having doubts that he would be able to sustain it long enough. He was worried it might drop before they get to the store because they were moving so slowly.

"Thanks, Tiger." Ryan collapsed the bubble into a dome and his shoulders rose in response. His breathing came a little easier and he could focus a little more on his surroundings, such as the worrisome number of guns attached to Jaguar's vest and the large duffel bag he was carrying.

"What for?"

"It's a half-bubble of nothing important, now. Much easier. I know I can do this."

Tiger snorted but said nothing.

Whether that meant that Ryan was forgiven or if it was just amusement, he decided either was better than the glare and tone he had faced earlier.

CHAPTER 15

This neighborhood allowed certain, specific access to the back of the abandoned grocery store that made it a desirable starting point. About a hundred yards from the cross street and behind a chain-link fence, a large concrete channel ran along the back of the neighborhood and continued beyond, but also ran all the way back west. The channel was twenty feet wide with sloped sides ten feet high that could easily be scaled by someone with a couple of steps to get up to speed. Whatever the particular reason that required it to be placed in the neighborhood, it was convenient. But not too convenient, because it stunk like something—something gigantic—was rotting. Rancid water,—likely leftover from the last storm that passed through—and garbage dotted the center of the channel as far as he could see.

The putrid smell began to insist upon Ryan and could feel his will slip away. It was difficult to ignore it because the stench seemed to pervade his entire body, but at the last moment, or at least he thought it was the last moment, he pushed the smell away and rededicated himself to maintaining their cover.

He heard something, the slight crackle of a radio, but tried to ignore it. Jaguar had offered him an earpiece, but he declined because it would be a distraction. As it was, something as simple as the smell of dirty water—and whatever else—was proving difficult enough.

"Lion says he just had the impression of something flickering in and out. Otherwise, he hasn't noticed us, though he should have us in his sights right now."

"Water stole my attention." Ryan pinched his nose for emphasis.

"Do your best to ignore it." Jaguar dropped the duffel bag, zipped it open, and pulled out something large and metallic.

Still trying to focus on maintaining the illusion, Ryan could see that Jaguar had produced what his old gym teacher called a "universal key." Used to cut locks off lockers, the bolt cutters made similar easy work of the padlock on the gate before them.

Ryan stepped forward enough that the bubble should overlap the gate and Jaguar yanked the chain off. The clatter that accompanied it was jarring, but those outside the bubble shouldn't have even noticed. Jaguar opened the gate and they started in. A block wall aside, they had a straight shot to the store.

The minutes ticked by slowly as they covered ground, and with each passing minute, exhaustion settled in a bit deeper on Ryan. It wasn't a physical tiredness, exactly, and it wasn't entirely mental, but a weird combination, as well as an emotional fatigue. Extending his will in such a way was a strain in a variety of ways and required intense concentration.

Ryan pushed it out of mind and focused on moving forward while still keeping the bubble active. Everything else could wait until they were done and back at Location B.

A beige-painted cinder block wall loomed before them a short time later, the grocery store alley on the other side of it.

While Jaguar jumped and pulled himself right up the wall, though it was a good ten feet tall, Ryan wasn't sure how he was supposed to get up there while maintaining the bubble, never mind the vest. It hadn't seemed like a big problem when they originally discussed it, but looking at the wall now, it was. They were right on top of Sikes's holdout, and now more than during the walk there, it was crucial they maintain their stealth.

Tiger hopped right up and pulled herself onto the wall as well. She sat and gave Ryan a little smirk. Jaguar and Tiger braced themselves with one hand while they leaned forward with the other.

"Jump." It was barely more than a whisper.

Ryan did as Jaguar ordered, extended his arms, and was hauled up the wall. It was a simple solution, one he should have foreseen, but with his attention so focused on the bubble, it surprised him.

Jaguar and Tiger hopped down on the other side. They both landed with guns drawn. After a moment, Jaguar turned and waved at Ryan. Ryan put his arms out and they helped lower him down.

"Thanks." He mouthed the word.

Jaguar led them onward, submachine gun in hand, while Tiger still watched their back. Ryan couldn't tell what Tiger was carrying, but at the moment he wasn't too concerned.

They were to make their entry via one of the side doors around the building. The first of the loading docks was about seventy feet away from them. A couple of vehicles, including a tractor-trailer with a forty-foot trailer, were parked farther down the alley toward one of the other docks.

Once they were inside, they only had blueprints to go on, and there was no telling how accurate they would be since they were fifteen years old. Outside, however, it was still quiet except for passing traffic.

Jaguar led them around the building to a small side entrance partially covered by the front of the building extending further out than the back. The instructions had been specific, that no powers except the mobile stealth device were to be used once they were within a hundred yards of the store. Certain abilities, especially those that disturbed reality, such as blinking, could be detected by some innate. Fisher, given his mental abilities, figured to be one who could detect such subtle shifts in reality.

That meant that Jaguar couldn't just blink himself in and open the door, so Tiger approached the door, put her pistol away, and pulled out a long, skinny, snakelike device out of a pack. She kneeled in front of the door and shoved one end of the snake under the door. She twisted the rest like a fun straw and looked into the other end. A dial was on the end she looked into, and she twisted it and turned it then pulled the snake back out.

Tiger shook her head.

They returned to the alley and stopped at a different entrance. Tiger ran the snake under the large panel door, and when she pulled the snake back, she shook her head again. The snake went back to the pack and she pulled out a couple of knives with black blades that seemed to swallow light that shone upon them.

Jaguar pointed to the loading dock further down the alley, near the vehicles, then led the way.

A bead of sweat rolled down Ryan's forehead and the edges of his vision wavered. He would be at his limit before long.

They froze as the headlights on one of the vehicles suddenly blazed like spotlights. It was blinding, and it was all Ryan could do to look away without losing his concentration on their cover. A moment later the blinding light was joined by the sound of a vehicle starting followed by its low rumble.

Jaguar quickly led them across the parking lot and to the loading dock. Jaguar held his gun in a way that suggested he was ready to use it, but the vehicle passed them without incident. It was a large van, something a moving company would have, but it was completely devoid of all markings. The van quickly disappeared around a corner and quiet and darkness returned, but only for a moment.

A crackle of a radio sounded out from behind the other vehicle, a van of the soccer mom variety. A man holding a radio in his hand suddenly walked around the side of it.

"Copy that. Delta three is on the move. Delta four will be ready in less than thirty minutes."

The radio crackled back something in return, but the man was already walking to the massive trailer. He paid them no heed.

Tiger and Jaguar exchanged looks then relaxed, slightly.

They covered the remaining distance to the next door and Tiger again pulled out the snake, put it under the door, twisted the knob, and then pulled the snake back.

She held up two fingers, then one, and pointed to either side of the large door, and then twirled her finger in the air twice. Snake returned to its pack, she drew a knife and passed it handle first to Jaguar, then drew two more for herself.

Ryan looked on in disbelief as Jaguar took the knife and set his SMG and duffel bag on the ground. Jaguar pulled Ryan to the door and indicated he should remain there, as close to the door as possible by pointing at him, then pointing at a spot on the ground. Ryan nodded.

Jaguar knew this likely wasn't a good idea, but he trusted Tiger. With the other doors inaccessible for whatever reason she had found, this only left doors that opened into the back of the store or the front doors. Entering through the front doors would be the epitome of folly so it had to be this one. Though he was risking announcing their presence, they had limited options.

He looked over at Ryan and took note of the sweat rolling down the young man's face. Ryan had insisted he could keep them hidden, and though Jaguar had his doubts because the young innate was untrained and unfocused, he had to admit Ryan had done an admirable job. But it didn't look as if Ryan would be able to keep the bubble going for much longer. If he thought Ryan might be able to hold on longer then maybe a roof approach would work, but that wasn't to be. This was it. Jaguar had to risk using his power.

The twirl of Tiger's finger told him that she had arrived at the same conclusion.

One of the problems with blinking into an unknown place was the danger of appearing on or in something unexpected. While it wasn't possible that one could embed themselves in stone — or at least Jaguar couldn't because some aspect of blinking that he didn't understand made it impossible for him to pass through such thick, dense material—one could still find themselves appearing on a slick surface, on an unstable one, or even in something. In moments like this, Jaguar recalled the story of another agent who could blink who managed to electrocute himself when he blinked inside a room that had an effective, and nasty, water trap waiting for him.

Tiger hadn't indicated there was anything in the way, so Jaguar took that to mean he had little to worry about. The door itself wasn't particularly thick, so it would be simple to go right through. It was just a matter of stealth.

Jaguar focused and blinked himself inside. It was darker inside the back of the grocery store than it was outside as candles and gas lamps left bouncing and unspecific pools of darkness.

Thirty feet ahead, two men had their backs to him by a large crate. Supplies glinted in the firelight and they slowly lifted and placed things in the crate.

To his right, a man looked at a portable device and looked to be ticking items off of a list. To the left, another man fumbled with the lock on the loading door. He swore quietly to himself while rattled a key in the lock.

All of this Jaguar took in when he blinked in. Not more than a second passed before he assessed every threat in the room, and in response, he turned to the man on his right.

Only a few feet away, Jaguar stepped right up, covered the man's mouth, and slit his throat. Two seconds now. Jaguar grabbed the small tablet from the man's hand, turned around and blinked himself to the other. When he appeared, he thrust his knife into the man's throat, yanked it out at a rude angle, and stepped aside to keep away from the blood. Three seconds. He slipped the tablet into a pocket of his cargo pants.

Jaguar turned and looked at the men loading the crate. They still had their backs to him and meticulously loaded away. They carried a large, heavy looking device to the crate and didn't appear to notice. The bodies at the door fell to the ground.

Jaguar held his breath, but the men were still oblivious, still loading the crate. True to his name, Jaguar crept forward, silent, and took in more of the storeroom. A closed door looked to lead further into the store while a small room was to the right, and a hallway to the left. He brought the blueprints to mind and remembered that the room to his right was an employee break room, while the hallway to the left led to the much larger storeroom. The door before him led into a hallway with a couple of offices and that opened into the butcher's area.

No one else was in sight, and Jaguar was quiet and merciful as he killed the two men. He waited for them to lower the equipment they carried before they died.

Jaguar was there one moment and simply gone the next. No fancy effects, no smoke, nothing to indicate that someone had been standing there. Jaguar just vanished. Ryan wanted to see inside the building, but he remembered that just running the bubble was a risk in itself, because while it was designed to bring them stealth, the act of using it meant that he was using power that someone might be able to detect.

Lion had tried to explain it, that the powers revolved

around modifying reality in specific ways. Powers such as what Malone and Warner used were rather obvious in their effect, but more subtle things, such as Jaguar's power or his own vision, were less definable in how they could be noticed. Certain innate, usually the ones with mental powers because that required a specific mental state to modify minds, were naturally more sensitive and perceptive. Considering that Fisher was an accomplished mental manipulator, and last they knew he had been with Sikes's crew, they had to assume he would be in the vicinity and would notice any powers being used. Although the nature of the stealth device was a power that modified reality, it partially concealed itself with its makeup.

For Ryan to use any other power, it had to be a last resort. Seeing inside the back of the store was not of vital importance at that moment. Jaguar was a trained operative, after all. Ryan resolved himself to patience.

Tiger held a couple of knives, one in each hand, and she twirled one around her fingers as though it was the most common, natural thing one would do in such a situation. The way she flipped the blade around her fingers was captivating. The knife danced through her fingers, constantly spinning, all the while she looked elsewhere. Ryan watched her then felt his own focus start to slip. He looked away, but not before she noticed him studying her.

She was still angry, he was fairly certain, but the smirk from earlier didn't seem entirely mean. Perhaps she was just messing with him. Either way, it was preferable to glares and derision.

The seconds ticked by, slowly, and gave Ryan ample time to investigate the alley. The tractor-trailer was backed up to the loading dock and the man was nowhere in sight anymore, nor could he be heard. The soccer van was still there and quiet, and now that he had time to study it, he realized it was plain like the large moving van had been. The truck was similarly devoid of any markings, except for the name B&S Trucking on the passenger door and the accompanying DOT license number.

Ryan pointed to the truck and air scribbled. Tiger looked over then nodded. The information on the side was likely bogus, or linked to nothing but a front, but it wouldn't hurt to look into. Tiger switched the knives to one hand and pulled a small box out of a pocket. She pointed it at the truck and pressed a button.

It was a spy camera, Ryan realized. He forced himself not to snicker.

Ryan brought his focus back to the bubble and he wondered, again, where Jaguar was when the man appeared in front of him with no warning. Just as suddenly as he appeared, Jaguar took his duffel bag and vanished. A few seconds later the door rolled up, slowly and quietly, and Tiger and Ryan ducked their way in.

The blood that spilled out of the bodies on either side of the door was the first thing Ryan noticed as he eased his way inside. Jaguar placed something in his bag then lowered the door and darkness, darker than the outside world where the night sky provided some illumination, greeted them and mercifully covered the evidence, the visual side of it at least.

Jaguar pointed at a crate some feet in the distance then down a hallway to the left. SMG in hand, Jaguar again led the way.

The candles and oil lamps in the room left the hallway in almost total darkness for its lack of illumination. Ryan reached a hand out for the wall once they turned a corner. It was apparent there were few windows in the back of the store because there was hardly any ambient light. Had they gone through the front, they would at least have some light from the windows, but they would also be illuminated like targets by the same windows, stealth bubble aside.

The hallway led left and zigzagged a short distance before it stopped at a door. Weather-stripping on the door prevented any light from coming through, but Ryan had the distinct impression there was light beyond the door. He realized that he was beginning to see the room and scolded himself and stuck to the bubble.

Jaguar waited while Tiger snaked under the door and waited for the report. It took some doing to shove it past the weather stripping, but Tiger held up a finger and pointed in the distance through the door.

The door opened slowly, but somewhat creakily, as Jaguar turned the handle and gently pushed. Light, firelight again, greeted them as it escaped into the hallway. Though the creaking was proving moderately quiet, a sudden loud chirp from the hinges gave them away. Jaguar shoved the door open and Tiger ran through first.

Ryan lost sight of Tiger, but he heard a whump and thump and Jaguar indicated Ryan should enter.

On the other side of the room, a man with a knife sticking out of his throat lay on the ground. Ryan looked at Tiger then looked away. With the bubble covering them, they likely didn't need to be so concerned, but Ryan decided now wasn't the time to remind Jaguar and Tiger of that. They were the professionals and they obviously had their own opinions on the best way to handle the current situation.

On a table in front of the dead man a laptop was open, the light of its display mingling with the candles burning next to it. Jaguar walked over, closed the lid, and shoved it into the duffel bag.

The room itself was split into two, though it was still a single, large room. A partition that extended up about eight feet sectioned off what looked like a small work area from the rest of a large storeroom beyond. Ryan couldn't see into the storeroom, yet he somehow knew that's what it was. He realized that he was again using his sight and chided himself for his lack of control. Ryan reeled his sight back in and focused, again, solely on the bubble.

He couldn't draw breath and was reminded that what he was doing was draining him immensely. The moment passed and Ryan drew a long, unsteady breath that rattled in his throat. Even though adrenaline raced through him, it wasn't going to sustain him long. He reached for Jaguar and motioned the universal sign of Hurry the Fuck Up. Jaguar nodded, made a brief tour of the room, and they left back the way they came.

Back in the small storeroom, they entered another door, this one leading straightaway from the loading dock door. Another hallway awaited them and ended at another solid door. Light flooded out from under torn weather stripping on the bottom of the door. This light didn't flicker.

Tiger again snaked under the door and retracted the

device almost as quickly as she shoved it under. Before she could say anything, the door burst open. The door ripped off the hinges and flew toward them with a thundering crack and screech of metal and wood being sheared apart.

Ryan, the farthest away from the door, had a split second to see the door bearing down on him. He threw himself against the wall and flattened his body against it. The door flew through the hallway and clipped him in the shoulder as it sailed past, but he didn't think it did any lasting damage. Ryan looked back down the hallway. Tiger hadn't fared as well and she lay unmoving on the ground. Jaguar was nowhere to be seen. Stealth, apparently, was no longer an issue, so he dropped the bubble and ran to Tiger.

Gunfire erupted in front of him though he couldn't see anything in what looked like an office beyond. The light was blinding to his eyes. Ryan ignored the room. He kneeled and rolled Tiger over.

Tiger was conscious, but her eyes had a faraway look that Ryan understood to mean she was dazed.

"Tiger! Get up! Jaguar is in there!" Ryan shook Tiger, lightly slapped her cheeks, but still Tiger stared past the ceiling. "Come on! Stop fucking around." Another round of gunfire erupted and Ryan looked up to the office. A person ran by the opening, but it was too quick and he couldn't make out anything other than dark clothing. It could have been the pope in a black bathrobe for all he knew.

Ryan shook Tiger again and hoped that he wasn't making things worse, that she didn't sustain a neck or back injury.

A crash echoed out from the room followed by the

sharp cracks of gunfire. Whatever was happening inside, it couldn't be good, and Tiger wasn't in any position to help. Ryan tried once more to get Tiger up, but she was completely dazed.

Ryan thought to grab a gun, but realized he might shoot the wrong person, so he went to the door unarmed and looked inside.

The slapping of fading footsteps came from the room beyond the door, and a fraction of a second later, the door creaked in protest as it ripped off its hinges. Jaguar dropped the duffel bag and blinked into the room just as the footsteps stopped and the door creaked. It was a total gamble because he had no idea what was beyond the door, but he knew he couldn't afford to stand there and be hit by it. He hoped that Tiger and Ryan would be able to react in time.

Jaguar appeared in the room and took it in as quickly as he could. It was a small workroom with a desk on one side and a table on the other. He ran to the left toward the desk.

A small computer tower and LCD monitor sat on the desk, and he shoved the chair aside far enough that he could get behind the desk. Secured with metal straps on a table on the other side of the room a shotgun pointed at the door that was now lying in the hallway. The shotgun's trigger connected to a tripwire just in front of the doorway. A portable electric lamp sat next to the shotgun, its LEDs throwing out blinding light in the otherwise dark room. In front of him, a dark hallway stood beyond an open door.

He knew right away that he was in a bad spot, but there were few options in the room. Worse, with the lamp on the table, it was like a spotlight that revealed his every move. Jaguar ducked behind the desk completely to figure out his next move just as bullets ripped through the room. The rounds slammed into the wall behind him and just overhead. Little puffs of drywall dust coughed out with each hit. He poked his gun out and fired a couple of blind bursts down the dark hallway.

Seconds ticked by in false silence. His gut told him something was wrong, so Jaguar fired a couple more blind bursts down the hall. He risked a glance behind the last burst. A man he knew, and disliked, was coming straight for him.

Malone threw his arms forward and Jaguar dove to the side, careful to avoid the wire in front of the door. Some unseen missile carved its way up the hallway and through the room to crash into the wall. Chunks of drywall and dust flew into the room forming a white cloud. He scrambled back to his feet and ran back to the other side of the room, firing into the hallway the whole time. Malone ducked into another room as Jaguar reached the desk, but part of it, including the computer and monitor on top, was missing. Jaguar coughed as he scanned for Malone.

They reached a stalemate and he popped his magazine out, turned it over to the other magazine taped to it, and shoved it back in. He chambered the first round and watched the hallway for movement. Tiger should have come in by now but hadn't.

Movement from the side caught his eye, but it wasn't Tiger at the door.

"Tripwire!"

Ryan heard the warning and his legs reacted before his brain could. His mind was encased in jelly, moving slowly and awkwardly and struggling to process simple observations and warnings. Maybe he should have stayed with Tiger.

Ryan half-hopped, but it wasn't enough and his toe caught the wire. He lost his balance and pitched forward, and the floor came up to meet him quickly. He met the floor with a grunt.

Ryan stayed on the ground and waited, but nothing happened. Whether he didn't set off the trap, or if it were only meant to trip whoever came into the room, Ryan didn't know and didn't care at the moment. Past the point of worrying about being embarrassed, he rolled over and shoved himself up to his feet. On the other side of the small room, Jaguar ducked behind a desk missing its side panel. Between the two of them, something had punched a large hole in one of the walls and sent a cloud of dust to hang in the room. That looked like something Malone might have done, and the thought cleared his mind.

"What's going on?"

"Malone, just ahead." Jaguar fired a burst down the hall as though to emphasize his point.

Ryan nodded and began to see. Almost instantly, far faster and more fluidly than he had ever experienced it, his mind's camera zipped away and panned out from his body. It cut through the space, down the hall and into a room off the side. Both the hallway and room were clear, so he moved forward and looked into another. Malone hugged a wall just inside the door, a pistol in hand. The same one he shot Ryan in the head with.

The sight of Malone, of that pistol, put him over the edge. Anger flashed hot and bright, but something hit his mind. Ryan reeled, physically reeled, as though he'd been hit and his vision spun away.

Ryan's head snapped back and hit the wall. He fell to the ground, only he didn't realize he had fallen until he opened his eyes. He was staring at the scuffed tile floor. Ryan blinked to clear his eyes and mind, but his head snapped back again. His ear burned with the movement, and dim realization set in that everything was ninety degrees off center.

Everything turned wavy and shaky. He couldn't focus on anything except to wonder why he was on the ground.

A wave of psychic energy, unlike anything he had ever experienced, flowed right past Jaguar. Jaguar wasn't normally so sensitive to such powers, but its passing was like a massive truck, or like something moving through Shamu's tank. The residual power overflowed and splashed him. He steeled his mind against what he could only describe as pure chaos. Had he not been trained to defend against such attacks, or had he taken the brunt of it directly, Jaguar was sure it would have overloaded his mind and left him little more than a gibbering sop on the floor.

The attack didn't come from Malone, because everything he knew of the agent stated that he had no psychic powers, but was instead telekinetic. The hole in the wall behind Jaguar confirmed that much, at least.

As the tail end of the wave passed, it was accompanied by an odd sound, like someone punching a wall. Jaguar sought the source of the noise and looked just in time to see Ryan crumple to the ground. A small indentation was in the wall at about the same height Ryan's head had been.

"Shit."

Tiger, I need you. Come on!

Ryan convulsed on the floor and fell into a fetal position. His eyes were open and his mouth was the picture of a silent scream while tremors shook his body.

Jaguar millimetered his way up behind the desk but ducked almost immediately. Gunfire erupted, but he got down in time. A bullet, if not two, passed him so closely he thought he could feel them brush his hair.

Malone would be moving closer soon, if not already, so Jaguar reached his gun around the desk and fired off another succession of bursts that echoed through the room.

Silence encased the back of the store following his bursts, but it was broken by a short series of thumps that echoed from the hallway behind him. A moment later, before he realized what the source of the sound was and that he should yell or say anything, Tiger burst through the doorway. Almost instantly, the shotgun roared. Jaguar cringed and looked over at Tiger.

Her left shoulder jerked back. Bits of clothing and buckshot peppered out behind her, but she came into the room, stopped to look at Ryan, then looked over at Jaguar.

"You started the fun without me? Selfish asshole."

Jaguar released a breath he didn't know he held. "You okay?"

Tiger looked down at her shoulder, slapped it once, then gave a thumbs up. "Armor stopped it just fine."

"You damn near gave me a heart attack."

Tiger pulled a machine pistol from behind her back, walked to the hallway as calmly as could be, and emptied the entire magazine into it. She walked back into the room and ejected the magazine with one hand while she slammed a new one in with her other hand. She hummed a tune as she chambered the round and looked back to Jaguar.

Tiger tapped her foot. "So what's going on?"

"Malone down the hall and Fisher must be nearby. Knocked Ryan the fuck out."

"On it."

Jaguar had known Tiger a long time—they were half-siblings, after all—but he was still amazed at how cocky and calm she could be in the face of danger. A cup filled to the brim wouldn't spill a drop if it rested on her stone-calm hand.

Tiger pulled another machine pistol out from behind her back and held them up, elbows bent, in true Hollywood action star form. "Ready?"

Jaguar nodded and Tiger smiled in response. Tiger jerked her head to the side and Jaguar popped up from behind the desk. He fired blindly down the hall, three bursts in the general direction he had seen Malone go. Tiger moved into the hall just as the third burst sounded. Miniature explosions of drywall filled the hallway as Tiger moved in, guns held in front of her.

Gunfire sounded out of the hall and Jaguar ducked and just caught sight of Tiger falling back. The long burst of shots that followed came from one of Tiger's machine pistols. Jaguar popped back up and aimed, but he didn't have a shot because Tiger was retreating in the hallway in front of him.

Tiger fired again, and Jaguar was surprised to see

Malone appear from inside one of the offices. Malone held his arms out in front of him. None of the bullets touched him as Tiger emptied both guns. The bullets fell to the floor and Tiger moved to draw a knife, but Malone thrust his arms forward and Tiger sailed back and into the wall.

She yelled in surprise then groaned when she crashed into the wall, leaving a Tiger-sized impression in it.

Jaguar ground his teeth and fired, but Malone put his hands back up and the bullets just stopped, as though absorbed by a gigantic mass of ballistics gel compressed into an impossibly small space. Malone thrust his arms out when the last bullet hit, but before Jaguar could duck fully, the wave of force knocked him over.

He gasped as it hit him. The power was silent, save that of the captured bullets slicing through the air, but its deadliness was without question. The power slammed into him, an invisible fist that threw him like chaff. His head snapped back and he cried out as it bashed into the tile floor. The bullets that Malone threw with the wave chipped away at the wall behind him and sprinkled him with more drywall dust. Jaguar struggled to get up, but clouds obscured his vision and consciousness began to slip away. With whatever remaining focus he had, he tried to blink himself away, to reload his gun, to do something, anything, but blackness overcame him.

He wasn't blind, and he could certainly see, but Ryan's mind was a mess. Like an earthquake, aftershocks shook his mind and made it impossible to focus. He tried to stand, tried to roll over, tried to pay attention to what was going on around him, but nothing seemed capable of pulling him out of the quicksand his mind had fallen into.

Thoughts were fleeting and random, scattered like pigeons when a child chases them. He knew he was in trouble, but he couldn't do anything about it. Then the realization hit him: if he could focus on that one thought, he might be able to get out of the mental paralysis.

Ryan drew every bit of will he had into that one thought, that he was in trouble, that he needed to do something. That thought was like finding the end of a knotted string, and he worked his way through it. It was slow, laborious, and it felt as though a great weight pressed upon him. He still couldn't move, couldn't process what was happening, but he understood that he was under attack. However, the source of that attack was mental, not physical.

It was as though someone was shooting at him and he needed to protect himself, but there was nothing around to use to defend himself. A wall, of course, would stop the mental bullets, but he was alone in empty space with nothing around. Ryan imagined a wall and it appeared. It was small, nothing more than a couple of flat rocks on the ground, but he focused on it, poured his will into it, forced it to grow.

He threw rock upon rock on it and it started to grow into a pile that reached his shins, his knees, his thighs, his waist. It was the beginnings of protection, of a wall, but there was no logic to it, no order. He forced himself to imagine it as a proper wall, not a pile of stones to crawl behind, and he pictured each individual stone and how it fit into the larger equation. The rocks ground and clacked together as they shifted and moved around. Within seconds, structure formed from controlled chaos, but even as the wall grew higher, it wobbled. It was uneven, tenuous.

Rocks weren't the answer, but blocks made sense. The rocks melted and reformed into long rectangular blocks, all the same size and shape, all even. The wall almost seemed to build itself before him but the mental bullets blasted through as though the wall was made of cardboard. The idea was right, but the execution was wrong.

The blocks melted again and this time took on a shiny appearance as they coalesced into long, thick, flat panels of steel. Some blocks reshaped into posts and the panels attached themselves to the posts. Ryan added to them, added sides to the posts. He built himself a house of steel and closed it off from every direction.

It was sudden, surprising, and it caught him completely off guard. His mind was quiet. With a sharp intake of breath, he realized that he could focus again, that he could think, that he could move. The mental knot fell away into a long, boring lump of string.

The outside world returned to him as he cracked open a window in his mental house.

A noise, loud, sharp, and angry boomed overhead. Ryan struggled to turn his head to see. He was still on the ground and everything was at the wrong angle, but the barrel of a gun hovered over the edge of the table beside him. The gun must have fired.

Someone stumbled into the room a second later, but they were nothing more than a tangle of dark legs. Voices, like whispers, came to him through the ringing in his ears. He couldn't make out words, but he thought he recognized their meaning.

With effort that left him panting, he forced himself to sit up straight and almost lolled over as his head pulsed. He might be able to think, somewhat clearly, but he was hurt. He understood that now.

Gunfire echoed out again and didn't help the ringing in his ears, though it had lessened some. Ryan blinked and just caught sight of someone rushing into the hallway several feet in front of him. He wasn't sure, but he thought it might have been Tiger. Ryan turned his head, slowly, and just managed to lean back and look down the hall they'd originally come through. Tiger was no longer there.

It was all starting to come together, then gunfire sounded again, long seemingly continuous bangs of rounds being expended. The gunfire ended and the brief silence was filled with a loud thump.

Jaguar unloaded his SMG down the hall and tried to duck behind the desk, but something unseen tore him from his feet and threw him back to crash headlong into the floor. Jaguar fidgeted, tried to do something, then fell motionless.

Ryan blinked in horror. "Oh, fuck."

Without consciously realizing it, Ryan's mind flew out to investigate. Just down the hall, Tiger lay crumpled against a wall, and a man Ryan knew stood over her. Just behind him, coming up the hall, was another that Ryan knew. The sore on his head trickled the slightest trail of blood and he stopped behind Malone.

"The young man is observing us," Fisher said.

"Let him," Malone said. "If he was capable of doing

260

anything but watching his friends die, don't you think he would have done something by now? It's not the first time, you know."

"Yes, yes, just make this quick and don't fuck up this time. You know that our time is limited."

"Yeah, yeah. I'll take care of these two and then give me a minute with the kid, okay?"

"No more delays, Mr. Malone."

Malone reached into his jacket and Ryan panicked. Malone was going to draw a gun and shoot Tiger in the head, just as he'd shot Ryan, only there was no way Tiger was going to stop it. Tiger wasn't innate and she looked unconscious. She was slumped against the wall, her hair a mess and her eyes closed. Ryan couldn't move, and there was nothing he could do except sit and watch.

Malone's hand seemed to move in slow motion as he reached into the jacket and his fingers curled around the black handle. The gun came out and slowly moved over until he aimed it directly at Tiger.

Malone thumbed the hammer, slowly, so slowly, and started to squeeze the trigger.

Ryan didn't know what else to do so he threw his will into a psychic attack aimed at Malone. It was raw, unfocused, amateurish, but Malone jerked back. The gun fired and ripped a hole in the wall just over Tiger's head.

Drawing upon reserves he didn't realize he had, Ryan readied himself for one more attack, but something caught his attention. Tiger opened her eyes and she blinked as dust from the wall rained on her, but her eyes were still glassy.

It was hopeless to throw another mental attack at

Malone because it wouldn't be as strong and Malone would be ready for it. Ryan did the one thing he promised Tiger he wouldn't do again. He invaded her mind.

Ryan psychically screamed at Tiger, ordered her to get up and save their asses, to do something other than lie there and be shot. Ryan sent the last of his will, pure command, into the scream and felt his vision start to float away.

It didn't leave him entirely, rather he seemed to lose control over it. Like a cameraman without a director, it spun away and turned left and right and eventually settled into a view from the floor in the hallway. He realized then that he wasn't seeing through his eyes, but through Tiger's.

Thoughts flooded him, images, sounds, memories, knowledge he couldn't possibly know and could never even dream to imagine. It was overwhelming and it was an incomprehensible mess. Like so many cards scattered on the floor, the thoughts were all over the place and Ryan could barely identify any of them. Thoughts, memories rained upon him, buried him in their relentless torrent. It was all he could do to maintain his concentration, but he knew he had to ignore all of it.

Malone stumbled and threw a disbelieving look over his shoulder then brought the gun to bear again.

Ryan—and Tiger—blinked. Tiger shot her legs out and caught Malone between them like scissors. Tiger turned her body over and Malone stumbled back. He fell with a shout of surprise. The gun went flying and careened into a wall and Tiger hopped onto her feet.

Whether Tiger or Ryan commanded the body, Ryan

wasn't sure. Perhaps it was both of them, but Tiger moved faster than anything Ryan had ever imagined and was behind Fisher in a second.

Something like a giant fist pounded against their minds, but Ryan was in the steel house and ignored it while Tiger drew a knife. She reached out with her other hand to grab Fisher's chin and pull it up, and cut the man's throat in one fluid motion.

Blood sprayed forward in an arc and Malone got up and turned just in time for it to fly into his face.

Malone threw his arms up and forward and invisible force slammed into Tiger and knocked her down. The knife went clattering away as it bounced down the hall. Ryan didn't feel it, exactly, but he felt something, an impact. Tiger shook it off and started to stand. Another wave slammed into her and forced her back down.

Malone wiped at the blood on his face. "Stay down, you fucker!"

Malone thrust again and again, but Tiger struggled against the bursts of power and even managed to draw another knife.

"Oh no you don't."

Malone sent another wave out and launched the knife from Tiger's hand. Malone threw out one more wave then turned to find his gun, but he suddenly ducked back into the hallway and threw his arms out the other direction. Gunfire rattled away and Malone backed off.

Tiger started to rise, but it hurt like hell. Again, Ryan didn't feel it, exactly, but he somehow just knew it. Tiger drew another knife, slowly and quietly, and still Malone backed up, his arms facing the other direction. Jaguar came into sight, SMG held against his shoulder as he fired burst after burst at Malone.

Tiger waited, silent, calm, and Malone was almost in range when he threw his arms out wide and turned a circle.

A wave of energy erupted from Malone and rolled out in every direction. Tiger, already woozy, couldn't stay up and fell back as the energy bowled her over. She hit the ground and Ryan could only watch as Malone ran by. Malone stepped right over Fisher's body and ran down the hallway. He vanished around a corner.

Quiet fell over the room and Ryan's view disintegrated into blackness.

Jaguar pushed himself up to his feet from his knees by bracing the stock of the SMG against the floor for extra support. He hurt. A lot. He was fairly certain he had a broken rib or two and his head pounded like a carpenter on cocaine. But he was alive, and it looked like Malone had run off.

The last wave of energy Malone threw out didn't hurt him, per se, but the fall, in addition to the previous injury, didn't do him any favors. As he stood and regained his bearings, he decided the office looked like a modern art exhibit with a bunch of small holes and one giant one to balance the appearance.

On the ground, Ryan groaned, but his eyes were closed and he breathed heavily. Hair clung to his face, his skin slick with sweat. He was crumpled on the ground in something resembling, but not quite, the fetal position. One leg stuck out awkwardly and had a slight shake to it, but he otherwise remained motionless.

Jaguar ambled forward into the hall, SMG held in front of him, and kept sneaking glances at Tiger on the ground. Blood had pooled under Fisher's body and was flowing around Tiger's boots and legs. Their bodies looked like large rocks jutting out of a sea of red.

Dust filled the air from the drywall having been tortured by guns and kinetic energy. Jaguar coughed as he stepped into a cloud of dust and took too deep a breath. He was helpless, caught in a coughing fit that left him doubled over. It passed quickly, however, and still all was quiet.

He kneeled to Tiger, gun still in hand, and put a finger to her neck. Her skin under his finger pulsed with a steady rhythm, but she was unconscious. He could hardly believe that Tiger had gotten up after Malone's kinetic assault, but she had. And more than that, she got to her feet and grabbed Fisher before the old traitor even knew what was happening and cut his throat as though she was peeling fruit. It was strange how she had gotten up and been so destructive and was now unconscious again.

But she was alive and breathing, and Jaguar decided that should satisfy him. They weren't prepared for what they went against. The normal soldiers, they were nothing. But other innate? Jaguar realized how dangerous they were and developed a new respect for what Sikes and his crew would be capable of.

And if there were two traitors in one office, it seemed possible, perhaps likely, there were others elsewhere.

Shit. That was a sobering thought.

Lion. I think they're gone. Can you confirm?

The radio crackled and he heard Lion in his ear.

"I saw a vehicle leave about two minutes ago. It may have been Malone, but I can't be sure. No luck on that one." That meant he'd had a shot, but it didn't go as he hoped.

Are you getting any other heat signatures?

"I see three near the offices and a few others outside. They're loading into a truck now. Mercenaries by the looks."

You have plates? It was a dumb question, but he knew Lion wouldn't engage with them. They were the rabble, after all, not the ones that mattered.

"Of course."

When they're gone, I think we could use you in here.

"Very well."

Jaguar turned and looked at Fisher. He normally reserved swearing in Swedish for special instances, and as he looked at the bleeding corpse of the traitor, this seemed to qualify.

"Jävel." He spit on the corpse and went back to Tiger.

Ryan awoke to Lion standing over him. It was a familiar experience and he wondered if he was at William's house and having a deja vu moment, but a quick look around reminded him that he was in the back offices of a grocery store. The bullet holes in the wall reminded him of the gunfight, and the giant section of missing drywall brought Malone back to mind.

The thought had him scrambling to his feet, but Lion restrained him.

"You must hold still. I am stitching your wound."

Ryan stopped. Stitching his wound? Now that he

looked up, he realized that Lion was doing something to him, and he felt a sharp, but small, bite and noticed the needle in Lion's hand. What the hell happened to him?

It only took another minute, and Lion pronounced the wound closed. Ryan tested a hand against it and felt he had a long gash on his forehead, then put his hand to the back of his head and felt another there. His hair had been shaved to reveal the wound for it to be stitched.

"Thanks. I didn't even know I needed stitches."

"Do you recall what happened?"

"Somewhat. I remember lots of gunfire, that asshole Malone throwing himself around, and then I think I remember cutting Fisher's throat. There's more, but it's jumbled, out of order."

A sharp intake of breath grabbed Ryan's attention. Tiger and Jaguar, unnoticed until now in his dazed state, stood a few foot away near the hallway. Tiger turned away sharply and stormed down the hall.

"What'd I say?"

Jaguar said something, gestured down the hall, then sighed and walked over to join Lion and Ryan.

"You took over her mind again, mate," Jaguar said. "She's not happy."

"I did?" Ryan looked from Lion to Jaguar, but neither showed any expression. "Shit, I'm sorry. I don't remember doing it."

"You did. She's not happy about it, but you saved her life. Maybe all of ours."

"What? How?"

"She was knocked silly but you made her get up. She was cognizant the entire time, but she couldn't get her body to work. You did something that jumpstarted her battery. She killed Fisher and took a shot at Malone, but he got away."

Ryan looked at Jaguar in openmouthed amazement then shut his mouth and looked away. What the hell happened?

Footsteps, or rather stomps, announced Tiger coming back into the room and Ryan looked over to see her come around the corner. Her expression was dangerously neutral and she stopped right in front of Ryan. She turned an intense stare upon him that Ryan found difficult to meet.

"You saved my ass, and I appreciate that. But I told you stay out of my head. You do it again, I'll cut your throat."

"I'm sorry..." Tiger walked out of the room before he could even get all the words out.

"I'll talk to her," Jaguar said. "Don't worry about it. Just glad you made it, mate."

Jaguar walked off after Tiger and stopped at the hallway. "Hey, thanks, too. For saving her." He started to walk away again then stopped. "And me." Jaguar vanished into the hallway.

Lion, who had been watching Jaguar and Tiger with interest, turned back to Ryan.

"Interesting. Tiger did not kill you."

Ryan's heart leaped in panic. "Has this happened before?"

"Once or twice. What is more interesting is that she did not tell you to, as she says, 'Fuck off and rot in a pile of shit.' I believe that means she likes you."

"But she said she'd cut my throat."

"That is her way of showing affection. It's endearing,

actually." Lion clapped him on the shoulder then walked off.

Memories came back to Ryan, jumbled images of thoughts he'd seen while in Tiger's mind. They were scattered, almost incomprehensible, but he held onto a fledgling thought that Tiger didn't hate him. However, there was little more to it than that. He wasn't sure what it meant, but it seemed like a good thing.

Ryan let out a breath he didn't know he was holding and put a hand to his forehead. Terrible was only the beginning of how he felt. He didn't hurt, head aside, but everything was tired. It was a slight play on the cliché of his hair hurting, only his hair was tired. With great effort, he got to his feet and leaned against the wall.

They were all alive, and bumps, bruises, and stitches aside they were in one piece, but he was upset and downright furious just the same. Malone had been there, and worse, Malone had gotten away. Though the specifics were still a bit hazy, Ryan knew that they had come close to Malone killing all of them. He knew he should be grateful to be alive, but he was angry.

All he wanted was a chance to get back at Malone and now the backstabbing manipulator was gone. Ryan slammed a fist against the wall and looked down in shame and disbelief.

"Hey." Ryan looked up. "You coming or what?" Jaguar pointed with his eyes and head down the hall, hands out in expectation.

"Now what?"

"We get the hell out of here."

Ryan took a final look around the room. Spent shell casings littered the floor and a thick layer of drywall dust had changed the floor from a dark industrial gray tile to white in most places. Ryan turned to see the hallway and immediately wished he hadn't. The person-sized hole in the wall bespoke of Tiger getting thrown into it, but his eyes were dragged to the bleeding corpse on the floor.

Blood had pooled around Fisher, his eyes still open in shock while his neck emptied his body of blood. Fisher's open sore on his head still trickled blood, a faint red against his skin. Ryan quickly turned away and followed Jaguar back the way they had originally come.

Lion and Tiger were waiting for them at the loading dock's door. Beyond the open door, the moon and stars shone like any other night. The vehicles that had been parked there before, the van and the tractor-trailer, were gone. The agency's black SUV, which Ryan had last seen in the neighborhood, was parked there now.

Without any word between them, they piled into the vehicle and started off. Jaguar started them out of the alley and took them back to the neighborhood where Lion left the vehicle for his car.

They drove back to Location B in silence.

CHAPTER 16

The last thing Ryan remembered was dropping off Lion to get his car before they started back for Location B.

Ryan lifted his head from the pillow and looked around. This was Location B, he was sure, though he hadn't been in this part of the house. Perhaps it was the starkness of the room and the plainness of the furniture. Maybe it was because he could hear familiar voices coming from another room.

Ryan forced himself to get off the bed and he went to the restroom. He caught sight of himself in the mirror, and though his hair looked odd because it had only been partially shaved, that wasn't what held his attention.

The face that met his in the mirror was haggard. Lines ran from his eyes like streams from an estuary. More than anything, his eyes looked tired. They drooped and there was no brightness in them.

Ryan moved his face closer to the mirror to and noticed something else. His shaved head wasn't the only change to his hair, but there were now a couple of gray hairs in front. They weren't gray all the way, but they were definitely gray at the base, as though someone had been painting them and stepped away before they could finish.

He took a step back, frowned, and stared some more. The face in the mirror had no intention of changing, so he went back to the bedroom. Voices still came to him from elsewhere in the house, but they were quiet and muffled.

Ryan pulled his phone out of his pocket, and after waiting for it to boot, smiled when he saw he had a signal. He flipped through the contacts and dialed home. He couldn't stand still and he forced himself to sit while he listened to the phone ring.

No one answered. Ryan stared at the phone as though it had somehow deceived him, but the answering machine picked up.

"Hey, it's me. Just calling to see if you're back and if everything is okay. I think I'll be home soon." Ryan ended the call and sighed. They must have still been out since they left a couple of days ago. The phone vibrated with new notifications, and after a quick glance, he decided none of them were important and they could wait.

Ryan left the bedroom and made his way through the house. Much like the house Malone had used, this was a small place with only a couple of bedrooms and it wasn't difficult to find where the voices were coming from.

The Debate Team was gathered around the same table they had used before for planning. Lion, still wearing a suit, sat upright, his back straight and posture ridiculously good as he consulted a tablet between looks thrown toward Jaguar and Tiger.

Jaguar leaned back in a chair, black BDUs replaced with more casual jeans and a printed shirt buttoned up except for the last couple of buttons. He and Tiger sat on opposite sides of the table with Lion at the head of the table. Jaguar and Tiger threw a tennis ball to each other as they spoke.

Ryan looked to Tiger and found she had also lost the

BDUs and had jeans and a baby doll t-shirt on. If he hadn't known it was her, Ryan would have never guessed it was the same person. It was the first time he had seen her look remotely feminine. He stared at her before he looked to the rest of the table.

The conversation stopped when Jaguar saw him walk into the far side of the room, and Jaguar caught the tennis ball and pointed with it toward him. Tiger leaned back in her chair and gave him a quick glance, but little more.

Ryan flashed a half-smile. "Don't stop on account of me."

"Come on in. We were actually just talking about you."

Ryan looked to each of them, though only Jaguar was paying attention to him at the moment. Ryan sat down in the chair opposite Lion, with Jaguar on his right and Tiger on his left.

"How are you feeling?"

"About how I look."

"Yeah, about that. There's something we should probably tell you."

Ryan lifted his eyebrows but said nothing.

"These powers we share, they don't exactly come free of charge."

Ryan thought about it and leaned back in the chair. He was tired and his mind felt like it was running through waist-high mud. "Using my powers did this?"

"Yes."

"Is it reversible? I mean, will this go away?"

Jaguar hesitated and Lion answered. "Reversible, no. Can it be lessened? With time. I'm well-versed in healing energies, but even I can't reverse the effects of time."

Ryan stared at Lion. "Time? It's been what, a week? I'm not sure since I've been in and out of consciousness, but it's not been that long."

"Time isn't linear."

"The hell it isn't. One is followed by two, two by three, and so on."

"That is correct, but that is not what I mean. It is possible for one to affect time, and for time to have an effect on one individually."

Ryan stared at Lion for several seconds now, his jaw and his brain trying to work out a response. "Are you saying I traveled through time?"

"In a manner of speaking, I am."

Ryan pushed the chair out and stood up. He turned away from the table and took a couple of steps while his hands went to his head. He turned back to face them. "Does this happen to all of you?"

They all responded at the same time. "Yes."

Ryan looked at Tiger. "But I thought you weren't innate. I mean, I don't see an aura."

Tiger shrugged. "I'm not, but that's not the whole story. I know you saw that." Tiger squinted, slightly.

Ryan remembered the way she almost seemed to shift in and out of sight, the way she moved faster than any normal person should be capable of. Yes, she was definitely not normal, but he still didn't understand it. "But you're not innate."

"No, I'm a half-breed. Half-normal human, half-innate, give or take."

"And so you're subject to the same price of time?"

"So they say. Lots of folks die young." She shrugged.

"But you look great." Ryan realized what he said

and could feel his cheeks grow warm. "I mean, you don't look like you're aging any more than anyone else." He looked to Jaguar and Lion and furrowed his brows. "None of you do."

Jaguar nodded. "It hits hardest at the beginning."

"But I bet you've all been doing this for years. Especially you, Lion, no disrespect intended."

Lion waved a hand at him.

"True, and that's the other part of it."

Now they all looked at him and Ryan felt his pulse quicken. He walked back to the chair and sat down, arms wrapped around himself while he looked expectantly at Jaguar.

"You're what we call an omni."

"I think I heard someone say that before. Does that mean my power is capable of multiple kinds of effects?"

"In a nutshell, yes. Omnis are theoretically capable of using all of the powers, only some require more training than others. Not all omnis find themselves able to use all of the powers, but most are capable of three or four.

"The different kinds of powers have different effects on the body. Teleportation is particularly unkind, though in my case, I limit its use where possible. Mental powers aren't so bad, and neither are bio-manipulation."

"You mean like what Lion does? Healing wounds and things?"

"Yes. Now telekinetics, they're kind of in between teleportation and bio-manipulation."

"What about seeing?"

"Yes, seers." Jaguar looked at the floor then dragged

his eyes back up. "I'm going to be straight with you: seers have it the worst. The mind isn't meant to experience life outside of the body. There are seers who have lived a long time. Many, many years, but they used their abilities sparingly."

"And I've been using it like a cell phone checking email." Ryan slumped back in the chair.

"Right." Jaguar stopped to look down again. "But you're an omni, and the price doesn't come any higher."

Ryan just stared at Jaguar while his mind turned circles. He had questions, but his tongue seemed paralyzed. Was he going to die early? How early? Could he do anything to counter it? Maybe there was a way that bio-manipulation could work and no one had figured it out yet.

Lion spoke up and the words hit Ryan like a physical blow. "Most omnis who discover their power at the usual time die before they're thirty."

"What's the usual time?" His voice was barely a whisper.

"Nineteen or twenty."

Ryan was twenty-six.

"So what does that mean for me?"

"I can't say. I have my doubts that a week of extended use would greatly diminish your life capacity, but most innate have their powers awakened early and learn to limit their use, both in frequency and in energy expenditure."

Ryan had been throwing whatever powers he had around with reckless abandon. With the exception of shrinking the stealth bubble, he had barely even touched upon the idea of using less power to accomplish the same task. Granted, he hadn't yet learned how to control that aspect, but he had been running around like someone stuck on overdrive.

Did that mean he wasn't even going to make it to thirty-six? Ryan didn't want to die early, wasn't ready to.

"Thanks for telling me." He mumbled the words as he got up from the table and walked away, his eyes barely focused on his surroundings as he stumbled back to the bed he had woken up upon.

The implications of the power were far more demanding than what he had imagined. How was he supposed to live with that knowledge? He supposed it was a little akin to being diagnosed with a terminal disease. In a way, that's exactly what it was, because he didn't want those powers to begin with.

How did people with terminal diagnoses cope with the knowledge that they were living with limited time? They had to accept it at some point and just forge onward, each day that they lived being a gift and not a guarantee.

Ryan collapsed on the bed and stared at the ceiling. How was he supposed to explain this to his friends and family?

Ryan opened his eyes, once again unaware that he had fallen asleep. Thoughts of his impending death returned with an immediacy that granted him no waking reprieve from his artificially-reduced mortality. A groan escaped his lips as he sat up and looked around the bedroom and tried to focus on something that would obscure the thoughts, if only for a moment.

It looked like it was daylight, so either he had only

fallen asleep briefly, or he had fallen asleep for a lot longer.

By the time he made it out to the kitchen, the chairs around the dining table were vacant. Ryan fished his phone out of his pocket. It was almost out of power and ready to die at any moment, but he had indeed missed a day. Shit.

Ryan found Jaguar seated on a couch in the family room just past the adjacent dining room. Jaguar and Tiger had conversed in this same room about the wisdom of bringing him along on their mission to get Malone and Fisher. It felt like a lifetime ago, but it was little more than a day.

Jaguar stretched out on the couch, a paperback in hand, though his hand obscured the spine and cover. Ryan wasn't sure, but he thought it might have been Bradbury.

"Hey, Jag."

Jaguar looked up from the book and slipped a bookmark in it. He placed it on the center of the plain wooden coffee table.

"Ryan. I was beginning to wonder if you'd wake at all." He said it with a smile and pointed at the opposite end of the couch.

Ryan walked over and took a seat. "I guess I was out a while."

Jaguar nodded. "How are you handling it?"

Ryan shook his head. "Not well."

Jaguar nodded. "It's difficult, I know. I can't imagine what you're feeling, but I can kind of relate."

"It sucks."

"It's not all bad. Once you learn to control things a little more, and with judicious use, you can live quite a while."

"Why didn't you say that last night?"

"Because Lion and I disagree on that point. There haven't been many omnis before you, and the last was twenty years ago. I only know this through stories because I was still too young to be in the agency, but they say he was a little gung-ho. He reveled in his powers and used them constantly. He burnt out in less than two years."

"'Burnt out?' Like burned out and died?"

Jaguar nodded. "That's what we call it when someone dies from their powers. Your heart just sort of gives out, as do the rest of your organs, all somewhat simultaneously. It's not pretty, and nothing can fix that."

Ryan grimaced at the thought.

"Most of the others burnt out around five, but there was one back in the sixties who lived quite a while. Fifteen years, they say."

"That doesn't seem long to me."

"But for an omni, that's almost unheard of. She could have lived longer, too."

"By not using her powers?"

"Bingo."

"That's a shitty deal."

"That's for each person to decide. Me? I figure I have another thirty years, if I'm lucky. I'm okay with that because I'm doing something I believe in."

Ryan stared at Jaguar. "How old are you?"

"Twenty-seven."

Ryan thought he looked thirty-five, but he didn't say anything.

"Tiger and Lion made the same decisions for

themselves."

"I think I need some time to think about all of this."

"Agreed. Don't make any rash decisions."

Ryan looked around the plain room and at last returned to look at Jaguar. "So what now?"

"Malone and Sikes vanished like a fart in the wind, so that's your call."

"I think I'm ready to go."

"I'll get my keys."

They pulled up alongside the curb and Ryan looked at the library. It was his first real view of it up close since the explosion. He had caught parts of it when he came to the square with Malone, but there were other problems at that time that made it impossible to make peace with what had happened, such as the fake clean-up crew and his inability to deal with the trauma.

Police tape still encircled the building and the square itself, and this time, Ryan was confident they were the real police, not mercenaries or cronies following Sikes's orders. Ryan hopped off the bike and left the helmet on the seat while he walked around to the front of the building.

The south-facing side didn't fare too badly considering a couple of large bombs had exploded. Sections of the building were patched with massive sheets of wood. The missing sections gave one the appearance that it could have been disrepair that was the source of damage. But when Ryan turned around the corner to the front, it was obvious that something big had shaken the building.

Where the big double front doors used to stand was now a gaping hole. The fascia next to the door was likewise MIA. Beyond the wooden sheets that now formed the front entrance, a white cloud drifted by far above where the roof had once been. Sunlight streamed in through missing walls. The lazy breeze kicked up dust inside the building, sent it spinning and dancing. The floor was somewhere under the dust and debris. And somewhere, buried under the roof and walls and other destroyed pieces of building and furniture, were the bodies of his coworkers.

He heard a voice somewhere behind him, and another join it, but he ignored them as he stared into the building. Ryan ducked under the police tape and moved forward, but he stopped at the edge of the rubble and peered inside.

The large pool of blood that had been right before the doors inside of the building was likewise covered in dust and rubble. Years of memories, good ones, bad ones, funny stories and wacky pranks, they were all gone now. Not the memories, at least, but many of the people who had been in them.

He wanted to talk to his other coworkers, the ones who had been lucky enough not to be there that morning, but he wasn't ready. Not yet.

"Goodbye, guys. I'll miss you."

Ryan bowed his head then turned around and left the library. Jaguar was waiting for him beyond the tape along with a police officer. The cop could have been angry, but Ryan didn't pay that much attention to him.

Jaguar joined him, silent for a few steps. "You okay?"

Ryan nodded. "As best I can be."

"Come on. I asked about your car and they said it escaped most of the blast. They haven't towed it yet, so you're in luck."

Jaguar and Ryan cut through the square, the police officer following a short distance behind them, and Ryan found his car at the far end of the parking lot. Just as Jaguar had said, his Honda had survived the blast, but a few chunks of something must have hit it because he didn't remember the softball-sized dents in the hood.

Ryan dug his keys out of his pocket and hit the button on the key fob. The car chirped in response and he opened the door. Hot, stale air hit him, but it was his car, something familiar and safe. Ryan climbed in and closed the door, started the car, and rolled the window down.

Jaguar strolled up to the window and leaned down. "Give it some time. Think about things. If you decide you want to learn a little about your abilities and maybe even help your country out, call me." Jaguar passed him a business card.

Ryan turned the card over in his hand. It was a plain, glossy black business card with white print on one side that simply read, "Jaguar: Problem Solver" and was followed by a phone number underneath.

Ryan put the card in the center console and stared at Jaguar. "Regardless of what I decide, I'm going to be watched, right?"

Jaguar smiled. "Of course. Word can't get out about these sorts of things. What would the public think?"

What would they think? Some things just weren't possible, even if they were. Just then, something hit him.

"What's with the hideout that you claim you don't maintain?"

Jaguar smiled. "It's complicated, but suffice it to say it's not a hideout as such, but a home. You might want to stop by some time, just in case."

Ryan nodded. "Perhaps. For now, I'm thinking school sounds like a good idea. Maybe it's time to get that MLIS."

"The offer stands."

"I don't think I'm the agent type. But I'll keep your card. Just in case."

"Take care, Ryan. It's been a pleasure, mostly."

Ryan thought about that then nodded. "Mostly." He extended his hand through the window and they shook.

Jaguar smiled and slapped the hood of the car and walked away.

Ryan rolled the window back up and started off for home. He couldn't wait to see his parents.

A QUICK WORD (OR 400) FROM KRJ

I could give you a sappy story about how I always knew I wanted to be a writer when I was a kid (I didn't) or how much it'd mean if you read my other books (a lot), but instead I want to you know that I write about a lot of different things. I have a small horde of short stories and novels that I've written over the years, and while I'm smart enough to know that they're not ready to be published, I do have something else that is ready to be consumed, and in fact, came out almost a year ago to the day after this book.

That's right. Through the magic of technology, even though this book came out a year before Reborn, you can still get a preview of it inside this here book.

While we could debate (no pun intended) all day about whether this book is science fiction or fantasy, there's no question about *Reborn*, the first book in the *Scourge of Kallandin* series. You see, that one is pure fantasy, though perhaps we could debate (again, no pun intended) on whether it's epic, dark, or just plain vanilla fantasy. Regardless, it's a timeless tale of a family doomed to bring ruin upon the land and the young woman who is everyone's last hope to save them.

There's a special preview of *Reborn* immediately following this shameless self-promotion. I'd appreciate it if you gave the book a whirl. And if you've already read it, then why aren't you pushing it on others to read? Just kidding... maybe.

I have some other things lined up, but for now I'm

working on finishing the *Debate Team* and the *Scourge of Kallandin* series. I may be bouncing around between the two until both are finished, so don't worry that I'll leave you hanging. I'm good for it.

Should you decide to give another of my books a shot, then thanks. I write because I think I have stories to tell that people will enjoy. A lot of effort goes into planning, writing, playing drums, revising, playing video games, editing, watching hockey, and polishing these stories, so any fears I may turn into a book factory (like you-know-who) are warrantless. (Phew! This almost turned sappy!)

Thanks for taking the ride. Cheers.

KRJ, October 8 2012

REBORN

1

Torches flickered in the Black King's hall. They did little to dispel the night's chill. Great pools of shadow cloaked much of the room in darkness, though what was illuminated was the fabric of nightmares: human skulls hung on the walls; twisted, macabre statues of bodies intertwined in sex and death; and a makeshift bed of cloth stained with blood. Chitinous corpses of corrupted humanoids and dead men littered the floor.

Morgan wiped sweat from his brow as his labored breaths crystallized in the air. All of his training as a child and a young man culminated in this moment. He stood triumphant over Acasul'Ra, the Scourge of Kallandin. The vile wizard, the kingdom's millennia-old foe, lay on his back, covered in cuts and blood, the corner of one lip turned upward.

Morgan had not escaped injury. Blood flowed from several wounds on his face and body, but he paid them no heed. The burning cut on his chest, where the wizard's sword had cut through his leather armor, did not matter now. This was the moment he had lived his life for, and for the fraction of a second he would grant himself, he would revel in it.

His excited heart slammed against his chest. Morgan only saw a defeated Acasul'Ra, and his own shining destiny, before him.

Blue flames danced along the blade of Morgan's

sword and he tightened his grip. Without further hesitation, he thrust it into Acasul'Ra's heart. Blood welled around the blade. Morgan ripped the sword out and raindrops of blood flew out in an arc and spattered on the ground around them.

The tyrant gulped in a breath and turned his gaze up to Morgan. The life in his eyes was already fleeting, almost gone, but a smile touched his lips.

"So foolish." Acasul'Ra spoke quietly, his voice little more than a rasp. Morgan leaned closer, his grip on his sword still tight. "Like all of the others before you. You think you know, but you don't. This is far from over. This is only the beginning." Blood flecked on the tyrant's lips as he let out a laugh that sent a shiver through Morgan's body.

Morgan jumped back in response, sword pointed at the dying man. "It's too late. You can't perform the transformation when you're dead. I'm beyond your touch now." Morgan smiled.

"As they all said. This is beyond you, boy." Acasul'Ra laughed again, bloody spittle spraying wildly.

Morgan quick-stepped back and held his breath. He scanned the chamber, but all was at it had been. Morgan released his breath and managed a smile. So much for the tyrant's threat.

Acasul'Ra laughed again, finality in the mocking sound. He took one last breath and shattered Morgan's life with four simple words: "I name you Acasul'Ra."

Justin Detrier lay pinned under the corpse of the horror he had just killed. The man, if it could be called as such, was massive. His large head was covered in black scales. The creature's tiny orange eyes no longer glowed. The monster had delivered what Justin was sure was a mortal wound with an axe. Blood ran freely from Justin's stomach, but it didn't matter. From under the corpse, he witnessed the fall of Acasul'Ra.

Suddenly red light suffused the horrible room. In the farthest corners, previously hidden statues depicting nightmarish visions towered over the corpses of foul abominations—drones, pawns, and other unidentifiable things—and men alike. Even the walls, black as an infinite pit, glimmered as though painted with blood.

Acasul'Ra had said something to his brother, and by the change in Morgan's expression, the message wasn't good.

Though he sustained several nasty wounds during the battle, Morgan stood tall and straight as he regarded the dead king before him. A slight frown marred his otherwise stoic face.

Despite his own predicament, pride filled Justin at the sight of his brother standing victorious over the Scourge of Kallandin. Morgan had done everything the Knights of the Crown said he would. His brother was a hero.

There was no jealousy and no envy as Justin watched Morgan wipe the blood from his blade with a tattered piece of cloth. Justin sought a breath to shout with, to cheer his brother, but a chill sprang forth with no clear source. The wind cut through everything, even his armor, and wrapped its cold embrace about his skin.

The wind exhausted the torches, and as suddenly as it had sprang to life, it left with a wheeze, the red light vanishing with it. Absolute darkness descended upon the room and Justin sucked in a hard breath, then another. Piercing red rays surged forth from the body of the dead king and Justin shouted in surprise.

The red light had been brilliant before, but the intense crimson was now painful to behold. Justin squinted and tried to see what was happening.

Morgan shouted in surprise and recoiled, but he froze in mid-movement as the redness became a living thing and coiled itself around him. His exclamation turned into a cry of pain as the coil tightened itself, first around his arms and legs, then around his torso. Morgan's hands went slack and his glowing sword clattered to the floor. The blue light of the blade, already overpowered by the intensity of the red, winked out.

Justin watched in silent horror, barely able to breathe, as the coil inched up his brother's body. Numerous shades of crimson swirled like a bloody fire as the unearthly coil made its slow, deliberate climb. The oddity wrapped its inky length about Morgan's head and twisted around his mouth before prying it open. Morgan's screams of horror and pain doubled as his mouth was wrenched open. His mouth opened wide, like a snake's, and Justin thought he heard the crack of bone reach him through his brother's cry of agony.

Terror ripped through Justin, and the shock and fear of what he was watching bestowed him energy he didn't know remained. He shoved the body of the creature off of him with a grunt. Fresh spikes of pain shot into his stomach and the rest of his battered body.

"Morgan!" Justin cried, scrambling to his feet. He

stumbled on one of the creature's legs and crashed to the floor. He struggled back up to his feet and shouted again, but his brother's cry was so loud now he doubted he could be heard.

Justin covered the fifty feet between them in a hurry, his stomach pounding in pain and excitement. He reached out, thinking to rip the crimson coil off of his brother, to pull it away as it continued to slowly, so terribly slowly, open Morgan's mouth.

Morgan looked like some sort of child's toy with a grotesquely comic head—here the head itself opened instead of the mouth. Justin reached for the coil. It was slimy and wet and smooth. His hands erupted in flames. He shouted and stumbled back in surprise as searing pain coursed through his entire body.

He slapped his hands against himself then dashed them against the ground. His skin sizzled under the crimson flames that filled his nose with the hideous stench of burning flesh. He collapsed onto his hands and rolled in agony, and after a moment, felt the pain lessen. The fire had been smothered.

Justin looked at his hands. They were crimson. His palms were also smooth, as smooth as the coil, all their lines and character gone.

A fresh cry brought Justin's attention back to his brother. The coil still entwined itself about Morgan. Though the touch of the sinister magic had burned him, it didn't appear to be burning his brother. That was a small consolation.

Justin picked up his brother's sword, the one that had been specially crafted for him by the Knights' master smith. Though he knew he was not a chosen one like his brother and couldn't wield the sword, Justin had to try.

For a moment, horns and strings sounded somewhere in the distance. Cyan flames burst into life at the base of the blade and rushed up to the tip along both edges of the longsword. Justin had seen the Fire of Justice on many occasions, but its appearance, sudden and unexpected, surprised him. The Fire shouldn't have responded to him. The weapon filled him with hope, made him feel as though anything was possible while its glorious music played and beautiful light shone before him.

As suddenly as the fire and the music appeared, screams of pain and horror overshadowed them. The coil pulled Morgan's mouth open even wider. Morgan's cry echoed throughout the chamber. Justin ached to end up his brother's suffering, but the sight of Morgan's mouth, hideous, bloody, and torn open beyond possibility, left Justin shocked and unable to move. The sword trembled in his hands.

Morgan stopped screaming and the coil fell still.

The sword became heavy in Justin's hands and he struggled to hold it out before him. The fire and the music, already foggy in his memory as he looked upon his brother, vanished. He struggled to raise the blade. The opportunity to free his brother was slipping away before him. The tip of the blade started to rise, and then it came down farther than it had already been. It kept falling. Confused, Justin studied the sword but didn't see anything except for the dim blade as he fought against whatever held it back. Sweat rolled down his forehead to mix with the blood and dirt crusted on his face. The tip of the sword fell with a clash to the floor.

The light of the coil changed. A subtle shift at first,

the red melted into black. It stayed black for a breath then shifted back to red. It continued to shift, each pulse coming faster than the last until only a confusing, cloudy combination of the two colors remained. The coil emitted black while still leaving everything crimson in its glow.

Justin struggled a final time to raise the sword, but the tip wouldn't rise from the floor. It was as though someone or something had taken the tip of the sword and held it to the ground with impossible strength. He realized what he had missed before: the coil had wrapped itself around the tip of the sword, black and almost impossible to see, as though it swallowed light itself.

The coil slowly climbed up the blade, slithering to and fro as it reached undulating tendrils toward the hilt. Justin gasped and released the sword. The weapon remained standing just as he had held it while the coil reached up and grabbed the handle.

Fear and horror forced him back a step, then two, and then four. The dead king, lying on the floor, started to writhe and jerk as though some unseen puppet master pulled on his strings.

Acasul'Ra's left leg moved first. The limb shot out to the left. His right leg jumped. Both legs jerked and jumped followed by his arms. Acasul'Ra's head snapped forward. His entire body gave a great convulsion and struggled off the ground, arms and legs akimbo until, at last, he stood in a horrifying mockery of life, limbs splayed every which way. The corpse lurched forward with stilted and exaggerated thrusting movements while his head fell back again.

The arms and legs danced and flopped as though

they had no bones. Bile rose in Justin's throat. A moment later, he vomited all over the ground in front of him. The bile touched the coil producing little flames and hisses of smoke. The coil still stalked him. Justin stepped back in fear.

The puppet that had formerly been the most evil and reviled man to walk upon Kallandin gave another sudden lurch and stopped. The dead king stood properly, though his neck and head hung at a sickening angle behind him. The head slowly started to move forward, bones grinding with each slow, exaggerated movement. His mouth fell open and his chin rested far below his head, as though it dangled on a wire. It reminded Justin of Morgan.

Justin turned away from the animated corpse and back to his brother as he took another step back. Only his brother's awful, hideously large mouth, blood issuing out of it, and his brother's eyes, were visible from under the coil. Justin looked at those eyes and he realized Morgan saw him. Panic, fear, and pain filled Morgan's eyes. Tears burst forth from Justin's own eyes at the terrible sight.

"Morgan!"

Justin started forward, but the coil forced him to stop. His brother stared at him then shot his eyes away before he turned them back to him. Morgan did it again, his eyes more insistent. Morgan wanted him to run, but how could he leave his brother to... to whatever horrible fate this was before him?

"Go!" It was Morgan's voice, only strangled and deep, but the command broke Justin's paralysis. He gave his brother one more look then bolted for the exit.

Acasul'Ra's black and red cloak of light pulsed with

a shudder as it shifted between the colors again. The transition was slow at first, but its rapidity increased until the light became a dazzle of flashing color. Justin stopped and turned around. Acasul'Ra grabbed Morgan by the hair. The Black King stepped onto the coil and climbed atop it until he towered over Morgan.

Though it shouldn't have been possible, Acasul'Ra thrust both of his arms into Morgan's gaping chasm of a mouth. Arms inside, Acasul'Ra shrunk, not in height, but in width, and shoved his head into Morgan's mouth. He inched forward, as though Morgan were a snake swallowing him. Justin couldn't watch and fought back another wave of nausea. He turned and stumbled over fallen creatures and men alike as he struggled to get to the door. He forced himself to only look and run forward but imagined with absolute clarity Acasul'Ra climbing into Morgan's mouth in pure defiance of all that was good and natural.

Justin burst into a hallway flickering with torchlight. Confusion, purpose, and nausea still waged war within him. It was a battle to place one foot in front of the other. If it wasn't for the trail of bodies they had left on their way to Acasul'Ra's chambers, he may not have made it out of the black fortress.

Justin stumbled through the dim hallways and, after time immeasurable, he reached the courtyard and drew in a long, ragged breath. The putrid air smelled of rotting and burned corpses, and the bitter wind was harsh and the sky dark with clouds. No matter. He was no longer confined in the same room with Acasul'Ra and no longer subject to the evil one's aura and the stench of despair.

Justin doubled over as he pulled in breath after

breath until, at last, his head cleared, revealing a new singular purpose: he needed to leave this place. But to what purpose?

His brother was still inside and was... what was happening to him? Justin half-turned back to the fortress but stopped himself when he admitted he didn't know what he could do, if anything, to save his brother. And hadn't Morgan told him to leave? But to leave Morgan...

Tears anew streamed down his cheeks, and Justin wiped them away with his hands, only to shudder when he touched his face. Something horrible made his skin shiver beneath his own hands. It was as though something rotten had touched his face and was still there, was eating away at him.

In the moonlight, Justin held his hands up and saw black lines on them. He pulled the sleeve of his jerkin up. The lines continued up his arm until they disappeared under the jerkin again. The patchwork of awful black pulsed, as though it had a hideous life of its own, only he understood it was him, that it was his veins. Acasul'Ra did something to him; the coil had left him unclean, cursed.

Pain shook him as flakes of skin began to fall down from his face. The fibers he touched on his jerkin joined his fleeing skin to create a perverted rain. The pain was forgotten at the bizarre sight. The jerkin rotted before his eyes. While the skin from his face stopped falling as suddenly as it started, Justin watched with horror as the jerkin rotted and fell to pieces until it was a patchwork thing that barely clung to his body.

He ripped it off with hardly more than a gentle tug and felt what little remained of its suppleness vanish in his touch. Somehow, he understood that in his hand, time greedily took from what he held.

The remains of the jerkin fell from unfeeling hands as Justin turned them up again. Black pulsed strongly at the fingertips and the palms. Those spots were darker, more cursed than any other. With a voiceless cry, he dropped his hands to his side.

Overhead, the clouds momentarily parted. In the moonlight that broke though, he caught a glimpse of dried blood on his stomach and he remembered the wound given to him by massive man with an insect's head. To his surprise, the wound had vanished. He put his hands to his stomach and searched for the wound. He ran his fingers over the drying blood, but there was only smooth skin.

Surprised, he looked around again but grimaced in pain as the rotting touch of death struck his stomach and sent convulsions rippling through his body. He cried out and fell to his knees. Immense pain tore through him and then faded. His stomach was wrinkled and dried, cracked and decayed where he had placed his hands, but healed itself as he watched.

Only a minute, maybe two or five, had passed, but by the time he regained his feet after watching in amazement, Justin was normal again, except for the black veins that coursed his body.

The clouds parted again. Below him, the horrible city of De'lu, the western arm of Acasul'Ra's kingdom, stood visible in the light of the moon and stars. A web of ramshackle buildings and piles of refuse, it was an insult to call it a city. Few fires burned in the city inhabited mostly by feral beasts and humans, but even as he watched, new fires sprang to life.

Justin watched the black city until the clouds closed ranks again. Though his view only lasted for a couple of seconds, hundreds of figures moved about in the city. Creatures and savage humans that somehow knew Acasul'Ra had died were preparing to honor their fallen king who would rise again someday. Rise again as Morgan?

Justin shuddered and started down the path. He was sure he would meet some of those creatures, some of those feral humans, but he didn't care. His brother was dead – was he truly? It hurt less to think so – and he was cursed, so what did he have to live for anyway?

ABOUT THE AUTHOR

KR Jacobsen lives in Southern California and dreams of visiting the Ice Hotel in Sweden. An eclectic fan of music, a drummer, and several other things that are likely too boring to mention, he is also the author of *Reborn*, a dark fantasy that is the first book in the *Scourge of Kallandin* series.

For more information about KR Jacobsen and to sign up to receive updates on new releases and promotions (not spam!), visit his website at: **KRJacobsen.com**. Be sure to check his blog for the latest ramblings about writing, reading, and whatever else comes to his mind.

If you would like to follow KR Jacobsen on twitter, you'll find him at **@KR_Jacobsen**. He's also on Google Plus and the dreaded Facebook. (He's not a fan of Facebook, in case it's not obvious.)

Omni
KR Jacobsen

Copyright 2011 KR Jacobsen
http://krjacobsen.com

Published by Crimson Blade Press

ISBN: 978-0983987918

Library of San Vicente Cataloging-in-Publication-Data:
Jacobsen, KR.
Omni/KR Jacobsen.
p.cm.
1.Sutter, Ryan (Ficitious character)—Fiction. 2. San Vicente (Imaginary place)—Fiction. 3. Conspiracies—Fiction.

Cover art by Igor Kieryluk
http://www.igorkieryluk.com/

www.ingramcontent.com/pod-product-compliance
Lightning Source LLC
Chambersburg PA
CBHW031555240626

47153CB00002B/516